D0246332

LARKINLAND

The only crime is being born, all the rest is self defence

LARKINLAND

Jonathan Tulloch

SEREN

Seren is the book imprint of
Poetry Wales Press Ltd
57 Nolton Street, Bridgend, Wales, CF31 3AE
www.serenbooks.com
Facebook: facebook.com/SerenBooks
Twitter: @SerenBooks

© Jonathan Tulloch, 2017

The right of Jonathan Tulloch to be identified as
the author of this work has been asserted in accordance
with the Copyright, Designs and Patents Act, 1988.

ISBNs
Paperback – 978-1-78172-395-1
Ebook – 978-1-78172-396-8
Kindle – 978-1-78172-397-5

A CIP record for this title is available from the British Library.

All rights reserved. No part of this publication may be reproduced,
stored in a retrieval system, or transmitted at any time or by any means,
electronic, mechanical, photocopying, recording or otherwise without
the prior permission of the copyright holder.

The publisher acknowledges the financial assistance of the Welsh Books
Council.

Printed in Bembo by TJ International, Cornwall.

As ever for Aidan and Shirley

Acknowledgements

Many thanks to Robert Kirby, a top man who never gives up, and to the Royal Literary Fund, who help me and so many other authors.

PART ONE

1.

The landlady drew back frayed floral curtains. 'This was Mr Bleaney's room.'

Barely space for two, Arthur Merryweather stayed in the doorway. He could see it all from there anyway: narrow bed, naked bulb dangling like a hangman's noose, chair bereft of its desk. The fourth room he'd been shown that afternoon, and not much worse than the others. 'How much?'

'Two pounds a week. In advance.' A shrewd look behind the landlady's horn-rimmed glasses as she took in the cut of the gentleman's jacket and tie, the trilby in hand, the educated voice, his *Antler* suitcase. 'Three quid makes you all-in. Laundry, bed and breakfast, and any little extras. My gentlemen find all-in most convenient.'

Merryweather poked his head further into the room. Not even a hook behind the door, he'd only missed the ashtray – some kind of garish seaside souvenir saucer. 'I'll take it.'

'There's no dogs. Or lady visitors. Not that I'd need to tell a respectable-looking gentleman like you that, Mr Merryweather.'

'Thank you, Miss Glendenning.' She means I'm ugly, he thought, as the pound notes were plucked away and secreted into the blue housecoat before he'd barely got them out of his wallet.

'Where did you say you worked again, Mr Merryweather? Just for my rates book.'

'The university.' The blank look told him she didn't know

the town had a university. Well he hadn't either until a few weeks ago. Had barely even heard of this place beached on the mudflats at the end of the railway line like a brick seal with a woodbine in its gob.

'Thought maybe you were in the insurance game.'

'No,' he said. 'I'm not in the insurance game.'

'You've got an air about you.'

'I shall be working in the library. At the university. I'm a librarian.' In the last word, his stammer, held back until now, partly revealed itself.

Adjusting a hair roller, the landlady scrutinised him as though trying to work out if a stammer was a good or a bad sign in a lodger. 'Never had no librarian before. Been teachers and clerks, and a scoutmaster. Commercial travellers in the main,' she said. 'One of my current gentlemen is in fur. Then there's Mr McCoist what does the seaside trade, fancy goods, you know, Scotch chap. We've a third in at present, travels in semi-precious stones but we hardly ever see him. He's in Leeds or Manchester more often than not. Since the coronation he's been that busy; well everybody wants their own jewellery now; you know, tiaras and such. And of course there was Mr Bleaney, him what had your room before. But I'll let you get settled in, Mr Merryweather. Bathroom's at the end of the landing. Mr Bleaney took his tub on a Sunday night, so if that suits. Washing's Monday, naturally.' Miss Glendenning's momentum took her down the landing to the banister before she doubled back on silent feet. After listening at the door for a while, she gave the ghost of a knock and re-entered. 'What would you say to a nice cup of tea?'

'I'd say, I'd prefer a horrible one,' Merryweather didn't say. Instead – 'Lovely.'

'Milk and sugar?'

'Please, two.'

The librarian waited until he could actually hear her descending the stairs before sighing with relief. He was mad to have accepted. This Glendenning woman (Miss – my arse), this blowsy, two-thirds slattern was exactly the kind of landlady he'd promised himself to avoid like the clap. Straight from the pages of *Punch* magazine. The way she'd stared at him on the doorstep should have been warning enough. No doubt she'd listen in on guests with a glass pressed against the wall, stare through keyholes until she went boss-eyed.

What was he letting himself in for, he wondered as he switched on the light. The unshaded bulb turned the box room into a police cell, and showed that the chair was rickety, and the wallpaper peeling. A splintered star marked the door where a high hook must have hung. The librarian grinned grimly. Obviously hadn't been strong enough for the rope when it all became too much for the last poor bastard who'd lived here. One supposed one ought to unpack.

A male cough on the landing. One of the other lodgers? The man in fur perhaps, or the seaside trader. Maybe a rare visit from that other one. The traveller in semi-precious stones – whatever the hell that meant. A floorboard creaked. A snatch of bumptious whistling: *La donna e mobile*. Perfect, some garrulous tosser come to intrude himself on the new arrival. Why did that always happen? The librarian waited for the inevitable knock. But none came. The whistling stopped, a more distant floorboard creaked and then nothing. Merryweather waited until the coast was clear before opening the door a crack to peek out.

'All aboard the skylark,' grinned the stocky cretin in a string vest standing on the landing. Hairy shoulders, daffodil bulb nose, he was almost as bald as Merryweather himself. Peering at the new lodger, the cretin's grin froze in confusion. 'Bleaney?' he faltered in bewilderment. The librarian opened the door more fully, allowing a flush of light from the bulb behind to illuminate his head. 'Oh, sorry, I thought you were… Strange that. You must be the new bod, eh?' Back to his jovial self, the cretin gave a mock bow. 'Greetings, fair traveller and welcome to the enchanted isles.'

'Afternoon,' the librarian conceded.

'So, she's finally taken a new prisoner, eh,' the friendly pratt continued, taking the librarian's hand before he could withdraw it. He had the grip of a warm swamp. 'That room's been empty for weeks. Another body snatcher are you?'

'Beg pardon?'

'Blimey, but you're honoured. She must have shown dozens of people round; none of them passed the test. Asked for it myself. Even offered a bit more of the old moulin rouge. Room with a view, you see. Mine looks over next-door's yard. Their outside bog fair whiffs on a summer's night. You can smell it in yours on a hot day but not as bad.'

'Well, better get unpacked,' said Merryweather, freeing himself from the swamp at last. Far from taking the hint, the windbag edged closer. The bugger will have his foot in the door in a moment, Merryweather reflected.

'I'm in fur, what's your load?'

Just a moment's pause. 'Books.'

Sweat beaded the other's forehead as though he was indeed dressed in fur instead of a string vest. 'The old *Encyclopaedia Britannica*, eh?'

'Well, amongst others.'

'Not my bag. Too much shoe leather. Listen, fancy a pint after tea? I'm off to a bit of a posh do later but I can always squeeze in a jar with a mate.'

Merryweather's lie was smooth with a lifetime of wanting to be alone in a world forever forcing itself on you. 'Sorry, I've work to do.'

'Oh. Until tomorrow then, maestro. Here at Chez Glendenning you'll find we inmates stick together. Which was why it was such a shock when doo-dah upped sticks without so much as a by your leave. Don't bother knocking, old man, my door's always open to chums. Name's Teesdale.'

'Merryweather.'

The man in fur grinned at the dour-faced librarian. 'Are you joking?'

'No.'

'Well, there's a nice little local up the way, *Merryweather, The Shoulder of Mutton*, but you'd better come with me first time to show you mean no harm; don't want the natives putting you in a pot.' A bray of laughter. 'By the by, word of advice,' Teesdale made a pantomime of checking for the proximity of the landlady. 'Make sure she doesn't do to you what she did to Old Bleaney, him who had that room before. Then again, maybe you might want her to.'

'What can you mean?'

'Put it this way, start worrying when she asks about gardening.' Teesdale winked over the fat finger plugged to his bulbous nose, then burst into another bray of laughter during which Merryweather finally made good his escape. Practically had to shut the door in the chatty bastard's face. As if Miss Glendenning wasn't enough, one of his fellow lodgers was a bad Music Hall turn.

The bed groaned as Merryweather sat, but it wasn't just the springs creaking. The librarian was laughing. His high shoulders shook; his crabbed ribs ached. *Dispatch from the edge of the known world*, he imagined penning this evening's letter to his successful friend, *have accepted a steerage in the third circle of hell...*

'Here we are; nice cup of tea.' Once again not waiting for her knock to be answered – a house rule? – the landlady entered rump first bearing a pair of teacups. The housecoat and hair rollers had been shed; about half a bottle of fragrance added. With no lock he'd have to think of a way of at least wedging the door. Blocking the keyhole too. 'Do you mind me asking you something, Mr Merryweather; do you like gardening?'

'Gardening?'

'Yes, gardening. Are you green-fingered at all?' Mechanically, Merryweather obeyed the landlady's gesture to join her at the window, and found himself looking down over a piece of waste ground slowly being devoured by the drizzly late afternoon. A couple of rods of weed barely contained by a crooked fence – a symposium of thistle and litter. Beyond that, the road. 'Mr Bleaney really took my bit of garden in hand,' she said. 'He was going to grow a bed of lobelias this spring, put in crazy paving, chop down that horrid thorn tree. Yes, he had ever such a lovely front garden planned.' Although it was now April barely a leaf showed on the hawthorn. 'I find a man much happier with a hobby, don't you, so if you want to…'

'I don't usually have the time for gardening.'

'Really?' Miss Glendenning appeared genuinely shocked. To hide his mounting irritation, the librarian took a sip of tea. Surprisingly refreshing. 'There now, you needed that, didn't you, Mr Merryweather?'

'Indeed.'

'You were spitting feathers, weren't you, as Mr Bleaney used to say. Now, we have tea, what you might call dinner, at six o'clock on a night, so you're just in time. Chop and chips tonight. Special treat.'

'Ah, not tonight.'

The landlady's perfume engulfed the librarian like a radioactive cloud as she edged along the sill towards him. 'I do the chops in Worcestershire sauce.'

'The thing is, I'm meeting some colleagues for d-dinner.'

In such a small room it was perhaps inevitable that two people turning from the window at the same time should brush against each other, but the librarian got the distinct impression that Miss Glendenning had done nothing to minimise their contact. More than just a hint of bosomy, perfume-sodden blouse in the momentary press. 'Oh, Mr Merryweather?'

'Miss Glendenning?'

'My room's just down the landing, opposite the bathroom.' Reaching the door, she turned. 'There's one other thing I ought to mention.' Her voice dropped conspiratorially. 'I don't know if you've met him yet.'

'Whom?'

'Mr Teesdale.'

'I have.'

'Well if I were you, I wouldn't spend too much time with him. Can't always take him at his word. Rather common actually. If you believed everything he said, you'd think he was a real top boy, and do you know, when he says fur, I've reason to believe that he really means hides. Animal skins, tanning, glue products, that line of trade. Even Mr Bleaney couldn't stand him, and that's saying a lot.'

As Miss Glendenning descended the stairs, a burst of bonhomieous *La donna e mobile* came whistling from the depths of the boarding house.

Once here, I may never emerge again, Merryweather planned writing in his letter.

2.

At the click of the front door behind him, Merryweather's spirits lifted. Such a strain talking to strangers; almost as bad as talking to acquaintances. He strode down the path that formed a causeway through the rising tide of thistle and rubbish comprising Miss Glendenning's 'bit of garden'. If this was 'taken in hand' what price 'left to fucking seed'? An evening alone stretched reassuringly before him. 'Oh, Mr Merryweather?' the landlady called from an upstairs window. 'The door is locked at ten o'clock on weekdays.'

'It's Saturday,' replied the librarian.

She'd already closed the window.

Merryweather had gone a few yards down the road before it occurred to him that she'd been calling down from his room. Tomorrow he'd have to make a few things clear. The rap of knuckle on pane made him turn again. Now Teesdale stood in the librarian's room miming the sinking of a pint whilst pointing up the road in the direction of an insalubrious looking public house on the corner. The *Shoulder of Mutton*. Merryweather strode on. Come Monday he'd get a lock for his door, but now, time for solitude. Solitude! He felt his shoulders relax, his lungs open like trees in a gentle breeze.

The stroll under the line of sycamores would even have verged on the pleasant if not for the piles of dog dirt one had to negotiate. The early Saturday evening queue at the trolleybus stop was long and gregarious. Working men's club and bingo bound no doubt. Most of those waiting seemed to know each other. Was he the only one wearing a trilby? The other men either sported the cloth cap of the locale, or despite the drizzle went bareheaded. Severe short back and sides for the most part, but a whole group of starkly luxuriant quiffs: teddy boys. The women favoured headscarves, those without were young, unmarried one presumed. Lord, how primitive we remain, Merryweather mused, despite everything – William Caxton, Thomas Hardy, the invention of Jazz – we're still just a study for 301. on the Dewey decimal system.

Dusk began to fall like damp smoke; the trolley arrived.

'Fourpence,' the clippie said. Merryweather only had a ten bob note. 'Broke the bank at Monte Carlo, did you?' grinned the clippie. Holding the note up for general inspection, he called down the trolley. 'Bloke here wants to buy the bus.'

'Tell him he can have it for nowt,' the driver called back.

'I'm Burlington Bertie,' the clippie sang.

14

'I rise at ten-thirty,' the driver replied not particularly melodiously.

'We don't have enough change, mate,' the clippie winked, handing Merryweather back the note. 'You'll have to owe us.'

So, Merryweather mused, that's how things are run under nationalisation. Piercing broad acres of corporation housing, the trolleybus took the librarian down its surprisingly straight couple of miles. Working his way through the bus, the clippie sold his tickets; the passengers chatted like hens; the teddy boys told a series of ever more apparently hilarious, certainly bluer jokes. An aroma of fish steadily brewed. Not for the first time, nor the last, Merryweather wondered how a path begun on the primrose lawns under Oxford's dreaming spires could have led him here at the age of thirty-three. His best friend, and chief correspondent, was already a successful novelist; other acquaintances were rising eminent in their fields: barristers bound for the bench, journalists, even a scribbler of detective stories; and here he was bouncing on a trolleybus. When had he chosen this life; made the momentous decision bringing him here and nowhere else in the great, big world? Fate, it seemed, was itself a trolleybus, carrying you where it must, following the wire laid down by some po-faced town planner in destiny's district council offices. Next stop a semi with a little wifie up the duff and one kiddie in the pram already? No, not that, never *that*. The librarian hid his grin in a cough. 'You all right, love?' the nearest headscarf asked.

'Quite, madam.'

There were a few titters, as much from the raising of his trilby as his accent.

'Not from round here, are you lover?' the headscarf asked.

Merryweather cursed himself for being without his usual shield of a newspaper.

Fortunately, an altercation at the back diverted attention. Jeers and catcalls. 'I've told you lot before,' the clippie was shouting at the teds. 'No ticket, no travel.'

A clear, high-pitched voice pealed above the disturbance: 'Calm down, pops, no need to lay an egg.' Merryweather turned to look at the speaker. It was one of the teddy boys. Baby face lined with some slum scrofula, he was a real short arse. Were many of the local people likely to be stunted? Lack of nutrition, coalmines and so forth, one supposed.

'Don't you sauce me,' the clippie said. 'It's a criminal offence, you little bugger – you got on here with no intention of paying.'

'*He* hasn't got a ticket.' All eyes followed the short arse's finger jabbing towards Merryweather. 'Why aren't you chucking *him* off?'

At the next stop, the teds were thrown off, but as the trolleybus started again, Merryweather could see them sprinting under the wire in pursuit.

'Want a bobby on here,' the clippie called up the bus. 'Them teds is running wild.'

'To think we fought a bloody war for them,' the driver returned.

'They want their arses tanned,' one headscarf said.

'They want sending to borstal,' another remarked.

Others chipped in. 'And to think there's talk of them scrapping national service.'

'Well you know who that young one is, don't you?'

'He's a proper toe rag, that's what he is.'

'Worst of the lot.'

'He's one of the…'

The bell clanged; Merryweather missed the information. A long queue at the next stop. Before the trolley could pull away, the teds were piling back on. The librarian stared resolutely forward. If there was going to be trouble, he didn't want to be involved: one of the few tenets of his sparse faith.

Without warning the town itself came into view, or at least a pocketful of lights was thrown at the fogged window. Rubbing the pane with the cuff of his British Warm, Merryweather was surprised by the sudden flare of a city. From the train all he'd seen of his new hometown had been the flotsam of slums and semi-slums and soon-to-be slums cast up on the flats of a tidal river. The search for lodgings, a list of likely addresses ringed in the classifieds of the local paper, had offered him more of the same mud-coloured houses, one of which had been Miss Glendenning's. Now, all at once – domes, spires, statues, the bold Parthenon of a Civic Theatre.

The trolley slowed, stopped.

'Is this the terminus?' Merryweather asked. 'I mean, are we here?'

''fraid so,' grinned the driver, climbing out from behind his control. 'Course *we'd* sooner be in Monte Carlo an' all.'

Through a stiff odour of fish, he followed his fellow passengers over the unexpectedly wide square, their temporary solidarity dissolving. At a fountain, the teddy boys formed a rugby scrum as they bent over a shared match, short arse in the midst. Riding a gusting wind, Merryweather gave them a wide berth.

Unable to find a single restaurant, and not fancying the queues at the many chip shops, Merryweather soon found he'd wandered back to the station. 'There's no dinners until eight,' a spotty youth asseverated at the desk of the Royal Station Hotel. 'We've a function on.'

Merryweather had noticed a cinema hard by the station. They were showing the cartoon version of *Animal Farm*. Cheered by the thought of loathing every minute of it, he bought a one and eight ticket for the six-thirty showing. Sparsely attended, a half dozen or so couples necked on the back row, whilst a contingent of pinko cranks sat bolt upright at the front, duffle coats no doubt fortified by copies of *Das Kapital*. The librarian indeed found himself laughing at the cartoon's destruction of communism, and was left suitably depressed by its account of human nature.

'You said eight,' Merryweather reminded the spotty and by now openly fractious young receptionist back at the Royal Station Hotel.

'Eight thirty.' A distant bell summoned the youth. 'We've the Wide River do on tonight,' he cast over a frazzled shoulder.

Disinclined to comb the streets in the wind and rain, not forgetting (how could one?) the bracing aroma of fish, Merryweather retired to the foyer bar. Port red carpets, countryside prints, plush wallpaper, cabinets of highly polished nautical instruments – clearly the Royal Station Hotel had pretensions to a kind of self-made exclusivity. He ordered a sherry and passed under high chandeliers to where deep armchairs were grouped in sociable quartets, each a different colour. Choosing a corner quartet, the librarian threw his British Warm on the red chair, trilby on the blue, briefcase on the mustard, and sat himself on the shit-brown fourth. That would stymie any windbag looking for a chinwag. A half-scowl at the distant sea roar of many human voices. A door leading off from the foyer had opened to reveal a function room heaving with humanity. The River Queen Ballroom was crammed with diners all dressed up to the provincial nines. Chunky black ties, aldermanic dinner jackets, wives in department store stoles. The door closed again and the storm of voices died to a remote hubbub. *Wide River Business Fraternity Dinnerdance* declared the sign outside the River Queen Ballroom in gold lettering. Odd word, dinnerdance, Merryweather mused, non-grammatical, distinctly primitive, on the cusp of annoying, yet not without its alliterative poetry. Well, the dinner portion of the evening was clearly in the ascendance, judging by the clatter of chatter, knife and fork. 'Your sherry, Sir,' said the bar steward.

'Should I give you my order for dinner?'

'Oh, it'll be more a case of what's left.'

Lighting a Park Drive cigarette, Merryweather brought out his slim *Lyflat* Memo Book, and, a society-discouraging frown on his face, set to filch another line of poetry from his meagre granary of inspiration. Easy enough to feel things, the hard part about writing poetry was not to sound like a prick.

'Mind if I park meself down a mo?'

Merryweather swore under his breath; hadn't noticed the interloper stealing towards him from the River Queen Ballroom. 'Sorry, it's taken.'

'What, all three chairs?'

'Yes. I'm… I'm expecting the rest of my party presently.'

'Give over. You'll want to hear what I've got to say,' boasted the intruder in a voice thick with Magnet ale and a wool town upbringing. 'Do I know you, cock?' the wool town wanker demanded.

Merryweather looked at the fatty, overbearing, pale face and thought of the pigs from *Animal Farm*. 'No.'

'Mebbes not. Know most folk. Round here they call me Mr Paper Products, what's your game?'

'Fur.'

For the second time that day, Merryweather moved too slowly to avoid a handshake. 'Funny that,' said Mr Paper Products. 'T'other fella I know is in the mink game an' all; didn't realise there were elbow room for two. He's a bit of a pipsqueak. Mebbes you'll do better.' Releasing Merryweather's hand, the salesman reached out for the blue chair just as the librarian drew it out of range. Losing his balance, the salesman stumbled forward. 'What the hell you laking at?'

'Beg pardon?'

'I asked you what you're laking at?'

'I'm sorry I don't understand what you mean.'

'You from bloody Lunnon or summat? Saw for yoursen I was sitting on't chair.'

'It's taken.'

'Oh suit yourself, baldy four eyes, hoity toity, miserable get.'

More and more people were coming out of the River Queen Ballroom. Two further attempts on the chairs had to be repulsed. Merryweather tried coaxing his muse with another couple of fags and a second sherry. No dice. Instead he began the anticipated letter to his successful novelist friend. Chuckling out loud, he'd filled two pages about the inimitable Miss Glendenning and the room of doom when he had to get up to piss. He crossed the foyer. The telephone standing amongst a thicket of potted plants brought him to a halt. After a few moment's indecision he went over. He'd dialled a couple of digits before seeming to change his mind about the call, and replaced the receiver. Walking away, he noticed a figure with a thick beard and patched coat dart to the phone. Didn't exactly look the type they'd welcome at the Royal Station Hotel.

In the bogs, a throat-clawing reek of disinfectant and a hectoring voice. Gordon Bennett! Mr Paper Products was hectoring some other poor sod over a urinal. '… some jumped-up Lord Snooty. When I asked him if…' Passing into a cubicle, Merryweather pissed as hard as he could to drown out the monologue, but his flow wasn't what it used to be, another sign of one's mortality if any further had been required. In lieu of that, he pulled the chain. 'You take a leaf out of my book,' Paper Products continued at his victim, on another, self-aggrandising tack now as Merryweather washed his hands. 'I started with nowt, and now look at me – '

Recognising the victim just in time, the librarian fled.

'Squire, squire!' Pursuing Merryweather from the toilets, Teesdale ran him to ground at the potted plants. The string vest had been exchanged for a rented tux and black tie, but he'd retained, even added jewels to his crown of sweat. 'Blimee, you've hit the ground running,' said Teesdale. 'First night and here you are. Not just a bean feast, this is where it all happens. Bunk up the greasy pole. Get the edge over the next fellow. That chap in the bogs? Only buys the stationery for every bloody Woolworths north of the river. Thought that would pull you up. He can make or break a chap. Just warned me about some bastard muscling in on my patch as it happens. But I can't stand in the greenery with you all night; I've other fish to fry. See that fellow at the bar, him in the coat?' Merry-weather peered through the milling bodies to where a man in an Astrakhan coat formed the focal point of a group of a dozen, a score of others. 'Biggest of cheeses, old man. Guess what he does?'

'I have no idea.'

'Guess.'

'Really, how should I know, Teesdale? Buys all the kippers north of the river.'

'No, no, you're off the mark there. He's the manager of this whole charabanc; yes, he only bloody well owns the Royal Station Hotel. He's next on my list tonight. By the by, I was only half joking, you know.'

'Indeed.'

'About your predecessor. Maybe old Ma Glenners really did…' Teesdale strangled an invisible neck. 'You know, afterwards, like a black widow spider. Then buried him in that bloody garden of hers.' The trademark laughter brayed out as though a donkey had got in amongst the Wide River Business Fraternity. 'Funny how he vanished though. Bleaney. He was an insurance agent, you know a door-to-door Johnny. Bit like you with your encyclopaedias. But he'd been doing very well of late. Trying to get a step up from your Man from the Pru. Moved into business insurance as a sideline. Even came to the last Wide River Do. Hired a dicky, and brought old Ma

Glenners. Should have seen her. If ever there was a double helping of a dog's dinner. Course he was out of his league. Well they both were.' And then Teesdale was elbowing his way through the now heaving foyer to where the biggest of cheeses was holding court.

After a five-minute wait at the desk, Merryweather saw the receptionist return from the kitchens. 'What now?' the receptionist demanded.

'Dinner for one, please.'

'If you must.'

The 'beef' Wellington was lukewarm (as well as tasting decidedly like a mixture of sawdust and sheep skin), the 'market vegetables' cold, two potatoes entirely uncooked, crumbs culled from next door's feast. Merryweather wouldn't have been surprised if his 'carafe' of wine hadn't been filled with the lees of next door's empties. The lone diner, he sat islanded in a glittering expanse of knives and glass through which the receptionist lumbered his way with the necessaries like a reluctant swineherd lugging swill. The librarian had graduated to an unappetising spotted dick when an orchestra of sorts started up next door. Evidently the dance portion of the evening's festivities had commenced. He brightened at the prospect of some jazz, Sidney Bechet perhaps or Louis Armstrong, but quickly relapsed into the depths of his almost contented discontent as a rather off-key, big band standard boomed out. The swineherd clattered the bowl away and carted over a tiny cup of coffee, which was quite clearly chicory. Merryweather was about to complain when the orchestra suddenly broke off. In the abrupt silence, voices rose. Not the annoyingly happy hubbub of earlier but a squall, a cackling of hyenas. Warning cries, the tinkle of breaking glass, and then a gang of smirking youths rucking past the open door of the restaurant. Teds. Amongst them the baby-faced short arse. No more than fifteen or sixteen, at the very oldest a stunted seventeen. Was childhood rickets common in fishtown?

3.

Mavis Glendenning stole silently over the landing. Even when none of her gentlemen were in, she moved soundless as a draught. Landlady's trade secret: overweight perhaps, with fallen arches too, but cat quiet. Opening the door without a creak, she slipped into Mr Bleaney's room. It would always be Mr Bleaney's room to her. No need for a light; she knew each inch of this room, every fibre of balding rug, secret harbour of dust, hill and dale in the dimpled ceiling, different note of the narrow bed's springs, which she brought to life now as she sat down. Closing her eyes, she breathed in deeply as though savouring a cherished, but fading musk. Entranced, she remained there, a hand laid where the head of a sleeper would rest.

Stirring at last, the lock on the new lodger's suitcase was easily picked. Two suits, a bottle of whisky, pair of carpet slippers, neatly folded underwear, dusty old books, files fat with densely scrawled-on papers.

At the sound of the gate swinging open in the garden below, Mavis darted to the window. Gazing through the gap between the frayed curtains, what she saw made her throw the window wide open. 'What you got?'

The figure on the path below stopped, and in the street-lamp's orange glow slowly went through his small bundle of letters. It was the Beckshaw boy from number sixty-one Coronation Road. 'Pools coupon and gas bill, Mrs Glendenning,' the youth replied. 'Letters for Mr Teesdale; postcard for Mr McCoist.' The boarding house was number sixty-one Corporation Road. Quite often the sorting office mixed the two streets up, and the halfwit boy would bring the misdirected post round when he got back from the Remploy factory and had had his tea. This evening he must have been at the church boys' club as well. It was well after eight.

'What about, Mr Bleaney?'

'Nothing for Mr Bleaney today.'

'Are you sure?'

Again, the laborious check. 'Pools coupon and gas bill, Mrs Glendenning. Letters for Mr Teesdale; postcard for Mr McCoist.'

'*Miss* Glendenning, how many times do I have to tell you?' she snapped.

'Miss?' laughed the person coming through next-door's gate, it was the headscarfed woman who had talked to Merryweather on the trolley. 'Then I'm sweet sixteen again and never been kissed before.'

Mavis frowned. Her feud with neighbour Kathleen Mealie was long running.

'See you've took a new lodger,' Kathleen called up. 'Proper posh and all. Flashing ten bob notes about. And after you wouldn't have that pal of our Stan.'

'I've got my standards,' Mavis said with some pleasure.

'You mean working men don't take their trousers off quick enough for you?' Kathleen's laughter sprayed the window like a handful of fish heads. 'That Mr Bleaney of yours wasn't so la-di-da when it came to the women. Haven't you heard what they're saying about him? Why he did off like the squits after a barrel of spratts?'

Having slammed the window shut with such force that the glass shook, Mavis retreated to the bed. For a long time she lay so motionless that had Merryweather come in he would not have noticed her. At last, she rose suddenly as though to a touch. Nodding slightly like one invited to dance, she allowed an unseen hand to steal round her waist whilst lowering her head to rest on a spectral shoulder. And then she was dancing to a silent orchestra, sailing up and down Mr Bleaney's room as though across the glittering reaches of the River Queen Ballroom at the Royal Station Hotel where she had waltzed one, magical night with Mr Bleaney.

4.

The teds had gone; the glasses they'd smashed had been swept up. In the River Queen Ballroom the dance was back in full swing. 'Aren't you going to buy a girl a drink?' The woman, who'd just taken Merryweather's arm, was neither a girl nor in need of another drink. It had taken twenty minutes to elbow his way to the bar, and he still hadn't been served. 'What you being like that for?' she shouted over the orchestra, as he tried to wriggle free. 'It's the Wide River do.' The wife of some senior sales director, she had the grip of a char.

Merryweather stared at the couples waltzing under the shifting constellations of mirror balls. A lurid spotlight tricked out a score of tawdry flirtations, half a dozen adulteries and a world of nonentities. And none more so than me, he reflected. Time to get well away from the bloody Royal Station Hotel. Was he tight? No, he decided, he'd only drunk a couple of sherries and half a 'carafe' of mixed vintages. Wrenching himself from the clutches of the pissed-up char, he waded through the morass of conviviality to where some revolving doors offered escape. Teesdale's bray, paying court to the biggest of cheeses, harried the librarian out through the spinning glass panes.

One was debouched directly onto the station. The evening express had just arrived, and heading for the exit to the trolleys Merryweather was caught up in the swirl of passengers. The human current carried him to the billboards. One poster showed a sun-kissed blonde opening her arms for a beach ball whilst kneeling on a cartoon riviera below the words *Come to Sunny Prestatyn*. If only he fucking had. Anywhere must be preferable to this place at the end of the tracks where the locals, apparently never having heard of the famous British reserve, were either at your throat or forcing unlooked-for intimacies.

Another garrulous queue awaited at the trolley. The thought of returning to the boarding house sent the librarian veering across the square. A whipping wind cleared his head, but made lighting a fag a Promethean struggle. Three, four, five matches flared and died before, head buried tortoise-like inside his British Warm, his Park Drive caught. Tongue bitter with match sulphur, Merryweather straightened up to find himself being interrogated by a giant. Readjusting his glasses, he saw that it was one of the statues he'd noticed from the trolleybus. What had this departed worthy done? Something great; something terrible? There was no clue on the plinth. Brought the railway here, profiteered from child labour, drew up the Factory Acts, repealed slavery? Ozymandias in the stink of fish.

The length of the Park Drive took him to a row of telephone boxes. They weren't the usual red affair but cream-coloured. Rather, wheat-hued. If it hadn't been for this oddity, perhaps he would have walked straight past them. Something in Merryweather was drawn to the eccentric, and he couldn't always fight it.

One booth was vacant. As in the hotel, he hesitated over dialling, but this time he did so. Coin swallowed, connection made. 'Arthur?' The hope in the voice on the other side of the line grabbed Merryweather by the throat. She always sounded so uncharacteristically lost on the phone. 'Is that you, Arthur?'

'Afraid so.'

'But I thought you weren't going to ring.'

'Bad penny.'

'Only I'm immensely glad you did.' Hairline crack in the adverb, forced jollity? Of course it bloody was. 'Where the devil are you, you terrible man?'

'Here. You know, up north.'

Oh, why the fuck had he rung her? Maybe he *was* a little tight. Two-thirds of the 'carafe' rather than half. After promising to leave her alone as well. That was partly why he'd come up here. A clean break, and now he was buggering it up. He let her talk without listening until he became aware of a question being repeated. 'Beg pardon?'

'I'm asking whether you've found lodgings, Arthur.'

'Lodgings? Yes, I have.'

'What are they like?'

'Rather dreadful actually. Truth is the whole place is spectacularly dreadful.'

'So you like it then?'

'I'm not sure that I don't.'

'Oh Arthur, can't anything be straight forward?'

'It would appear not.'

'I miss you so much.'

'I really wouldn't, you know.'

Yes, he was an ass to have rung. Worse, sheer cruelty – playing with the puppy you're no longer prepared to feed. Not that you could call her a puppy. What *could* one call her? Well, whatever it was, he couldn't expect her to keep bailing him out of his loneliness, on his terms, always on his terms. 'The money'll run out any minute now and I haven't got any more,' he lied, fingers fluttering at the little babel of coins piled by the slot. 'Gave all my change to a fellow singing on a street corner.' The lie was too extravagant; she knew him well enough to know he would rather have a tooth extracted than toss a copper to a street performer.

'What's your number, Arthur? I'll ring you back. And your address so I can write.'

Be firm, Merryweather told himself; selfish to give false hope. 'What was that? I can't quite hear. Bad line.'

'I thought we might go to the cottage one weekend once you've settled in,' she said, not entirely able to hide her desperation. 'You know how you love it there, we'd both feel better for a weekend away; oh, Arthur…'

'Oh Lord, there's the pips…' Merryweather could barely believe it when he heard himself imitating the sound of the pips before replacing the receiver. When had it come to this? There was no sodding excuse.

A tap on the window from someone waiting. The tap became a rapping fist. 'Hold your horses,' Merryweather barked. 'I've only been in a couple of minutes.' A third knock. Sheer bloody rudeness. The librarian thrust the door open on – a tramp. Bird's nest beard, patched coat, felt hat on a shock of hair, the sort of character you'd expect amongst mangolds, not a town square. Was it the fellow from the phone at the Royal Station Hotel? The tramp pushed past Merryweather and clawed the refund tray for coins. Extricating himself from any possible scene, as well as the acrid stink, the librarian strode away.

Crossing from the brightly lit square, he stumbled down a half-lit cloister of department store windows. Stopping to look at a display of ladies nightwear, he glanced over his shoulder. The tramp was following him. 'Shit,' he hissed, and hurried on. The civic grandeur dwindled further to a dusk of betting shops, tattoo parlours and a first-floor billiard hall whose stooping figures silhouetted the Venetian blinds. And still Mr Wurzel Mangold was coming. Aiming to loop back to the square, Merryweather merely succeeded in plunging deeper into a backstreet twilight, deserted except for thronged, throbbing, sudden corner pubs. Already out of breath, he was wondering whether he should actually begin running when he realised that the tramp had stopped following.

'Got a fag?'

Startled by the closeness of the voice, Merryweather swung round to see a drunk propped against a wall. 'No,' he replied, already walking on.

The answer seemed to stun the lush. 'Haven't got a fag?'

'That's what I said.'

The librarian shot down an alley. 'How can you not have a fag?' the drunk shouted after him in outrage. 'Got to have a fag. What's bloody life without a fag?'

Merryweather hastened on. Didn't want to admit he was lost, yet the smell warned he must be close to the docks, as did the sudden, restive call of a seagull. He looked up. Hundreds of the birds were roosting amongst the vertiginous chimney pots of the semi derelict area in which he'd drifted. The wind whipped ever sharper. If one came to another pub why not pop in for a quick snifter just before last orders? Well, for a start, because these were the kind of establishments from which a stranger would be lucky to emerge with his life, let alone the shirt still on his back. Lifting coat lapels to their furthest extent, and freshly amazed by the personal fecklessness that had brought him to this godforsaken, herring-boat town, the librarian carried on.

At first Merryweather thought that the jangle of voices was a pub door opening. Ahead, beyond the ken of the single streetlight, a group of figures milled. One broke away, and sprinted towards him. The rest gave chase. A pack of baying hounds. Teds. The librarian pressed himself into a doorway. The quarry was overhauled not five yards away. 'Not trying to run away were you, Clive?' a high-pitched voice asked. In the midst of the bullying pack, Merryweather saw a slight figure with a gnarled baby face – the short arse ted from the trolley and the Royal Station Hotel.

'I aren't the one you want, Titch,' Clive gasped, clearly terrified. 'I swear on me mam's grave I aren't.'

'Go and tell that to the marines, pops,' returned Titch. Scrofulous cherub face mooning, Titch turned to his accomplices. 'Clive's been a naughty, naughty boy, haven't you, Clive?'

The librarian shrank deeper into the doorway. What sounded like a slap was followed by a cry.

5.

Sugared mug of tea brimming at his elbow, the desk sergeant was congratulating himself on a nice, quiet shift when he heard the station doors open. 'Just you is it, Amos?' he said, relieved at the sight of the bearded tramp in a patched coat being led in by a young constable. 'Been at them phones again?' he added in the avuncular tone he adopted with the more or less harmless chaff of life. A celebratory swig of tea. 'Happen you'll be glad of a roof over your head tonight, with that wind.'

'It weren't just the square tonight, Sarge,' said the young constable. 'Amos has been at the Royal Station Hotel.'

The mug slopped as the desk sergeant put it down. 'What you do that for, you daft beggar? You know what they're like at the Royal Station Hotel since that office of theirs was turned over. We'll have to book you in properly now.'

'Amos isn't the only one,' said the constable. 'Titch Thomas' crowd paid it a visit an' all. Caused a bit of a rumpus. Broke some glasses. Gone by the time I got there. They weren't very happy about it at the Royal Station. Well, you know who the owner is, don't you, Sarge?'

The sergeant sighed. 'Chief constable's brother.'

Car lights slid across the window. 'Happen that'll be him,' said the constable. 'He said he were going to pay us a visit. Not just about tonight but last month's robbery there. He said he wants to know what progress we've made.'

'None,' sighed the sergeant.

It was at this moment that Merryweather, having narrowly avoided being knocked down by a Rolls Royce, walked into the police station, voice unsteady, heart clanging. 'I've come to report a crime. Or an incident at least.'

The desk sergeant peered at the librarian. 'Do I know you?'

'No,' returned Merryweather in confusion. 'I've just witnessed a gang of youths...' Recognising the matted beard and felt hat of the tramp being led down to the cells by the constable, he broke off.

Before Merryweather could continue, the station doors were thrown open Wild West saloon style. 'I want something doing about it,' demanded a man in an Astrakhan coat. 'And I want it doing now.' Teesdale's biggest of cheeses was flanked by flunkies. 'Sending one bloody, wet-behind-the-ears bobby's no good to man nor beast.'

'Take a seat, Sir,' the desk sergeant murmured to Merryweather with a sigh. 'Be with you just as soon as I can. And what seems to be the trouble, Sir?' he asked, turning to the owner of the Royal Station Hotel.

'Trouble? I'll tell you what the bloody trouble is...'

Half listening to a tale of teddy boys crashing one of the year's most glittering social occasions, cheeking guests and even urinating in the aspidistras, Merryweather replayed in his mind what he'd just witnessed himself. After the cry, he'd leant out from the doorway to see 'Clive' being led away, stricken with fear. The librarian had seen too the grin on Titch's infant phiz.

'Now what I want you to do,' the biggest of cheeses demanded of the desk sergeant. 'Is to birch Titch Thomas. Tonight. Now. What's the matter with you, man? You're standing there as though nothing's happened. Tonight's the Wide River Do, I've guests from all over the north of England, and that dirty little street arab...' Shaking with rage, the big cheese turned puce as a Red Leicester. 'And what about that robbery? We lost five hundred pounds, and are you bloody plods any nearer to an arrest? Like hell you are.'

'Shouting won't help anyone, Sir.'

Rising to the boil all the while, the words spurted forth. 'Do you know who I am? Look here, if you don't do something right now, I'll get on the phone to the chief constable and you'll be out on your ear quicker than you can scratch your balls.'

When the big cheese and his minions had left, accompanied by two constables and the promise of two plain clothes, Merryweather rose from where he'd been obediently sitting. 'Excuse me.' He may not have inherited much from his mother, but he had her deference for the police in full.

'You still here, Sir?' the sergeant replied wearily.

Fighting a tightness in his throat, first sign of a bad fit of stammering, Merryweather recounted what he'd witnessed. 'And the thing is, I think it was this Titch Thomas and his crowd.'

'Did you actually see anything?'

'I'm pretty sure there was a slap.'

'A slap?'

'Then they took him away. Someone called C-Clive. Only I felt I ought to report it because, well, they may have hurt him. Perhaps he's lying somewhere in a pool of his own blood.'

'Have you been drinking, Sir?' Merryweather was beginning to regret going to the police. Even more so when the desk sergeant narrowed his eyes and added, 'it's a serious offence, wasting police time.'

6.

He must have been a *bit* on the squiffy side of things, Merryweather decided, because all at once he was ball breakingly sober. Way past midnight, and the last bus long gone. Neither hide nor hair of a taxi. What else to do but find the trolley stop at which he'd alighted earlier that evening, and follow the wires home? Home? Tall figure stooped, shoulders rounded, the librarian trudged up the copper trail. The police simply hadn't been interested. For a good mile a stray dog latched onto him until a stone persuaded it to bloody well sod off.

The door to Sixty-one Corporation Road was locked. Timid at first, gradually, Merryweather's knock grew louder, until – 'Bugger off.'

'I'm locked out,' the librarian apologised to the heavily bearded head poking from an upper room, not his at least.

'And I've had a hard week flogging 'lucky ducks' and other bloody seaside tat,' the bearded head growled in best Glaswegian. 'And you woke me up.'

The window was slammed shut. A few minutes passed with Merryweather hovering sheepishly on the step. Suddenly stung by both the other man's rudeness and the ludicrousness of the whole situation, he'd raised a fist to knock again when the front door jerked opened. 'You coming in or no, you bloody, lanky Sassenach?' The traveller in fancy goods, McCoist, – who else could it be? – stamped back up the stairs, grousing all the way.

One couldn't say the omens on his first day in the town at the end of the line were exactly favourable, to say the fucking least. In his room, Merryweather went straight for his whisky.

As suspected, the bed, shunted right up against the wall, was about as comfortable as a berth in Reading gaol. To boot, his feet dangled over the end, and the springs shrieked if he so much as farted. Wanking would be a ticklish business, not that he remotely felt like that tonight. With no glass, he supped his dram straight from the bottle. The unshaded light too harsh, he lay in the darkness and waited for the sharp edges of the evening's events to blunt – the police station, Titch Thomas the baby-faced hooligan, 'Clive', the tramp, the phone call, Mr Paper Products, Sixty-one Corporation Road, the whole bloody town...

The next thing he knew, Merryweather was being woken by a blinding light. Someone had turned on the bulb. A fumble for spectacles revealed only a bright dazzling. Slowly, like a religious apparition, Teesdale materialised from the flaring light. He was pissed as a newt. 'Just thought I'd check in, old man, as promised; I say, is that whisky?'

Before the librarian could reply, his fellow lodger was sitting on his bed sucking at the scotch. Merryweather felt the urge to punch the intruder's bulbous nose. 'What time is it, Teesdale?' he demanded.

'Night's still young.'

'I was asleep.' Merryweather reappropriated the bottle.

'Get caught up in the trouble?' the man in fur asked. 'Ruffians at the bloody Royal Station Hotel, what's the world coming to?' A drunken swipe at the air. 'I was a worm's fart from flogging some sozzled cow a silver fox when those ruddy hooligans came in and queered the pitch. A guinea in commission gone south. Had to sort them out before things got nasty.'

'*You* sorted them out?' said Merryweather, his sense of the ludicrous drawn despite the ungodly hour.

'Ex-paratrooper, old man.'

'But there was a whole gang of them.'

'Tush! Old paratrooper trick. You go for the biggest one. Like this.' Flourishing a hand in Merryweather's face, Teesdale reached out and snatched the whisky back with the other. 'Does the job every time.' Despite the intrusion of the whisky-guzzling, irritating homunculus with the bulbous nose, Merryweather began to laugh. 'Got a lift home with a chap I know,' Teesdale went on. 'Has his own Humber Hawk. Someone big in the knitted-sock game. Only thing is, he was sick. All over his own socks as it happens. Why he wasn't wearing his shoes, I do not know.' Teesdale drank; Merryweather's laughter began to hurt. 'By God but this is living,' the man in fur blazed, sweat standing on his forehead. 'Thought you were a po-faced Charley at first like that Bleaney bugger. You know, him before you. Ma Glenners thought the arse shone out of his sun, but I'll tell you something, Bellweather, in the whole year I've been here, never once sat like this with him setting the world to rights. Truth be told – pain in the arse. Sodding sobersides. Bloody cups of tea like a Methodist. Queerest of fish, think he wouldn't say boo to a goose, but went bloody mad if you so much as looked at his sauces. Practically took a swing at me once for using his Lea and Perrin's. Course old Ma Glenners gave him the best cuts of meat. Smug get. Always doing the pools. Had some system. Won them too. Well, he must have. Why else throw it all up and vanish like that after all those years? Up sticks without a forwarding address? Me smell money. Don't worry, he didn't leave anything behind. Believe me, I've turned this place upside down. Talking about rhino, don't s'pose you could loan me a couple of quid? Those ruddy teddy bears snatched the bread from my mouth…'

'Teddy bears?' Merryweather's mind was filled with all sorts of confusion that for some reason was devastatingly hilarious. He only just managed to take back the bottle.

'Bloody hooligans that pissed in the ferns.'

'Oh, you mean, teddy boys.'

'What?'

'The correct nomenclature is teddy boy. Not teddy bears.'

'Me no savvy, old man. Pass whisky.'

Despite a drunken tussle over the bottle, the librarian's pedantry asserted itself. 'One says teddy boys not teddy bears.'

'Not the foggiest what you're blethering on about, Penny-feather. But you gassing on about teddy bears reminds me. What would you say if I said to you, giant hamsters? Comic eh? Not so bloody funny if they made you a millionaire. A hamster has one hell of a nap.' Fishing in a pocket, Teesdale brought out a scrap of gingery fur. 'Cop a feel of that. Now if I could just get a partner. Might fancy it yourself. Let's say a tenner for starters. A fiver. Ten bob even…'

Merryweather must have fallen asleep again because once more he was being woken. The naked bulb still burnt Gestapo bright but Teesdale had gone. As the librarian sat up, the half empty bottle of Glenlivet scuttled off the bed. Why was he awake? Oh yes, a phone was ringing. No one answered it. It kept ringing. Just when he thought he couldn't stand another scan of its pealing spondees, it stopped of its own accord.

The arms of his Westclox semaphored a disgusting hour. The shabby floral curtains twitched with a sharp-wristed draught. He switched the light off, and lay there. The moon shoved its nose into the shabby box room. How many heads had rested where his was, counting the sheep of their failures? This was the kind of place you wandered into on an unlucky day, and found yourself caught fast like a fly. This Bleaney character had got out, but would he? Bleaney. What kind of a name was that? What kind of name was Merryweather? And the phone was ringing again.

'Do you know what time it is?' he barked into the phone when he'd gone down the stairs to where it stood on the rickety hall table. The line crackled, flickered, died.

The librarian was back on the landing when the ringing restarted. Hard to credit he was the only one awake. No sounds of stirring from his fellow lodgers, just a braying donkey: Teesdale snoring. He strode down the cold lino to the landlady's room. 'Miss Glendenning,' he called. 'The telephone is ringing.' Enraged by the facile rhyme, he rapped against her door. Nothing. 'Do you realise it's the dead of night?' he demanded into the receiver, having descended the stairs once more. 'What? No, he's not here. What the buggery are you ringing at this hour for anyway? I've told you, no. He used to live here, but… how should I know where? I've never met the man.'

Tongue swollen, eyes burning in their sockets, not drunk, yet not sober, he lay in bed feeling like a salted slug. Fumbling for a pen he began adding one of his celebrated postscripts to his successful friend's letter. But how to capture the full horridness of the wee hours boarding house? Dazzled by the bulb, he wrote by moon and fag light until the room was so smoky, tears streamed down his face. Then he lay there blankly. Drink was supposed to help one sleep. Insomnia, what a sleepy word with its pillowy vowels and divan consonants. Was there a term for the opposite of onomatopoeia? He went to the window. The moon picked out a rash of beaker rings dotting the rotting wood of the sill. Night didn't improve the view. In the garden, last year's thistles were an encamped army. Whatever else he might be, this Bleaney was no Capability Brown. The neighbouring roofs stretched like a prison wing. The librarian was just about to turn back to bed when a movement under the tree caught his eye. Someone stood under the hawthorn. A girl! Well, young woman. What the hell was she doing there? She was staring up at his room. He stepped back. Was she the one who'd just been on the phone asking for Mr Bleaney? Asking? Pleading. She'd sounded desperate.

Had she seen him? Merryweather crept from the window. All he needed now was to be dragged into some ugly, early hours scene.

Out on the landing, a floorboard creaked. Dander up, Merryweather shot from his room. A bedroom door was just closing, which he couldn't tell. Three separate snores now competed: Teesdale's donkey, what must be McCoist's death rattle, and the landlady's walrus-like barking. *I have heard the mermaids singing each to each*, as T.S. Eliot certainly didn't sodding well say about a boarding house at night.

7.

'The telephone? I didn't hear a telephone.' Miss Glendenning dropped the plate of kippers before Merryweather. 'Did you hear a telephone in the night, Mr McCoist?'

The bearded Glaswegian across the table was bullying a dollop of HP sauce from its bottle. 'If I had, I'd have hoyed it against the wall.'

'Mr McCoist didn't hear anything, Mr Merryweather. Did you hear a telephone ringing in the middle of night, Mr Teesdale?'

Teesdale shook his head. 'And I sleep very lightly.'

'Who on earth would be ringing at that hour?' the land-lady said. 'Unless it was for them Mealies next door. You wouldn't believe what they get up to. No phone of their own, people ring here and expect me to fetch them. Just ring the pub, I always say, that's where they'll be. I wouldn't mind but there's a public phone box just up the way. Anyway,' Miss Glendenning peered at Merryweather part disapproving nanny, part hands on hips fishwife. 'Expect you were a little confused after the Royal Station Hotel. Can I remind you of our house rules, Mr Merryweather. Gentlemen are required to be back for ten o'clock; no drink is permitted on the premises. I'll overlook it this once. Now, what's your sauce?'

'Sauce?'

She gestured at the bottles arranged on the checked tablecloth like outlandish chess pieces. 'Ideal, Daddies, Henderson's Yorkshire, Gentleman's Relish, Tomato Ketchup, Goodalls, HP and of course Lea and Perrins.'

The massed rank of condiments threatened to tip Merry-weather's queasiness into something worse. The late night whisky session had been a grave error. 'Oh, I don't really like sauces.'

'Don't like sauces?' The landlady appeared aghast.

Teesdale shook his head as though with disbelief, and McCoist, who had a permanent, constipated scowl, glowered yet more grimly.

Even without any sauce, and *with* a hangover, the kippers were excellent, cooked to a turn, but his hangover goaded on the usually cautious librarian. 'She wanted to speak to Mr Bleaney.'

'Who did?' demanded Miss Glendenning.

'The girl who rang.'

'What did you tell her?'

'That he didn't live here any more.'

As Miss Glendenning glared at her new lodger and then strode back into the scullery, it occurred to Merryweather that her horn-rimmed glasses were sharp enough to blind someone. McCoist demolished his kippers, drained his teacup, belched and departed.

'I shouldn't take that line with her if I were you,' Teesdale said sotto voce through a mouthful of fish liberally anointed with *Ideal* sauce.

'How do you mean – line?'

'You know, making jokes about Mr Bleaney. I'm all for ragging, in the right place, but – '

'I wasn't joking.'

'What, some dolly ringing up for lover boy in the middle of the night?'

'Oh, I didn't say dolly. I can't believe no one else was woken. The phone rang for ages. And then when I looked out the window there was a girl – '

'I'd steer clear of Mr Bleaney altogether if I were you,' Teesdale interrupted. 'Made the same mistake myself. If ever the phone rings, best leave it. As for girls in the garden, well, just don't look out the window.' Again sotto voce: 'Not as gentle as she looks, old Ma Glenners.'

Unwillingly, Merryweather found his own voice lowering. 'Who's the girl in the garden?'

'One of Bleaney's bints.'

'But how old was he? This girl can't have been much more than nineteen or twenty.'

'Your age, you know, mid-forties. And another thing, old man; just choose a sauce, easier in the long run, believe me.'

Sunday morning but no one at sixty-one Corporation Road seemed to be going to church. On his way out, Merryweather found the front door blocked. 'When I first started in the guesthouse trade, Mr Merryweather,' the landlady said, arms crossed, face set. 'There was this chap what lodged here. Come to town to see about building a bridge over the river. He held his knife and fork like a duke as well; *he* didn't like sauce. But let me tell you this, he wasn't all he thought he were. His breath weren't either. Soon found out you don't make Mavis Glendenning the butt of a joke twice. Tell you something else for nowt. Next time you're at the river, take a look; know what you'll see?' Merryweather shook his head schoolboy style. 'The ferry – that stupid bridge of his never got built neither.'

Outside, the sun shone; the smell of fish was almost mild. No teddy boy quiffs at the trolleybus stop, Merryweather was with the churchgoers. Headscarves put aside for the Sabbath, a confectionery of mill town millinery was on display. Blanc-manges, soufflés, even a black forest gateau. Gloved hands gripped handbags. Contrary to all other arrangements in the animal kingdom, by contrast the men were subdued, drab: clean cloth caps, woollen ties and faded but immaculately brushed suits. Empty of work, their great hands seemed an error of evolution. Churchgoers, far fewer this morning than in the Saturday night revellers' queue. Far fewer than he remembered from his Midlands childhood. Far fewer than in the novels of Arnold Bennett. Sign of the times? Those around him were just remnants of the great Wesleyan era, beached driftwood of non-conformity's heaving... Removing his glasses, Merryweather passed a hand over his face. He was still far too hung over not to be nauseated by his own imbecilic cleverness.

They didn't sell the *Sunday Times* in the corner shop. Having bought a copy of yesterday's local paper – snubbing the offer of a chat from the newsagent as inoffensively as possible – Merryweather stood at the trolley pretending to read it. He could feel the spread pages fairly crackling with the respectable folks' curiosity. The trolley, one of a reduced Sunday service, eventually arrived. 'It's Burlington Bertie,' the clippie greeted him. 'Got any more ten bob notes?'

'That's him I was telling you about last night in the *Shoulder of Mutton*,' Kathleen Mealie explained to the clippie. Merryweather turned to see one of the few head-scarved women smiling at him. Catholic, he decided, social antennae reading the signals, not to mention the tribe of kiddies spilling over into the seats around her. Was it the woman who spoke to him on the bus yesterday evening?

'What, that's old Ma Glendenning's new fella?' the clippie grinned.

A vowel of protest from the Presbyterian contingent, Methodist murmurs, Congregationalist consternation, entire chapels of disapprobation heaped on the librarian. 'Lucky bugger.' The driver's grin revealed a set of cuddy's teeth.

'Language,' the clippie winked. 'God squad on board.' Merryweather felt a stubbly chin broach his newspaper. 'Tell you what, Burlington,' the clippie whispered. 'Let you off *another* ticket if you fix me up with your Mavis.'

Kippers repeating, the librarian paid for both the morning's and last evening's tickets, and burrowed deeper into his paper. Elsewhere in the world, subject peoples were agitating for independence, empires were falling apart; here fish prices were steady, both professional rugby teams had lost again, and so forth. What was this? Still no leads in the worst crime spree ever to blight the city. Hundreds of pounds taken, four safes cracked – the last of which had been at the Royal Station Hotel – and not a single clue.

Getting out at the square, again Merryweather found his spirits lift at the surprise of a city. The banging in his head grew less insistent. The municipal baroque might even be called pretty if one were accustomed to the fish honk. Last evening's tramp was dozing on a bench by his domain of cream telephone boxes after a night in the cells. At his feet lay a half-starved mongrel; the same one that had followed Merryweather last night? Some admixture of whippet and basset hound if such a monstrosity was possible. Eyes down, Merryweather skirted by the sleepers. Presumably the short arse they called Titch Thomas would have been dealt with. They hadn't seemed to need his help; and as his mother said, the police always know what they're doing.

His aimless wander took him to the almost grand façade of last night's hotel. Evidently, all roads led to the Royal Station Hotel in Haddock City. Despite the advertisement for morning coffee with the papers, Merryweather walked on. However, his quest for a newsagent selling a quality national Sunday paper and a suitable café to match drawing a blank, he was obliged to return to the hotel with its vertiginous chandeliers and vomit-making upholstery. Mercifully, no sign of teds. Once again he chose the brown seat.

Having ordered a pot of tea, he was just reaching for the *Sunday Times* in the pile on a table when a hand pushed his aside. 'I'm sorry,' said Merryweather.

'Don't mention it,' said the man, who'd snatched the *Sunday Times* and proceeded to carry off his prize to another quartet of coloured chairs.

'I was reading that actually.'

The thief turned at Merryweather's sharper tone. It was the overbearing tosser from last night, Mr Paper Products. Before the librarian could slink off, the Woolworth grandee had made the connection too. 'The newspapers belong to all the guests,' he said, 'not just you and the rest of your party.'

Deciding to avoid a row, Merryweather made do with the *Sunday Express*. On ordering a second pot of tea, he saw that

the other man wasn't even looking at the *Sunday Times*. The
librarian went over. 'Excuse me, mind if I…'

'Still reading it.'

Once more the kippers repeated on the librarian.

When Mr Paper Products finally left, he bequeathed the
Sunday Times to another of his ilk, a steady stream of which,
like bilious trout, were rising late at the Royal Station Hotel.
In the course of the morning, Merryweather read every paper
except the one he really wanted. Gradually the percussion in
his head had eased to a distant tom-tom. Despairing of the
Sunday Times, he rang the bell at reception. 'Excuse me,' he
said when the receptionist came at last. 'Do you have a guide
book?'

'What?' It was the spotty swineherd from last night.

'You know, a book about the area. Things to do, what to
see, where to go.'

'There's nothing like that.'

Clearly it was no Baedeker resort, yet there must be
something of note in the locale. Deciding to forgo luncheon, a
decision made easy by the lingering kippers, Merryweather
set out to explore for himself. Avoiding last night's back lanes,
the librarian soon found himself wandering through a forest
of cranes, and inching over narrow, bouncing bridges, which
arced disconcertingly over deep, froth-flecked canals. The smell
of fish thickened. A sudden ship loomed over a terrace end
like a beached whale, and then there was the river itself, a
wide grey mile, and beyond that the indistinct infinity of the
sea. He'd reached the docks.

So, the place was practically an island, bound by river, sea,
railway line and those shallow lagoons of wheat he'd sailed
through on the train. Even had its own paddle ferry, which
Merryweather, with boyish excitement, was soon aboard. Up
on deck, he watched the docks fade and the far coast slowly
loom. A rag tag of boats could be seen chugging in from the

sea. Gradually they grew bigger. The fishing fleet returning. The sun came out, and the herring boats were transformed by the brilliant white of the gulls thronging them. All at once not herring boats but Egyptian Dhows. Merryweather almost smiled. Then the sun went in.

The far bank was reassuringly dismal. Coal heaps, coal spoils, and a coal staithe. No self-respecting shithole was without its coal staithe. As the librarian picked his way over the shingle, valiant thoughts of an infant Alfred Lord Tennyson rockpooling hereabouts on a visit to his grandfather did little to turn the shore's sullen scowl. The idea of Andrew Marvell sitting on these banks composing to his coy mistress just seemed silly. It was a place that had seen its own arse. A train stood on the stilts of an absurd pier. For a moment he was tempted to catch it and throw himself at the unknown miles of fen and wold beyond, but he had work tomorrow. One oughtn't turn up to a new job *completely* unprepared. Ah yes, the necessity to earn a livelihood hunkering down on one like a farting toad.

He could still barely believe he had the job. The interview had been a twenty-minute chat in the British library reading room. The panel, well, the pair interviewing him had practically begged him to take up the post. They'd waxed lyrical about his growing reputation in academic circles, felt confident he could continue his innovative and intellectually rigorous librarianship up north, and basically licked his bibliographical arse. How an earth did he come to have a bibliographical arse, let alone a reputation in librarianship? He'd only become a librarian in order to keep out of khaki.

The librarian with the growing reputation was examining a spectacularly dead fish when the ferry hooted. He looked at his watch. The return journey commenced in five minutes. Lord, think of being marooned here!

'Sorry, Sir,' said the official blocking the companionway when Merryweather arrived breathless. 'The ship's sailed.'

'No it hasn't,' rasped Merryweather.

'Well it should have, according to the timetable.'

'But it's still here. Look, the companionway's still in place. I could just step onto it.'

'No, you couldn't.'

'Yes, I could.'

'No, you couldn't.'

'Yes, I could.'

The pantomime ended with Merryweather lifting a leg to mount the companionway just as the official, British Rail insignia glinting on his forage cap, uncoupled it. Falling, the companionway head-butted the quay. 'I told you, you couldn't,' said the official.

So, the unions were spreading their kingdom into rivers and sea too. What next, nationalise the bloody sky? Quarter of an hour later, in a screeching hoot and a belch of smoke, the Royal Princess pulled out minus one of her passengers. Sitting on a rock, Merryweather watched the ferry labour toward the distant fish dock. The tide crept in; shorebirds fed; the train on the pier left. It took an age for the ferry to return; really, one would think it was traversing the Malacca Straits not this grey, mud creek. It was late afternoon by the time he got back to his digs. 'Now you've done it,' Teesdale pronounced, appearing at the front door just as Merryweather was opening it.

'How do you mean?' the librarian asked.

'Only gone and missed Sunday dinner. She made it specially for you. Roast, horseradish, Yorkshires, the works. I don't know how she does it with the rationing.' Merryweather was halfway up the stairs when Teesdale called after him. 'Woah, Tonto, where do you think you're going?'

'I have things to prepare for tomorrow,' the librarian replied, irritated that he'd dignified Teesdale's impertinence with an answer.

'How's that fair on the rest of us? You don't seem to understand, she even made gravy. Likely you've set her off for the rest of the week. No, no, no, old man. Fair's fair, you can't leave her to stew. Go and talk her round. That was one thing Bleaney was an expert at.'

Miss Glendenning was in her 'private parlour', the downstairs room opposite the dining area. She didn't look as though she was stewing. Lying in a nest of cake crumbs, doilies, an emptied two-pint teapot, a filled-in pools coupon, and enough balls of wool to cross the river and back a hundred times, she was snoozing contentedly. For a moment the librarian wondered why she reminded him of an overfed anaconda. Then he realised her false teeth, protruding from a wide, slack mouth, gave the look of a python's gymnastic jaw. Far more seriously, he wondered why the bloody hell he wasn't creeping away, packing those few belongings which he'd unpacked, and letting himself out the frigging front door. He could spend the night at the Royal Station Hotel and choose one of those other lodgings. The place with the outside bog would be preferable to this. Mind made up on this course of action, he was just tiptoeing away when he heard a distinct hiss – false teeth being sucked in. 'Oh, hello, Mr Merryweather.'

'Sorry for bothering you,' Merryweather mumbled. 'Come to apologise. About Sunday dinner.'

A chubby hand waved exoneration. 'Oh, these things happen.'

'You see, I just didn't realise,' Merryweather continued, cursing himself for bothering to explain instead of getting the hell out of it.

A smile tipping into a simper as she sat up. 'I won't hear another word. Come and sit down.' Knocking aside the balls of wool with a cavalier elbow, she gave the spot beside her a mischievous spank. Full of misgivings, he obeyed. The give in the two-person sofa took him by surprise, as did the sudden alignment of thighs. 'Been getting to know your new congregation, Mr Merryweather?' For some reason he nodded. 'I like a man with religion. Methodist?' Again, a fatuous nod. 'As a youth, Mr Bleaney was strictly chapel. You know, you remind me of him.'

Then followed a discourse on the habits of her erstwhile lodger, not the least uninteresting of which was the fact that he varied the times he rose of a morning. On Mondays, she explained, his Westclox rang at twenty past seven so that he might be at the breakfast table for twenty-five minutes to eight and could therefore trick his body into thinking it was still the weekend; every other morning a quarter past alarm brought him down for half-past seven, until Friday when he set his alarm clock at ten past so that he could be ready for his kippers at twenty-five past seven, thus guarding against any sloppiness of thinking it was already the weekend. 'Everything done just so, on the dot, nothing left to chance, well, that was Mr Bleaney's way.'

Only the landlady's bladder saved Merryweather further torture. Retreating upstairs, he found Teesdale sitting on his bed. The man in fur rose anxiously. He was crowned with sweat. 'How goes it with the lady of the house, old man?'

'Nothing the matter with her,' Merryweather replied tersely.

Like a character in some restoration farce, Teesdale heaved a gargantuan sigh of relief. He seemed only a step away from kissing Merryweather's hand profusely. Instead he took a fag from the librarian's spare box of Park Drives lying on the chair; by the famished look of the packet, and the smoke-filled air, he must have been helping himself all day. The sound of the toilet chain being pulled was followed by the clangs and hissing swills of the plumbing that fretted the area above Merryweather's ceiling like the web of an iron spider. 'Wait a bit,' said Teesdale, holding up a finger until the chain was pulled again, followed by the sluicing and banging of pipes. 'McCoist,' the man in fur explained. 'His Sunday sessions take a bit of shifting. If I were you I'd stay clear of the bog for a good half hour. And whilst we're on the subject, wedge the bathroom door.'

'Beg pardon?'

'When you have your tub tonight. Sunday was always Bleaney's night in the hot tub. Not that he bothered to keep it closed. Up to you of course, if you don't mind a visitor.'

'Are you trying to warn me that Miss Glendenning will attempt to gain access to the bathroom when I'm in the tub, Teesdale?'

'I'll leave that up to you to decide, boyo. Only make sure you *do* have your tub. Nothing annoys her more than playing fast and loose with her immersion.'

Later, in the (not so) hot tub, reading a detective story written by another one of his Oxford friends, Merryweather was glad he'd taken Teesdale's advice. The lockless bathroom door handle turned. 'Hello?' Merryweather called. The chair he'd used to wedge the door creaked as a shoulder shunted the other side. 'The bathroom's engaged!' the librarian cried.

Footsteps receding down the landing. A stifled giggle? Heaving himself out of the bath, Merryweather towelled off as quickly as he ever could.

Lying on the Reading gaol bed he wrote to his successful friend, *this place may be even worse than I thought.* To his mother he wrote, *the lodgings are mainly clean.* Knowing how she worried he crossed out *mainly*.

That night he was again woken by the phone. Having nearly fallen down the stairs, he fumbled for the receiver, only to find no one on the line, unless he could hear light breathing, yes, he could. Was it the girl again? Pressing down the cradle, he left the phone off the hook. It had nothing to do with him. Don't get involved.

The others' snoring reverberated round the landing as Merryweather ascended the stairs and passed down the lino to his room. He climbed into bed. At last, curiosity getting the better of him, he stole to the window and lifted a curtain corner. 'Bleaney's bint' stood under the hawthorn, staring up at what had been Mr Bleaney's room. Good god, was she there every night?

The librarian was a long time falling asleep again. No sooner had he drifted off than the Westclox was summoning him. He was at the breakfast table for seven-twenty-five on the dot. 'I like a man who's regular in his habits,' approved the kipper-bearing landlady.

8.

Hiding behind his (local) morning newspaper on the trolley, Merryweather felt as though he were going not to a library but a hospital for the prognosis of some lump. The Monday morning breakfast table repeated on him as much as the kippers: that barrage of sauce bottles, chewing jaws and bad breath.

Contrary to expectations, a pleasant surprise awaited him at the university. Instead of the utilitarian, redbrick barrack rising from a raw building site his successful novelist friend had led him to expect, he found half hidden in lawns and willows, a country house brocaded with ivy. A post box was quickly located, and the weekend's letters dispatched. At the Aide to the Vice-Chancellor's office he had to wait for half an hour. 'What does he want?' he heard the administrator ask his secretary.

'Something about the library, sir.'

'Library? What does he want with the library?'

'You appointed him as the new head librarian, Sir.'

'Did I?'

Throughout their brief cup of tea, the Aide to the Vice-

Chancellor continually rearranged pens on his desk as though working out some enigmatic puzzle. His curly beard and fringe gave him the look of a merino sheep. This ovine resemblance reminded the librarian that the man on the other side of the desk had been the silent partner in the interviewing panel at the British library, though he clearly didn't remember Merryweather. 'Found digs yet, Merriman?'

'Yes, thank you.' His mother's son, in the face of authority Merryweather demurred from making correction.

The Aide to the Vice-Chancellor paused in his pen arranging. 'The town does have *some* good areas; I've always maintained that. How do you find arrangements on the river? Yes we are rather out on a limb. Where the train runs out, the land too, wot? And we're just left with the mud and the sky. The natives, well you might like them or you might not; on the whole the students can sometimes be keen. Not a bit like that dreadful novel doing the rounds.' Merryweather suppressed a grin. His friend, and chief correspondent, was the writer of the deliciously scandalous academic novel doing the rounds. 'Well, no doubt you'll be anxious to see your little fiefdom. Very good of you to come in today, Merriman. Above and beyond…'

Was *everybody* off their rocker here? The librarian puzzled as, interview over, he headed in the direction the Aide to the Vice-Chancellor's secretary had pointed out.

Merryweather's fiefdom was yet another surprise. Had his luck changed? Leaning out of some children's story, a pair of manorial gateposts offered a secretive avenue of chestnut trees. The avenue graciously ushered the librarian to a brownstone building bearing the simple sign: Library. In summer, that dead wood adhering to the walls would be rambling roses; spring, when it arrived, promised bluebells. For now, a robin piped the melancholy carol of a T.S. Eliot April; all that was missing was a gardener's fork for it to perch on and begin conducting the way to a secret garden. And there was the garden fork!

Not a city sound to be heard as the new head librarian mounted his library steps for the first time. Above the door, a sculpted stone figure in the art deco style reclined on lintel. The figure – reclining or hovering? – peered down at him. Was it an angel? Art deco, the final and least expected touch. The ghosts of Evelyn Waugh's bright young things. Et in Arcadia Ego blah, blah, blah. That was one thing about librarianship, it might be sexless and bloody boring, but, like a convalescence from a good bout of measles, it gave one plenty of time to read.

The angel watched Merryweather push and pull the entrance door, shunt and shove, thrust and shoulder. All in vain, it was locked. No sign of anyone within. No lights. Nose pressed against the glass, all the new man could see was a darkling, marble vestibule. Skulking in the shadows like a Neanderthal peering from his cave, the bust of some beetle-browed philanthropist frowned at the disturber of his peace. Knocking unanswered, Merryweather got on his knees and called through the low letterbox.

'Oi!' A shout from the chestnuts. The librarian struggled to his feet. Was it directed at him? 'Yes, you, you lanky sod. What's your game?'

For a moment, he thought the person breaking from the undergrowth, all whirring arms and neck, was a policeman. Only when the official reached him did the librarian realise his mistake. 'I'm trying to get in,' Merryweather explained.

'Oh you are, are you? Well you're not going to.' Not the sprightliest of men, the college porter was out of breath. 'Can't you see it's closed?' Merryweather's trilby, tie, briefcase and British Warm seemed to mollify the custodian. 'Thought you were some grubby student.'

'Actually – I'm the new head librarian.'

Torn between suspicion and a professional sense of caste,

the porter took off his hat and scratched his head. 'Didn't they tell you? Nowt's open today. No students. Nothing.' Suspicion reared to the fore. 'How do I know you're who you say you are? No one told me. I didn't even know the last one had gone.'

Feeling rather ludicrous, Merryweather opened his briefcase to bring out a copy of *The Library*, the journal of the Bibliographical Society. The porter flipped through the pages with a yawn. 'No, I don't suppose you'd read something like that unless you really were a librarian.'

'Well exactly.'

The porter fell back on the eternal sigh of his breed, as well as the habitual mix of pronouns. 'Better come with me, sir, and I'll see if we can't sort you out for yourself. I'm Harry. Harry Oxley.'

Harry led him back up the chestnut avenue and across a chain of secluded lawns to where a more municipal, Winifred Holtbyish building stood. A hushed maze of parquet floors contained the porter's lodge. Merryweather was installed on an ancient chair beneath an enormous dovecote of pigeonholes. Smelling the lodge's varied woods and listening to the porter on the phone, he felt gratitude for having missed both the war and national service. Easy to imagine a rifle range, wet feet, and the porter, a sergeant major, explaining how to strip a Bren gun for the hundredth time. Four separate phone calls had to be made, two of them trunk. At last the hugest bunch of keys Merryweather had ever seen was plucked from a hook. 'If you'd like to come along with me, Mr M.' Jingling like some Dickensian turnkey, the porter led him back through the parquet labyrinth, over the lawn, through the enchanted gates and down the chestnut avenue to the library. 'That wants taking down,' Harry declared, looking up at the angel as he unlocked the door. 'Or one of these fine days it'll come down and crush a student flat.'

Passing through the philanthropist's marble gaze, they entered the library proper. After the imposing entrance and almost grand vestibule, the first impression was frankly underwhelming. Something about the size of a real tennis court presented itself. Less fiefdom than corner shop. Well, not quite that bad. As Merryweather's eyes grew accustomed to the half-light, he saw that the shelves were almost spectacularly tall. They towered into a shadowed silence bound by a lofty gallery. Above that, high windows. Following Harry, Merryweather found that the premises had a second, identical room, which gave access to a couple of smaller reading rooms. In total, the whole concern was on the scale of a thriving branch library. The high windows gave the vague feel of a mausoleum. Merryweather felt half at home. When Harry switched a flick, the gruelly light barely thickened. 'Bloody bulb's gone again,' he said, voice amplified to a giant's timbre by the cavernous emptiness. 'Pardon my French.'

There was another surprise. Following his guide between tight, dark shelves, the new librarian stepped into a well of light. A dome rose high above him. It had been hidden from him by the tall stacks. A metal staircase wound steeply up the side of the dome. 'Careful coming up here, Sir.' The steps creaked as the pair mounted them, the echo rippling through the several deeps of the library. 'They all like this?' the porter asked, stopping halfway up.

'Beg pardon?' asked Merryweather, not sure the stairs were exactly safe.

'Are all libraries so loud?'

'I've never really thought about it.'

'They're supposed to be quiet, but they're not, not when nobody's in them. It's only when they're full that they're quiet. What do you make of that?'

'Interesting,' said the new head librarian only quarter lying.

The winding stair led to a smoked glass door marked *Head Librarian* in rather skittish swirls. The porter opened up. By some architectural sleight of hand, instead of the storeroom attic Merryweather had been expecting, the room was commodious to the point of extravagance. Decorous cornices, oil paintings, armchairs, and, wonderfully incongruous, a chaise longue. Two pairs of generous windows to boot. After the crypt-like library, the view – chestnut avenue, gateposts, a lawned middle distance bound by tree-lined road – opened up like the vista from a headland. 'Its acoustic is the opposite of a theatre,' Merryweather said, without turning from the window. 'That's what makes them so loud. Libraries. Paradoxically so, given all the signs for silence.' His eyes narrowed as he continued to gaze at the view whose limit was described by a bicycle trolling through a tracery of leafless branches. 'A theatre is designed for projection, a library, introspection. On stage, one seeks to be heard by hundreds, a library has a far greater ambition. It aims to reach…' Merryweather broke off. He could see Harry making off under the chestnuts. 'And so forth.'

Shoulders easing with this unexpected bonanza of solitude, Merryweather sat at his desk. Solid as a tug. Just as well, more than likely it would be required to haul him into the waters of middle-age. Perhaps beyond. It offered all the tools of the trade. Ink bottle, ink well, blotting paper, telephone, in and out trays, an ashtray (plain), pen holder (rather decorative), enough drawer space for concealing a dismembered corpse let alone a bottle of Glenlivet, paper too, sufficient thereof for the writing of a novel. Except his novel-writing days were over, that was a business best left to his successful friend. Merryweather suppressed a belch of regret, but it was that morning's kippers not the brace of his own unsuccessful novels, which had found little favour with the reading public when published just after the war. With the nearly pleasurable air of being a ship's captain finding himself alone not only on his bridge but on the whole vessel, Merryweather lit the fire from the ample basket of logs, and then his first Park Drive of the day. A relatively exciting though not entirely trustworthy feeling flickered with the flames as he sat on the chaise longue: he'd be able to write poetry here. Reaching into his breast pocket, he felt for his *Lyflat* notebook

Wouldn't want to be pissed coming down these, the new head librarian mused an hour or so later descending the winding stairs. Stroke of luck arriving on a day when there was no one else. He wandered the book aisles. One by one pleasures dwindled, but not this; to be alone in a library was the nearest he would ever come to happiness. Alone – how did Shelley put it? A good library provided one with the choice society of ages. These deceptively quiet shelves housed a bustling city: lovers, murderers, cheats, frauds, heroes, villains, swashbucklers, losels, loblolly men, the lot. Humdrummers too and downright failures. No doubt Merryweather's own fictional counterpart was hiding here on some obscure page sucking the lemon of his bad luck. Every emotion, prayer, thought, deed, disappointment, hope, victory, disillusionment. Life, without having to go through the shit yourself.

He'd just reached his beloved 800. aisle when Merryweather stopped dead. Had the porter come back, or was someone else in the library? No, just the slowly sifting motes of dust. Still gloriously alone, he looked up at the poetry. There was Thomas Hardy. Top shelf; pity for a man who suffered vertigo all his life. Wheeling over the mounted stepladder, he slowly scaled the precarious rungs to about the height of Juliet's balcony. The copy of Thomas Hardy seemed to rise to his hand. 'What are you doing here?'

At the sudden voice, Merryweather nearly fell. 'I – I,' His stammer trespassed on his explanation as he searched for the woman speaking.

She seemed somewhere up on the gallery in Ancient History, but when she spoke again, appeared to have wandered down into Economics in the adjoining chamber. 'We're not open you know.'

'Mr Oxley let me in.' The stammer obliterated the porter's name.

'Who?'

'Porter. I'm M-Merryweather.'

When he finally saw her, he realised the library acoustics were not to be trusted. All the while she'd been just on the other side of the shelf from him in Myths and Legends. Also up a ladder, she was now leaning round the end of the bookcase, peering at him.

'Mr Merryweather, the new head librarian?'

Pale in the frail frame of light, she was still beautiful. Way beyond my league, he knew instantly. The thought helped him to a self-deprecating smile. 'Mr Arthur Merryweather. The new…' A modest cough. 'The new bod.'

'Oh.' Her sudden blush made her seem lovelier, as did the preposterous yet somehow magical transaction of their leaning out and shaking hands. 'I'm so sorry, Mr Merryweather. We weren't expecting you until the middle of the week.'

'So I gather.'

'I'm Miss O'Leary.'

They both descended their stilts, and met on the junction between Myths and Literature. The new head librarian's heart leapt all the higher whilst his head grew more certain of their disparity. Salmon do not shoal with chubb. 'What must you think of me, Mr Merryweather?' That blush again. 'It's just I thought you were an intruder.'

'No, I'm not an intruder. At least I hope I'm not. How does one go about making a cup of tea in these parts?'

The water slowly heated over a gas ring in the frigid, windowless cupboard that didn't even try to pass as a staff room. 'Let's take the pot upstairs. There's a fire up there,' said

Merryweather. He'd long since schooled himself into acting confidently, almost debonairly when he was certain that he couldn't exist romantically for a woman. Thus he was now able to mount a flight of steep, twisting, creaking metal stairs with a fanciable girl like Miss O'Leary whilst carrying a tray of full teapot, cups and saucers, and little milk jug, without spillage. 'Please sit down,' he said, placing the tray on the desk.

'Thank you,' she said, sitting opposite him. He poured her a cup, and handed it over – hand free from shaking. 'Thank you,' she said again. Watching her new boss stir in her sugar, Niamh O'Leary stopped herself from thanking him a third time and wondered whether she ought to offer the digestives in her string shopping bag. She thought not. After all she was only an *assistant* librarian. Then she wondered what he'd been writing in the notebook, which had been open on the desk, and now lay under the tray. It had looked like poetry.

Ought one to offer her a cigarette? Merryweather wondered. He decided not. 'Well, it all seems very nice,' he said. 'The library, university and so forth.'

'I hope you're going to be happy here, Mr Merryweather,' she said.

A half grin. 'Oh, I doubt I'll be happy, but I may well be a little less unhappy.'

Her sudden laugh, taking flight in the airiness of his office like a charm of goldfinches, astonished him. 'Oh, I didn't mean to imply…' she began, but his grin, three-quarters full now, showed her that he hadn't taken offence, had in fact *meant* to be funny. Everyone had said the new broom would be stuck up, but even though he'd been at Oxford and was at best a Protestant, *and* he hadn't even come up for an interview making *them* go down to London, this balding, somewhat gangling, jam jar-eyed man wasn't stuck up at all. 'I'm sorry I was so sharp downstairs, Mr Merryweather. It's just with the robbery.'

'Robbery?'

'Hasn't anyone told you?'

'No.'

'Broke the safe in the University finance office. They took over three hundred pounds. There was a whole spate of robberies in the town. At the Royal Station Hotel, a billiard hall, and a jewellers. Quite the biggest thing ever to happen in this town since they invented battered fish, and...' I'm talking too much, Niamh admonished herself. 'And – they still haven't caught them.'

How lovely she is, Merryweather reflected. Catching the lights of the fire and windows, her fair hair sparked with ginger flames – didn't one call that strawberry blonde? Set firmly by some lady's product, nevertheless it seemed just waiting to catch a breeze to be cast loose. When she talked, her eyes sparkled like the sun on a raindrop. A nauseatingly sentimental observation, but in her case bloody true. 'The whole place seems ship shape,' he said when she caught him staring. Stumbling over the words slightly, he was profoundly relieved not to have said 'shit shape'.

'Yes,' she said. 'It's a good library.'

The new head librarian was on his second cup before he dared a glance at his companion's breasts. A crucifix was on guard. You won't need that with me, he reflected sadly. He strode over to the window. 'Really is a lovely view.'

With her new boss at the window, Niamh tidied up the tea things, and managed a quick peek at the notebook. It *was* poetry. He was a poet! Ever since a little girl, Niamh O'Leary had dreamt of meeting a poet. True, they hadn't looked like this in her dreams; hard to imagine Mr Merryweather shouldering a calf from the byre all crackling with frost like P.J. Kavanagh; or, like Yeats, staking (and ruining) his life on an infatuation. Hard even to imagine him falling helplessly and irredeemably in love with an unlettered milkmaid like Thomas Hardy. But he was a poet, that's all that mattered. Her crucifix rose and fell with excitement. A good type of excitement, or not? Niamh had reached the age of twenty-eight and still couldn't tell the difference. Not the kind of thing you asked Father Carrick.

When Merryweather turned, he found her eyes, lamb large, fixed on him. He rode a moment's confusion. 'Look, would you show me round the place, Miss O'Leary?' he asked, quickly composing himself, after all he was supposed to be the boss round here. 'Guided tour sort of thing. Show me the ropes and so forth.'

'Of course, Mr Merryweather,' she replied, deciding that his slight stutter was suitable. Poets ought to have a wound, like Byron and his club foot.

9.

If Merryweather had been requested to outline in advance the events of the first day at his new job, short of Niamh O'Leary actually being naked, he couldn't have come up with anything better. The bright Monday morning dimmed to a foggy afternoon, but the sun remained shining in the library as she 'showed him the ropes'. Under the drifting silences of the library, they went through everything from 000 through to 999, and back again. He even managed to hide his fear of heights as she led him round the gallery. At lunchtime (she called it dinnertime) they shared her sandwiches. 'I always make too many anyway,' she laughed, 'and end up giving half to the sparrows.' They even left work together. He felt a pang when they parted in the fog, each catching a different trolleybus. 'It's ten past six, Mr Merryweather,' his landlady said confronting him in the hall as he returned home.

'So it is.' All afternoon Merryweather hadn't so much as glanced at his wristwatch.

'Ten *past* six. The others are waiting. They aren't best pleased.'

Merryweather found himself being manhandled into the dining room. The fog of overcooked cabbage was as thick as the peasouper outside.

'Where the hell have you been?' McCoist demanded, beard looming from the vapours.

'Play the game,' said Teesdale entirely invisible. 'Tea is at six sharp.'

'I apologise, I wasn't aware of the hour.' Merryweather pulled off his British Warm. 'I've just got back from work. We were busy. Then there was the fog–'

'Means we all have to wait, old man. She won't dish up until all her guests are here.'

The librarian was rammed – there could be no other word for it – into his chair. 'I do not run a roadhouse,' spat Miss Glendenning into his ear. 'Or an all night café.'

'If you're late again, I'll bray you,' said the Scot.

A tea-towelled tornado tore through the kitchen and came back bearing three plates of bubble and squeak. They were dropped before the three diners. A furious battery of sauce bottles. 'Here.' Merryweather flinched as the landlady lunged at him, but she'd merely picked up his cutlery. For one absurd moment he thought she was going to start feeding him. Instead, she thrust the knife and fork into his hands, and strode into the kitchen. Slowly the fug cleared to reveal – pigs at trough, the other lodgers were already well into their meals. 'On your tatties?' Miss Glendenning reappeared to upend a gravy boat over Merryweather's plate. 'It's *Bisto*. Well, with you turning up your nose at sauce.'

'Ah – thank you.'

Treacle pudding and custard for afters, both as delicious as the bubble and squeak. 'Now come on, Mr Merryweather,' the landlady smiled, her mood lightening capriciously. 'Clean your bowl like the other gentlemen, otherwise I'll think you don't like me. Show him, Mr Teesdale.'

Teesdale held up an empty bowl. 'What says you to a foray to ye olde local?' the man in fur asked, finger pressed against his nose when the landlady had started to wash up.

'I've work to do,' said Merryweather.

Alone in his room, coat and hat hanging on the bed knobs in lieu of a wardrobe, Merryweather lay on the bed, ashtray on heart. How much less ugly would he have to be for Niamh O'Leary to look at him twice? Let her skin lose three-quarters of its clarity, her bosom two-thirds of its lift, let her teeth yellow and her voice grate, and he would still fall for her. Burn much less brightly, and the assistant librarian would yet dazzle. He scored out the line of poetry he'd been writing. It was true but unworthy of its subject. Again the eternal problem of the poet: how not to sound like an arse.

'Oh, Mr Merryweather, I'm glad I've caught you,' said the landlady after the merest of knocks. Stepping into the room, she closed the door with a swing of her hips. Her hair, beribboned and combed up high, sat up on her head like a performing poodle. Her mood had lurched to an arch playfulness. 'Did I startle you? No, don't get up. I've brought you your laundry.'

'Oh, I haven't given you any yet.'

'What's this then, Scotch mist?' She placed a pile of freshly laundered clothes on his chair. Shirt, trousers, and underwear. 'No, don't worry, it's all part of the service – for good little boys.' She was at the door when she turned. Oh God, what now, Merryweather thundered within. 'Are you partial to music, Mr Merryweather?'

'A bit.'

'Knew you would be. Like Gracie Fields, don't you? Mr Bleaney did.'

'I'm a jazz man,' he said, working out how best to make it clear he couldn't have her coming in and out of his room.

'Jazz? Oh.' A flicker of familiar boredom. 'Well, just to let you know there's a radiogram downstairs in my private parlour. Some evenings I allow one of my gentlemen to join me. Can be you tonight, if you like. The *Showcase* is on. I find Archie Andrews a caution, don't you?'

'I wouldn't laugh at Archie Andrews if you held a knife at my goolies,' he didn't say, picturing the hideous ventriloquist's dummy. 'I've rather a lot of work to do,' he did say.

'Oh dear, is Jack going to be a dull boy?'

A simper like a pot of porridge, Merryweather noted for the next letter to his successful friend, *one moment a cabbage-cooking harpy, the next…* Well, if one required any further evidence here it was, God was British. Lo it came to pass, for every Niamh O'Leary there has to be a Mavis Glendenning. Tell her now, he urged himself, tell her to keep the fuck out of your room, or she'll be forever in and out. 'Miss Glendenning I – '

'That won't cause a fire will it?' she demanded.

Merryweather followed her stare to the handkerchief he'd contrived to shade the bulb's glare.

'It was rather bright you know.'

'Mr Bleaney never complained.'

'Is there a spare shade somewhere? Or I don't mind purchasing one myself.'

'Mr Bleaney didn't need a shade.'

'My eyes are rather sensitive.'

'And you're saying his weren't?'

'I have no idea, I didn't know him.'

'No. You didn't know him. Now, is there anything else you wanted, Mr Merryweather, only I'm very busy.'

'One thing actually. Do you think you might be so kind as to not just – '

'So odd coming in here and not finding Mr Bleaney,' she interrupted him again. 'Best room in the house, he had it the whole time he was on the Bodies, right until – they moved him.' The top two studs of Mavis Glendenning's housecoat paffed open as she sat beside her new lodger. The springs positively shrieked. Her thigh stole in against his like a cat. 'The others are going out tonight,' she whispered. 'So it'll just be little old me all alone on the lovely soft settee listening to Archie Andrews. Oh, I understand. Took Mr Bleaney time to come out of himself too. He was a loner an' all. You get to spot the type in my trade. Truth is he'd have spent the rest of his life moping up here if I hadn't brought him out of himself. *You really brought me out of myself, Mavie.* His words, Mr Merryweather. His words. Are we going to have to take you out of yourself?'

'I'm really very busy.' Merryweather tried to rise. A hand restrained him.

'You know something, Mr Merryweather, Arthur? You've a look of him. In a certain light, it can catch a body quite unawares.' Striking with the speed of a snake, she took off his glasses. Befogged, Merryweather lurched away from a trespassing hand, and staggered to his feet. The ashtray was sent tumbling. A crack underfoot; a crack in his landlady's voice. 'Now look what you've done.' When he'd found his glasses, the landlady was pressing the souvenir ashtray saucer to her breast like a Wagner contralto her dead warrior. 'You stood on it.'

'If I've broken it, I'll pay,' Merryweather said. 'You know, replace it.'

'*Replace* it?' The word vibrated in the box room like the top notes in an aria. Two handed, she lifted the saucer above her head. Catching the light, the ceramic blazed into life. It was a seaside scene. A sweep of glazed sands meeting a cerulean sea under a flawlessly blue sky. Seagulls tumbling over a varnished pier. *I'm from Frinton-on-Sea, please make good use of me,* decorative lettering rhymed round the rim. A crack had sundered the seasidescape, and when the landlady dropped her hands, each held half of the painted resort. 'Replace it? This couldn't be replaced for all the money in the world.'

The librarian knew he'd regret it but: 'Why not?' After all, it was the kind of knick knack produced in its thousands.

A gulp. 'His.' Another gulp. 'Souvenir.' A third gulp as she relinquished the broken ashtray. The pieces dropped to the floor. 'Mr Bleaney went to Frinton every July.' Despite the immensity of her loss, a memory seemed to trick a smile. 'He lived for that fortnight. Thought about nothing else for weeks before. And afterwards. Well, that were him all over, if Mr Bleaney took a fancy to something, he took a fancy to it. Like with the wireless radiogram. Went on and on until I bought it. Should have heard him. Oh, when it came to that radiogram he could have sold ice cream to the Eskimos. *With a radiogram you're never alone, Mavie; with a radiogram you've got the world in your private parlour, Mavie; with a radiogram you've an ear pressed to every wall, Mavie.* Wouldn't countenance records being played on the turntable on a Sunday, mind you. Not with his Methodist upbringing. That radiogram was as much his as his ashtray. Only I don't think he'll be coming back for either of them, do you?' Good God, was she actually waiting for an answer? Instead, Merryweather took out his wallet. There was a ten shilling note. Before he could find some change, she'd snatched the note.

The landlady finally gone, there was hardly time to put the halves of broken ashtray on the windowsill, and, taking out the latest letter, slip in a couple of extra paragraphs about the insuperable woman before once again the door handle was turning.

'Did you say you had a newspaper?' a string-vested Teesdale demanded.

To get rid him of him, Merryweather tossed across his paper. But opening out the local rag over the bed, Teesdale sat down, and having helped himself to the Park Drives on the chair under the washing proceeded to give a commentary on all the news of the river town.

'I've read it for myself actually, Teesdale.'

The man in fur continued with his local digest. Both rugby teams lost again, bad for business, but at least fish prices were steady. 'You'll soon find that fish rule the roost in this neck of the woods.' More talk of a bridge, 'the bridge from nowhere to nowhere as I call it.' An annual bill of a hundred pounds to wash all the municipal windows. And then, 'Good God, how long's it going to go on for?'

Merryweather held out against the bait as long as he could. 'How long's what going to go on for?'

'They still don't know who did it, you know.'

'Did what?' the librarian asked, cursing his vapid curiosity

'Oh I keep on forgetting, you're new to the Wild West. It was big news in these parts. For weeks you heard of nothing else.'

The bait knocked aside at last. 'Someone been fixing the fish prices?'

'Even bigger than that. There were four of them in a fort-night, you know, safe cracking jobs, and they still haven't got anyone for them. Last one about the same time Bleaney vamoosed. Maybe that's why he did off. Old Bleaney a safe cracker!' A short bray of laughter. Then, 'Hello, hello?' Reaching over to Merryweather's pile of neatly pressed laundry, the man in fur lifted out a girdle. 'I see old Ma Glenners has left a calling card. No doubt she'll be back later to claim her lost property. Anyway can't sit here all night listening to you gas on.' Having broken wind, Teesdale left the room. Through the open door Merryweather watched him head for the toilet. 'Say what you like about this place, old man,' his fellow lodger opined. 'An indoor shitter is one of life's necessities.'

Merryweather had only written a page to his mother when his door was opened again.

'Ready, old man?' A sports jacket, broad check cloth cap, and a cravat had transformed Teesdale into a golf club barstool bore.

Whether Teesdale was being deliberately obtuse or not, it took Merryweather fully ten minutes to satisfy him that he really wasn't going to the *Shoulder of Mutton*. Alone again, Merryweather continued with his mother's letter: the library is small but compact… good food at the lodgings… a laundry service… I'll come home for a visit once I've settled in…

A laundry service. Picking up Miss Glendenning's misplaced 'smalls', he tiptoed to the bathroom, and hung the girdle from the pendulous clothes-horse – a rather grand name for the flimsy rack dangling from the mouldy ceiling. Back in his room, he heard a volley of hysterical laughter from downstairs. Laughter? It could equally be the screams of a massacre. The floorboard began to bounce with banal music. The famous radiogram had been switched on.

Even with cotton wool in his ears, Merryweather could hear the demented jabbering. How could one concentrate? Impossible to read, write (neither a letter to his sister nor poetry), or even think. Driven to bay, he snatched up the pieces of ashtray as though to hurl them against the wall. Something stayed his hand – *I'm from Frinton-on-sea, please make good use of me.* Frinton, where had he heard of that before? Wasn't it that godforsaken place on the Essex coast, the seaside town with no pubs? Yes, the dry resort. Good God, think of that. Not only had this Mr Bleaney lived in a fusty box the size of a police cell, entertaining himself with old Ma Glendenning and Archie Andrews, but he'd holidayed at Frinton to boot. The letters to his novelist friend were off mark. He'd strayed not into a comedy but a tragedy.

Lying on his bed, the two broken halves of the ashtray on his heart, Merryweather stared at the dangling bulb barely tamed by the hankie. Then he gazed at the laundry on the rickety chair. After this he studied the hookless door, followed by the pieces of ashtray. Periodically a draught bellied the curtains so that an overactive imagination might suggest someone trying to get in, or out. Then he began at the bulb again just as Mr Bleaney might have done before *you really brought me out of myself, Mavie.*

This thought drove the librarian from the room.

He crept down the stairs. The parlour door was ajar. The librarian couldn't resist a quick peek. Obviously the Scotsman had changed his mind about going out, or had had it changed for him because there he was on the settee with the landlady. All three gas fire panels bubbling, two heads close on the anti-macassars. A mirror on the wall showed each face caught in the net of the radiogram. Mr McCoist's grin was massive and piercingly childlike: a giant entranced by fairies. Knitting without looking down at what she was doing, the landlady was Madame Defarge at the guillotine. 'Is that you, Mr Merryweather?'

How the flying frig had she heard him? 'No, it's the ghost of your precious Mr Bloody Bleaney come back for his ruddy ashtray,' Merryweather didn't say. 'Just going for a constitutional,' he did say. 'You know, given one's sedentary job.'

Her reply was drowned out by the tossed caber of the Scotsman's (and wireless audience's) laughter. '… and the door's locked at ten.'

'And this bloody time, it'll no be opened again.'

Looming suddenly out of the fog, a cream of wheat telephone box waylaid Merryweather as he made for the *Shoulder of Mutton.* Was this the one used by the girl under the hawthorn? He'd already piled his coppers and lifted the receiver when he thought better of it. His lady friend wanted a wedding ring, he wanted comradeship with occasional sex, and ne'er the twain should mate. Those doomed to drown ought not to clutch at others, lepers should wander the hinterland alone, and so fucking forth.

The fog made the *Shoulder of Mutton* almost picturesque in a Jack the Ripper's Whitechapel kind of way. It was more crowded than Merryweather would have liked. Teesdale had his nose deep in some reading matter. Without looking up, the man in fur gave an imperious gesture and called over, 'mine's a pint of best.'

'Well, look who it isn't,' the barmaid greeted the librarian with a grin. It was the headscarfed woman from the trolley.

'It's Burlington Bertie,' the clippie sang from down the bar.

'He's risen before ten-thirty,' added the driver at his elbow.

'That's what they call you round here,' the barmaid explained. 'You know, the old music hall song, I'm Burlington Bertie…'

'I rise at ten-thirty,' Merryweather finished wanly. He thought for a moment about ordering wine, but didn't want to draw any unwelcome attention. 'A couple of pints please, and whatever you and your friends want.' He indicated the clippie and driver, his natural nearness tempered by the old drinkers' adage to be on good terms at the local. 'Since it's my first time,' he added by way of caution.

'You're a gent, Burlington. Port and lemon for me. Pints for the boys. I'm Kathleen. We're next-door neighbours.' She winked. 'And how are you finding the woman of the house? You just be careful. Or she'll get her claws into you like she did with that last poor bugger. Pity, he was all right at first. Not a relative, are you? Brother, cousin?'

'No.'

'That's fast moving,' said Teesdale grudgingly when Merryweather joined him. 'In with Kathleen already.'

'I'd hardly call it "in with".'

'Took months before she knew my name.'

'I'm not actually called Burlington Bertie.'

'Well, you've certainly caught her eye. Another ladykiller, eh? No offence, but who'd have thought it at first dekko? Same could be said about Bleaney I suppose. Anyway, with you in two ticks, sahib.' Teesdale returned to his booklet. A brochure? The local commercial directory, Merryweather ascertained through his professional ability to read upside down. Teesdale's moving lips, intent face, and finger doggedly following the print line, just as surely revealed his reading type to the librarian: *Sunday Express* by obligation, *News of the World* by inclination, comics by choice. If forced into the world of adult books, Sapper or similar. 'The bible,' Teesdale announced, holding up the directory whilst tapping his nose in the way that was already beginning to irritate Merryweather. 'Anyone who's anyone is in here.' The pub fire roared, and the jewels of sweat on Teesdale's brow formed a tiara. 'Even our old friend's in. Look.' Teesdale turned the pages of the beer-soaked, dog-eared, glorified pamphlet. 'In the Bodies section. Say what you like about him, he knew how to sell himself, listen to this: *Life is full of uncertainty from unfortunate accidents to untimely death…* (Well he's right there, old man.) *…allow Mr Bleaney, sole agent of Riverside Life Assurance, to give you piece of mind no matter what calamitous and sadly tragic events wait in store, be it a broken ankle or massive heart attack. Businesses catered for.*'

'Is that why one calls it the Bodies?' Merryweather asked, not quite able to squelch a yawn. 'Life assurance I mean, because it deals with death?' No answer. Teesdale was thumbing through the directory with such doglike determination that the librarian was driven to ask: 'What are you looking for?'

'Old commando saying. Know thy enemy. Remember I was telling you about some bugger muscling in on my patch?'

'No.'

'Try to keep up, Merryweather. Little birdie at the Royal Station Hotel told me I've got a rival, and the fur world's not big enough for two. Especially in pleb town.' Teesdale's eyes glinted like a skinner's blade as he continued to search, before closing the directory to become the genial hail-fellow-well-met irritant again. 'Not in here whoever he is.' He accepted a cigarette. 'Actually, since you ask, I'm thinking of doing a Mr Bleaney myself.'

'You're thinking of a doing a "safe-cracking job"?'

'Hey?'

'You said before that maybe this Mr Bleaney was behind the safe jobs.'

'No, no what I mean is this, I've got big plans. Don't know about you but I'm not here to stay. Going to bugger off just like Bleaney. I've a toe in a consignment coming from foreign fields. Whole new way of doing things.' Finger to tulip bulb nose again. 'All I'll say is, goodbye mink, say farewell sable.' Teesdale reached into a jacket pocket and produced a small sample of fur. 'Give him a stroke, old man, won't bite.'

'Another one of your giant hamsters?'

'Hamster no; what gave you that idea? This is rat.' Merry-weather removed his hand. 'Think about it, millions of rats in the world, nobody wants them,' Teesdale continued. 'In fact the opposite. But what many people don't know is that the rat carries a lovely pelt. The only glitch is the bald patch where the tail was. Bit like your pate, old man.'

'Did *he* have a toe in a foreign field?'

'Who?'

'Our Mr Bleaney?'

'No, strictly a home bird.'

'Yet he disappeared.'

'Look here, why are you so interested in Mr Bleaney?'

'I'm not, it's just that everyone else seems to be. Mr Bleaney and his remarkable vanishing act.'

'Rather a dramatic way of putting it. Next you'll be saying old Ma Glenners really did do him in. Actually I was the last one to see him. *I might be some time.* That's what he said when I met him on the stairs carrying his suitcase. A real Captain Oates job. *I might be some time, would you mind cutting the grass when necessary?* I told him to sod off. Truth be known, old Bleaney was bit of an oddbod. Had this system with the pools. Like a mania with him. Something to do with away wins for the East Anglian teams and sea temperatures. He was a crank really. Stiff as a parson, then all of a sudden he went off the rails.' For an instant Teesdale was reflective. 'Supposed to be bad luck isn't it? Crossing on the stairs.'

'Funny name,' Merryweather mused.

'What is?'

'Bleaney.'

'Still harping on that, old man?'

'It's a sort of food. A kind of pancake. They eat it in Poland. A blini.'

'What are you wittering on about? Now, a pal of mine said he was a college walla, not from these parts.'

'Who, Mr Bleaney?'

'For Pete's sake, you and Mr Bleaney. I'm talking about this fellow muscling in on my patch; my chum said he was a real posho. Talked like Charles Laughton, you know when he played Quasimodo. *Do you think you could ever love a man like me?*' Teesdale's imitation of Charles Laughton was surprisingly compelling. '*No, I didn't suppose you could. The bells, the bells!*' The two lodgers' laughter brought stares from the whole pub.

A gallon of ale later, arms around one another's shoulders, the fellow tenants were rolling home through the thick brume. Drizzle made the fog worse. 'Gonna find him,' the man in fur was snarling drunkenly. 'Gonna find that Quasimodo muscling in on my patch. Gonna show him nobody messes with a Teesdale.' He swung a punch at the night and came off second best.

'And I'm going to bloody well ring somebody up,' the librarian slurred.

A King Lear of the fur trade, Teesdale shook his fist at heaven, and raged against the fate of a luxury goods seller in a fish town. At last Merryweather managed to persuade the heavy telephone kiosk door to let him in. Seemed to take an age to dial. He'd only managed two numbers when a fist rapped the glass. 'Making a private phone call,' Merryweather cried with passion. Shaking his head like a dog emerging from water, Teesdale continued trying to get in. 'Bugger off!' yelled Merryweather. 'Got to apologise. She's a fine woman, and I'm a stinker. Don't deserve to be her friend.'

'No good,' declared Teesdale, succeeding in poking his head round the door. 'Didn't leave a phone number.'

'Who didn't?'

'Mr Bleaney.'

Even as he fell to his knees helpless with laughter, Merryweather could hear his mother's childhood warning about the habits of the lower classes in public telephone boxes. What would she make of her bright-eyed boy if she could see him kneeling in a pugwash of fag ends and urine? What would his father think, looking down from his blackshirt heaven? But the idea of ringing Bleaney was just too funny to let him rise. 'Teesdale,' Merryweather said, suddenly and unaccountably finding himself back out in the fog. 'Do you believe in love at first sight? You know, meet a girl and that's it.'

'Thunderbolt job?'

'You see, I was ringing the wrong person. There's someone else I'd much rather talk to.' Merryweather peered up at the stars. There weren't any. 'One look,' he marvelled, 'and – stamp! Your book's on loan forever.'

With supreme bad grace, McCoist let them in. No, I'm not that pissed, Merryweather decided back in Mr Bleaney's room once more. Just merry, just Merryweather. A giggle. At least the wireless had been turned off, no doubt Mr Bloody Bleaney liked to be asleep by twenty-five past ten. Sensible drudge.

The librarian was woken by the telephone. Already the *Shoulder of Mutton's* camaraderie had become a head-thumping misanthropy. Once again no one else was awake. Knocking on the landlady's door did nothing. Coming close to twisting an ankle, he stumped down the stairs. 'Do you know what bloody time it is?' he demanded into the receiver. 'Look, I told you the other night he doesn't live here anymore. I haven't the foggiest idea where. I don't know him from Adam. Now will you bugger off and stop ringing.' Having disconnected the line, he left the receiver off the hook.

Back in bed, Merryweather watched the ash lengthen on his fag, and then drop into the freshly glued ashtray.

Divert them as he might, his thoughts ran to Niamh O'Leary. She was lovely. O, gargantuan understatement. Being with her was like playing postman's knock with Rosalind in the forest of fucking Arden. What poetry could be written about a girl like that? But not by him. Balding, inch-thick specs, increasingly given to bad breath, his were the attributes of a librarian not a troubadour. Slowly the replacement Frinton ashtray filled. Handfuls of rain rattled the windows. He'd have to plug that draught. Once again the snorers competed. Was the girl in the garden again? Nothing to do with him. Yet curiosity eventually provoked him to the curtains. Yes, 'Bleaney's bint' was there, staring up at Merryweather's room, intent as a ghost. The street lamp showed that her hair was bedraggled with the drizzle. He went back to bed. The last thing he wanted was to get involved with a ghost. He had enough trouble avoiding the living.

10.

If Merryweather had been hoping for another cosy day alone with Niamh O'Leary then he should have sodding well known better. Next morning the rest of his staff showed up. 'And so,' he concluded at the end of his first staff meeting. 'One hopes to continue the wonderful traditions of learning and knowledge and so forth, so ably established by my predecessor.'

Through the jute sacking of yet another hangover, the new head librarian dared to glance at Niamh as she left with the rest. Four qualified members of staff, eight unqualified, and one muse. Well, on the whole they all seemed pretty decent. The usual mix of matron, old maid and pedant. Docile. Although one could never tell. Contrary to public opinion, libraries were hotbeds of rivalry and enmity.

Alone in his office, Merryweather was just contemplating what to do next when he heard someone toiling up the metal staircase. Like a third-rate repertory Agatha Christie play, the foot on the stairs took a while to reveal itself. It was Harry Oxley; he was carrying a bulging postbag – well, sack really. 'Shall I send Miss O'Leary up?' the porter asked.

'Beg pardon?'

'Only I expect you'll be needing assistance.' The porter dug a hand into the sack and brought out a sheath of unopened mail. 'Some of your backlog. Been weeks since the last head left. And Miss O'Leary's the fastest typist.'

'What an excellent idea, Harry.'

Did the porter wink as he left? Merryweather had the feeling that that man was going to be a distinct asset.

What might have been a testicle crusher became one of the loveliest mornings Merryweather had ever spent. Clearing a space for Niamh on the other side of the desk, logs crackling on the fire, together they dealt with enquiries from publishers, printers, stationers and booksellers; batted away overly exacting requests from elderly researchers and cranks; apologised to electricity and water boards, and remitted all manner of outstanding bills. Niamh was just finishing the last of two dozen replies on a brand new Olivetti *lettera 23* found in one of the office's many nooks under an avalanche of dusty box files, and Merryweather was standing at the window, fingers tapping to the jazz scats of Niamh's typing whilst enjoying her reflection deep within the glass, when he realised she'd stopped and was staring at him. 'Do you really like Thomas Hardy?' she asked.

'Beg pardon?' he replied, as flustered as he'd ever been.

'I saw you with a copy yesterday, you know when we were up the ladders.'

'Of course I like him; don't you?' he returned, not knowing what else to say.

'He's like a wet weekend in purgatory.' As soon as she'd spoken she regretted it. After all, he was her boss. To her surprise though, Mr Merryweather was nodding.

'Yes, he is rather.' The new head librarian's heart gave a curious lurch as he added: 'In his defence he also happens to be our tenderest love poet.'

At that unexpectedly exciting moment the tête à tête was breached. Someone was standing at the bottom of the stairs singing – of all things – the Red Flag. 'Ernie's here,' beamed Niamh, flushing with pleasure. 'May I go for my dinner?' The flush became a blush. 'I mean, I'm on earlies, Mr Merryweather, may I go to the refs?'

'Of course you may,' said Merryweather, his simple words hiding a Mariner's trench of disappointment – and foreboding.

From the top of the stairs, Merryweather watched Niamh descend to where the baritone singer waited. Muscular arms held in wide appeal, blond hair rippling like wind buggering through the barley, the square-headed bastard was Kirk Douglas down to the cleft in the chin. Still singing the communist anthem, Ernie whisked Niamh away through the 123. shelves, and beyond the fiefdom of the library.

The fly in the ointment, began the new head librarian's postprandial letter to his successful friend, *is some wooden top cunt from the sociology department.*

Lunch had been dreadful. Cold hotpot in a crowded cellar with all the acoustics of a greyhound track. He'd sat alone; Niamh with the blond arsehole. This Ernie, another lone diner informed him, was the university's rising star. Youngest ever lecturer to publish, Oxford and Cambridge were fighting over him but he scorned them as elitist. Not only that, he was a concert hall standard pianist, and the best rugby back on the river.

'Does he always sing communist anthems?' Merryweather had snapped, feeling his demon of indigestion stirring.

That afternoon, realising the folly of feeding any budding feelings for Niamh, the new head librarian returned his assistant to her usual duties and threw himself into other pressing organisational tasks, such as reading Thomas Hardy. Our tenderest love poet? Well, yes. Our most miserable too. And what was wrong with that? After all, only halfwits and tossers were happy.

Despite his resolution, Merryweather found himself inventing a task that took him to the periodicals, a small, panelled area deep within the library over which Niamh presided. Peeping through a thicket of *Times Literary Supplements*, he watched her for a few moments – a nymph in her glade. Then, unwilling to play the balding Centaur, slipped away unseen.

The rest of the day passed somehow. Another meeting, with heads of departments this time, and a 'personal chat' with each of his staff until at last the library was closing, and he was left alone in the office. Normally a connoisseur of solitude, as the cold afternoon lengthened to evening beyond the windows, Merryweather could feel himself tipping into an uncharacteristic loneliness through which the boarding house loomed like a U-boat. A vision of the unwifed, unloved future seemed to mock the stiff senility of his own stooping shadow cast by the fire. Was he really going to spend the rest of his life in a rented room, working in a library, arranging the words of dead men like pinned moths in a collection? Would he ever know love? Weigh a son in his hands; lead a daughter to market on the cockhorse of a knee? Well, he fucking hoped not, and yet how deep the ice of singletude bit this evening. 'Hello,' he said, having picked up the phone and dialled. 'How are you? Yes, it's Arthur, the bad penny. Me? Oh, it's still rather dreadful up here. You know how you were saying about going to the cottage? Well I was thinking, it's April, the leaves will be coming out and the little birds will be singing from every tree. One will be able to have the most marvellously gloomy time in the country. Yes, how about this Friday?'

11.

Between letter writing, reading, smoking incessantly, penning occasional lines of teeth-pullingly bad poetry, some pretty unsatisfactory wanking, and fixing a bolt on his bedroom door, Merryweather made it to the end of the week. Not forgetting the ever faithful Glenlivet. At the library there was almost enough to do to keep his mind off Niamh, especially when the students arrived on the Wednesday. Friday lunchtime loomed at last, and he was just putting on his coat to catch the train when he heard light footsteps on the stair. A knock. 'Come.' Slightly out of breath and bearing a book, Niamh entered the head librarian's office. Beyond civil nods and greetings, they'd barely talked since Tuesday. 'If you really want to know about tenderness,' she said. 'Read this.'

'Thank you, I will,' said Merryweather, heart catching as he accepted the book.

Book under arm, he went to the station. The midday train was heaving. No chance of a compartment to one's self, let alone a seat without neighbours, but when the loose-limbed joker in the duffle coat sitting beside him dug his elbow right into the librarian's ribs, unusually Merryweather didn't elbow him back. Too busy thinking about the Gerard Manley Hopkins book Niamh had given him. Not that he liked the Jesuit poet, good Lord I mean what next, read G.K. Chesterton's Father Brown stories without gouging one's eyes out? No, what he was pondering was why she'd given it to him. Was it a signal; semaphore to show him she sensed he'd backed off and didn't want him to? A sign that Kirk Douglas couldn't give her what she wanted? Balls, balls, balls – *do you think you could ever love a man like me? The bells, the bells!* As Teesdale's berkish Hunchback of Notre Dame said. Knowing that they both enjoyed poetry, it was no more than an impulse for friendship. And wasn't *that* something? Yes and no.

He met his lady friend at a mutually convenient mainline station where they shared a late lunch and the latest news. Or at least she did, telling him all about her recent research work for the English department of a Midlands university. He told her nothing about Niamh of course. It was too late to realise that he oughtn't to be going to the cottage.

Chugging them free of industrial smoke, blighted trees and pinched, proletarian faces, a branch line engine lifted them onto moors. 'But don't you think Shelley's a bit of a tosser?' he asked, digging up an old chestnut.

'Not as much a tosser as Thomas Bloody Hardy,' she grinned, horsey teeth showing in their full glory, ponytail a frayed rope thrown over her shoulder.

Chuckling, he looked at his companion. The telephone lent her a vulnerability she actually lacked, like de-horning a cow.

Easier repulsing her advances in person, easier too to see why she was such a valued friend, in spite of her tendency to talk a load of crap. She spent most of the journey telling him about some characteristically clownish Romantic poet, someone even more ghastly than Shelley; not remotely interested Merryweather felt no need to pretend to be so. From time to time he even permitted himself a sigh. 'No dogs allowed, you know,' she said. 'So kindly set that black one of yours down at the next station.'

'Oh, I couldn't do that. I'm lost without him. He's a guide dog for the misaligned.'

'Oh, that's rather good.' Fumbling for a notebook, she scribbled his words down. He grimaced. 'You'll be glad when you're famous, Arthur.' One of her most persistent lines of attack was through the wide gates of his vanity. 'All the same, I wish you'd cheer up.'

'Oh, sod off.'

He thought for a moment about whether to tell her that her electric green dress didn't set off her complexion to perfection, then decided not to. That wasn't friendship. He allowed her to continue telling him about her Romantic buffoon without howling, which most certainly was.

By the time they arrived at the absurdly remote country station, even Merryweather was ready for the walk. The black dog certainly was, and romped ahead happily savaging some newborn lambs. The wind, untainted by cities, or fish, roared over them. 'Breathe in Britain,' his friend declaimed from a theatrical molehill. 'Absorb the Angles, suspire the Saxons, inhale the ancient Britons.'

'Smell the sheep shit,' said Arthur, regretting having played the gentleman by offering to carry her weekend bag as well as his own. What the hell did she have in there – the skeleton of that Romantic nitwit?

Clearly in one of her 'inspired' moods, she threw out her

arms and yelled into the gale. 'Blow winds and crack thy cheeks! Come cataracts and storms!' Stepping down from the molehill, once again she was only a five foot nothing, rather plain, plumpish Jane Austen in an unbecoming electric green dress. 'I do love a gale,' she confided. 'Makes one feel so alive. Like Cathy in Wuthering Heights.'

'Balls.'

Watched by a lamb, the librarian relieved himself behind a wind-shriven bush. Blow winds? Well, she'd got the King Lear bit right. If ever there was a blasted heath. The only sign of life on these skull-bald hills was the lambs, and they were doomed for the plate. Merryweather had been bracing himself for the whole Rabbie Burns experience but any little bird singing from a tree here would be tossed away like dandelion seeds. Avoiding the backwash of his own piss, he watched it pool in a mossy cup. Imagine if spring stopped coming. That would put a poker up the cheeks of the Wordsworth brigade, no more fucking daffodils and violets. Wouldn't make any difference to his poetry. For a start, he'd hardly written any, and in those poems, which he'd actually finished, and were one part decent, it had already happened. Increasingly he sensed his was to be the poetry of a place where spring had forgotten to come. A permanent late winter. A Mr Bleaney's room. A… Balls, balls, balls. Zipping himself up, he stared at the moss cup. The piss had soaked away without trace. How to catch that level of non-existence in a poem. No, one had to dress life's awfulness; too much to take viewed in the buff. Like seeing your own father with an erection. What an idiot he was, wearing a mac instead of his British Warm in this wind. When was he going to stop believing that things would turn out better than he feared?

Merryweather picked up the luggage. Gordon Bennett, forget the bones of a Romantic poet, felt like there was a bloody slaughtered pig in there. 'Oh for fuck's sake.' A genuine howl as, scaling a tussocky knoll, he saw her on the bridge below. Twice previously she'd proposed to him there. And here she was now waiting halfway across.

Feeling uncomfortably like a Billy goat gruff, the librarian stepped onto the wooden bridge. As suspected, she did not move. Beneath them the young river raced. 'I'm no good, you know,' he said, beginning the speech rehearsed for just such an occasion. 'In the marital stakes, I mean.' But he hadn't got halfway through his exposition of personal worthlessness before she interrupted.

'Arthur, let's play pooh sticks.' They both laughed. What else could one do? 'What's this; levity, Sir? And I thought you'd got out on the wrong side of bed again this morning.'

'There's only one side of the bed in Mr Bleaney's room.'

'Cryptic.'

'Literal. The bed's pushed up against the wall. The room would flatter a coffin.'

'So that's why you chose it.'

Dutifully he went to the riverbank to collect sticks. Losing his balance, he stepped into the water. Scattering icy drops, he kicked at his black dog. Ernie would never make a pratfall like that. Some are born to be easy Ernie, others to lose their balance. Every day that week, Ernie had taken Niamh to lunch.

At last, Deepghyll Cottage. Grey of slate and stone, drain-pipes askew, all wood warped, moss rampant, Hansel and Gretel's cottage after a few years in the British climate. It took Merryweather half an hour and a whole box of matches to get the fire burning. 'Don't use all the kindling, Arthur.'

'It's so bloody damp.'

The fire took eventually. In its growing glare more of the living room became visible than could be seen in the light permitted by the Lilliputian window. Heavily laden book-shelves dominated. A mantelpiece packed with (to Merryweather) dreadfully silly 'ornaments' picked up in the local environs by his lady friend – bird's nest, rusty sickle, sheep skull with pheasant feather through the eye socket etc. And, in front of the fire, an old settle with bolsters. By arrangement the farmer had left milk in a churn. Tea and cake was most welcome. Turned out that the heavy grip had contained the luxuries as well as the necessaries; along with the tea things, he'd been carrying the complete works of Dickens, which were somehow squeezed into the already arse-tight book-shelves. 'What a relief,' she said. 'To have Charles here with us too.'

'So, you don't like children,' she said, reiterating his speech delivered on the bridge. 'You don't like toddlers, you don't like babies, you don't like christenings, you don't like weddings, you don't like the idea of living with someone else, you don't like –'

'Well, I don't like people much, really,' said Merryweather, reclining on the settle.

'You prefer being lonely?'

'Oh, loneliness is their word for doing what you want.'

'Now it's my turn to say it – balls.' She shook her head. 'Aren't you frightened of being alone? Don't you worry about one day looking at yourself in the mirror and finding a lonely, old man?'

Occasionally friendship required the truth. 'I worry about that every day.'

'Well, don't you want to do anything about it?'

'I *do* do.'

'What?'

'Avoid mirrors. Assiduously.' This time neither could raise a laugh. 'Look, it's just your bad luck that we happen to be friends,' he said. 'And my good luck, I suppose. But none of it will alter anything, fear of the future, feelings for others, friendship, warmth. You see, I don't know why, but almost always I want to be alone.' Words so often felt, had never seemed apter.

'What are you doing here then?' She smiled, but he knew she was serious.

'I don't know.'

'Chivalrous as ever, Arthur Merryweather.'

'I suppose if I can't be by myself then you're the next best thing.'

A few minutes later, as he stood browsing at one of the bookshelves: 'Another thing I meant to ask you, Arthur. Since when did you start reading Gerard not so manly Hopkins?' She was holding up the copy Niamh had given him.

After persuading the village pub to burn them a mixed grill and dust off a bottle of wine, they returned to the cottage, and read the rest of the evening away, she quoting reams of the deadly Romantic in a penetrating voice, no telephone to mellow those brittle glottals now, he thrown on the resources of a detective story penned by one of his Oxford friends. At midnight they went to their bedrooms. At half past he watched himself put his book down, get up and go to her door. A single knuckle knock, and then he entered. A lengthy attempt to turn off the paraffin lantern on her bedside table, a lifting of the coverlet, and a lanky Charles Laughton climbed into bed with Jane Austen, not exactly the bright young things.

About halfway through, Merryweather became aware of himself grunting and groaning. He pushed harder to drown the noises but they reached such a pitch of ridiculousness that he was forced to break off. 'What's the matter now, Arthur?'

He gaped into a darkness temporarily warmed by their bodies. Beyond the cottage, lambs keened on the night. 'Beforehand, you know, pre-coitally, one feels certain things,' he said. 'Fondness, affection, compassion, warm-heartedness, and so forth. Even tenderness.' A slight trip on the last word.

'And then, during play so to speak, one becomes like, well like Fred Truman.'

Sighing, she reached out for a cigarette whilst still beneath him like one used to such an arrangement. 'Fred Truman?'

'A fast bowler, a savage, just trying to get the wicket, doesn't matter how.'

'God, Arthur, you're such a romantic.'

'Like slaughtering a lamb.' He rolled off. 'My landlady does that, you know.'

'Does what for God's sake?'

'Knocks without really knocking. Like I did. Comes down to the same thing as just walking into another's room, you know. She's not happy about me fixing a bolt on my door. I had to pay *her* extra just to keep it. And she took a ten bob note for a bloody ashtray worth a shilling.'

'Is this boarding house really as grim as the picture you paint?'

'Old Ma Glenner's radiogram is never off. Floods the place like a blocked drain.'

She passed him the cigarette. 'The dreadful proprietresss?'

'Lady Bracknell of the kippers.'

'Madame Vauquer of the fish dock.'

'Don't bloody well bring Balzac into it.'

'What are your new chums like?'

'There's this character called Teesdale. Snores like a donkey. Got a hide like one too. Another one's a bearded psychopath. A third's never there. He travels in semi-precious stones. I know, it's a hell of a lot less exciting than it sounds. Then there's Mr Bleaney.'

'Who?'

'We share a room.'

'That sounds wildly unlike you, Arthur.'

'Not literally. He had it before me and the way everyone goes on about him, you'd think he was still there.' He passed her the fag back. 'The phone rings in the middle of the night for him. Constantly. Got into a frightful row with Old Ma Glenners for leaving it off the hook.'

'Unerringly you have found the worst possible establishment in the world.'

'The postal service is dreadful as well. That letter you posted on Tuesday didn't reach me until this morning.'

'I've written twice. I had to ring your mother for the address.'

'I'll have to move.'

'Boarding houses?'

'Towns. I've heard Frinton-on-Sea is pleasant.'

The fag was exchanged again. 'You've obviously never been there.'

'Have you?'

'Frinton? God yes. Had an uncle who lived there. Ended up killing himself. That happens a lot in Frinton apparently.' He sat up to listen. 'Can't get a drink for love nor money,' she went on. 'Everyone's either a Methodist or old. Walking sticks, palsied step takers on death's bleak promenade type of thing. In fact, precisely your idea of hell. Or should that be heaven?'

He nodded. 'So that's where I knew it from. Harwich for the continent, Frinton for the Incontinent. An old music hall joke my father used to tell.'

'They have this impeccably ghastly shopping street that they call the Bond Street of East Anglia. But why this interest in Frinton? It's two hundred miles away.'

'Mr Bleaney.'

'I'm beginning to think I shall hear a lot about that name.'

'Who had the room before me – '

'I've gathered that much.'

'Spent every summer holiday at Frinton-on-Sea.'

'Is that a haiku? What else do you know about this chap?'

Merryweather began to chuckle. A giggle flared into a

rasping, gurgling, shoulder shaking. Incapable of speaking, the librarian made several false starts, the words lodging in his throat like a toad. 'Mr Bleaney… Mr Bleaney…' Aggravated by this repetition, his hilarity became helpless, the kind in which you suddenly realise that if you don't stop laughing soon you might die. At last the toad was spat out with the words, 'least likely lady killer…'

'Not literally I hope.'

At last, the hysteria had passed. 'Actually he might have been a kind of bank robber. His greatest love was for Archie Andrews.'

'What, that ghastly ventriloquist's dummy?'

'He had a foolproof system for the Association football pools. He haunts the lodging house. Sends the women wild. Young and old. You'd think I was making it up, but there's a girl, no more than twenty, who waits for him in the garden at night. Well, I call it a garden. Not much of a horticulturalist old Bleaney.'

Reconciling herself to sleep, she turned and snuggled into her pillow. 'And just where is the famous Mr Bleaney now?' she yawned.

'That's the mystery. Gone. Vanished. Disappeared. Nobody knows whence nor why. Or at least they're not saying.'

'So that's why you came here, to get away from Mr Bleaney.'

But he hadn't got away from him; of all people Mr Bleaney had followed the librarian to Deepghyll Cottage. As his companion slept, Merryweather lay there, cigarette a cat's eye on a night road, and imagined joining his predecessor on the annual excursion to the East Anglian Essex coast. Except, since this was England, instead of the pastel blaze of the saucer ashtray – a rainy fortnight on a windswept esplanade. Alone or with a domineering elder sister? Perhaps an exacting mother with a slow growing cancer. A homosexual lover with a penchant for nervous breakdowns. Or as part of a Methodist mission. Merryweather foresuffered it all. Distribution of tracts along the Bond Street of East Anglia, teatime hymns on the prom, endless evening beetle drives fuelled by lemonade and dyspepsia. A fortnight. Just imagine it. A frigging fortnight. Trips to the ice-cream kiosk the highlight; then eating your cone with the pallid sands below and the sense of your own extinction blowing in from the East Anglian Essex sea. And everything as inconsequential as a sandcastle built by somebody else's child.

At last sleep lapped over the librarian like the tide over Frinton sands. In their slumber, the ancient cottage provided the pair with an unconscious intimacy. A buttock to buttock tryst in the dell of the bed's sag.

To his surprise, Merryweather slept if not like a king then at least like Burlington Bertie. Did indeed rise at ten-thirty. Lunch of – roast lambkins of course – at a surprisingly accept-able 'otel, broke the back of the day. That night there was no single knuckle knock on his lady's chamber, no becoming 'like Fred Truman'. Sunday was dealt with by a trip to the local sheep fair, and then it was a matter of trains and stations again. Somehow things were always easier when in transit. Better to travel hopelessly than arrive in despair. And so forth. Ensconced in window seats, his friend continuing her panegyric for her odious new poet, he alternated between the view and trying to herd a word or two of poetry into the fold of his *Lyflat* Memo Book. *Note Bene: must stop thinking in terms of such insipid, wankerish imagery as herding.* Gathering the toe-nail clippings of one's inspiration would be more suitable. Or emptying its chamber pot. By the time they were sharing a farewell pot of tea in the ornate provincial train station tearoom, aside from the three pages of doodling, he'd succeeded in writing a single line: 'This was Mr Bleaney's room.'

'How fares the bard?' she asked.

'Actually I've just written a poem. Shall I read you it?'

'Honoured, Sir.'

He turned to one of the pages of doodling.

> 'There once was a man called Bleaney
> Who rented the room before me
> Couldn't take any more
> Hung himself from the door
> But that *wasn't* the end of old Bleaney.'

'A very poor limerick indeed. And here's something for you to consider: aren't you frightened of becoming just like your Mr Bleaney?' After assaults on his vanity, his friend's second most common attack was through the roomy cellars of his insecurity.

'How do you mean?'

'I mean, is that all you want from life, to be a half mystery left behind in a rented room?'

'I forgot to tell you something else about him. Old Ma Glenners told me. She closes for three days over Christmas. Where do you think he goes?'

'I have no idea.'

'Stoke. And why do you think he goes to Stoke?'

'Because he's an avid devotee of Arnold Bennett?'

'No. Because he has a sister there.'

'Really, Arthur, you're becoming fixated.'

'The funniest thing is, apparently I look like him.'

'Oh now you're being preposterous.'

'On the contrary, when I arrived the people in the house mistook me for him.'

They parted. 'You're destined to be great,' she declared, threatening to shanghai his stiff-fingered handshake into an all-out embrace. Merryweather stepped back briskly. Partings were her speciality. 'Your writing I mean. Your words will be celebrated.'

'Oh.' Relief, and yet no relief. 'I gave up the third novel, you know. Didn't even want to read it myself.'

'At last,' she murmured fervently. 'Haven't I always said that poetry is your true metier? Now it will all start.'

He tried to remain pleasant since they were parting, though he felt like she'd kicked him in the bollocks. How he'd wanted to be a novelist like his friend. Not to be. For him, novel writing had been a bout of constipation, strain as much as you like and the best you can hope for is a few ounces of shit. 'Oh, I shall fail at poetry too no doubt. Here, boy.' And tapping his thigh, the librarian headed for his platform, followed by his faithful black dog.

Merryweather's train was late. Newlyweds just returning from fucking each other for a whole weekend in Scarborough, or some other moth eaten, honeymoon Xanadu, took up an entire coach. Avoiding them like the clap, Merryweather was just congratulating himself on securing a compartment to himself when someone entered. The trespasser proceeded to open the window. A glare of mutual recognition; no time to get away. Pig faced, it was the Woolworth King, Mr Paper Products from the Royal Station Hotel. 'It just lets the smuts in, you know,' the librarian said. 'An open window in a station.'

'You're rationing fresh air now, are you?' An ironic hand picked out the empty seats. 'Mind me sitting, or are you expecting the rest of your party?'

Merryweather took out his copy of Gerard Manley Hopkins. Best way to tough out the hour or so ahead was being bored shitless by the Jesuit priest. He hadn't even opened the book however before his fellow passenger moved to the seat directly opposite, and leaning forward, was casting for his eye. The librarian steadfastly refused to look up. Didn't seem to matter. 'Do you know the best-selling writing paper throughout Great Britain and the Commonwealth?' the salesman asked. There followed an exposition on social stationery that required neither response nor reply, and showed no sign of reaching a natural conclusion.

With a finger flourish powerful enough to swing a hefty gate, Merryweather opened the volume and slipped into Gerard Manley Hopkins's poetry. But there was no way through the scrub of adjectives and rank rhythms. Searching the pages for a less overgrown entrance, all he could find was a kind of paddock poetry about shaggy ponies, felled trees, and, possibly, kestrels. No wonder Hopkins never published a single poem in his lifetime, the librarian mused, and died more than half a nutcase.

At last, stumbling out of Hopkins' 'weeds in wheels', Merryweather looked up to see that the world had become full of seagulls. The train was drawing alongside the river. Seagulls and the river's levelling drift, the far bank's unbeckoning netherland. The dreary, liminal beauty tugged at Merryweather. He was back. Back home? Hardly that. Yet could one really be feeling some attachment to this Trades Union Venice on its kipper lagoon; or was he just excited at the thought of seeing Niamh again? Either way, madness seemed to lie.

12.

'Funny how it always happens when the wife's cooking me a steak,' sighed the desk sergeant. 'Last week we had all that carry on at the Royal Station Hotel, and it seems we're to have another to do tonight.'

'What's happening, Sarge?' the young constable asked, his excitement making him look even younger.

'Inspector Drax is making a move on the safe-cracking jobs. That'll mean overtime for me and you.'

'On a Sunday night?'

'Tactical. Catches them off guard. Even your criminal fraternity observe a Sabbath of sorts.' Sergeant Edmundson glanced over his shoulder at the smoked glass door of Inspector Drax's office. 'As well as that, the Chief Constable's been on the blower twice this week. The press still ring every day. Can't wait any longer. He's got to collar somebody.'

'Won't it be dangerous, Sarge? The Thomas gang use coshes and all sorts, don't they?'

'Chair legs with masonry nails. Nasty. But it's not the Thomas brothers we're bringing in.'

'Why not, Sarge?'

'Still not enough evidence.'

'Who we bringing in then?'

'The only line of enquiry they've got. Chap by the name of Bleaney.'

'Who is he?'

'Don't know. All we've got is a name and an address. Some rented room.'

A broad silhouette loomed in the smoked glass, and then took stunningly obese flesh as the door opened. 'Want to drive for us, constable?' Inspector Drax demanded in his deceptively soft voice.

'Yes, sir,' said the constable.

A stench of bay rum as Sergeant Edmundson lifted the counter for the mountainous Drax. The inspector's clean-shaven face glistened; a nick caught the electric light. During his service as a black and tan in Ireland, Inspector Drax had got into the habit of shaving with a knife. Sergeant Edmundson, who'd served with the inspector's unit in County Cork, recognised the chin nick for what it was. That hand was always unsteady at the decisive moment. 'Arbuthnott,' Drax called back into his office. 'Let's get busy.'

Unhurried, Detective-Sergeant Arbuthnott passed under Edmundson's lifted counter. The uniformed man winced at the cloud of foul breath in his wake. The station called Arbuthnott corpse breath, but only when he wasn't there. Less than half the body weight of Drax he looked oddly similar to Himmler, even down to the severe short back and sides. 'Do you think there'll be shooting, Sarge?' the young constable whispered.

'Hurry on now, lad, don't keep the inspector waiting.'

Headlamps flashed at the window as the black Wolseley 19 pulled out of the car park. The sergeant barely had time to put the kettle on when the station's Wild West saloon doors opened again to admit a tramp with a patched coat and felt hat. 'I was wondering when you would show up, Amos. You're a right stormcock. Always singing in the teeth of a gale.'

13.

'No use knocking like that. Not nobody's in.' Heart sinking at the double negative, Merryweather looked across the littered garden to see his next-door neighbour at the crooked fence. 'They've all gone out, Burlington love,' Kathleen Mealie added. 'Tell you what, pop into ours.'

'Oh, really I couldn't impose – '

'It's no bother.'

After a weekend in company the librarian would perhaps have given a little finger to be left alone. He was just about to bolt when his neighbour headed him off at sixty-one's front gate, 'come on in then, Burlington. I'll get you in next door.'

Great relief. 'Have you got a spare key?'

'Aye, summat like that.'

If Merryweather had thought Miss Glendenning kept a shabby home, next-door was the hungry 'thirties all over again. Stark as a potato knife, poverty cut him everywhere he looked. Uncarpeted floorboards, doorless doorways, walls smeared with dirty hands and margarine, murals of damp, ever-hungry gas meter prominent as a gibbet – a page from Orwell's *Road to Wigan Pier*. And the smell. Yes, as Orwell knew, it was the smell that always wrinkled the bourgeois nose.

All at once Miss Glendenning showed herself in a new light. Valiant warrior in the struggle against poverty and dirt.

'Cup of tea, Burlington, love,' decided Kathleen.

'I really need to get in next door,' said Merryweather, breathing through his mouth. 'Work to – '

'Kettle's on.'

It was the kind of place where the kettle was never sodding well off. The ill-lit scullery bore such resemblance to a hencoop that he wouldn't have been surprised to find a cockerel eyeing him from the grease-encrusted sink, or an egg laid in the open packet of Co-op 99 tea. The kettle was of an age to interest an antiques dealer. Huge copper sides glinting as it laboured to the boil, it belonged in a folk tale, as though any moment it might pipe forth advice or a warning. Under the rancid stench crouched a smell of gas to give Merry-weather's mother nightmares for the rest of her life.

'Three?' Kathleen asked spooning sugar into the slop of curdy milk.

'Four, please.' How else to stomach it?

'Have a nice time with your lady friend then, Burlington?'

Taking his glasses off, Merryweather rubbed his eyes. So, there really was no such thing as privacy on the river.

'What's *he* doing here?' a child's voice inquired from the shadows. 'You said Mr Beans had varnished.'

'An't Mr Beans,' Kathleen told her daughter. 'It's Uncle Burlington. Met him on the bus last Sunday, remember?' She turned to Merryweather. 'Mr Beans is what the nippers called Mr Bleaney.'

'How much do we owe?' another child wanted to know from somewhere dangerously close to the kettle as the librarian put his glasses back on.

'He an't the tally man,' their mother pointed out. 'Uncle Burlington just lives next door. He's taken Mr Bean's room.'

'Do *you* not know any jokes either?' a third kiddie

demanded. He didn't seem surprised at the shake of the librarian's head. 'Mr Beans didn't. Bet you don't like dogs an' all.'

By the time Merryweather was sipping at a chipped enamel mug that showed suspicious signs of having been used to store paintbrushes, he was hemmed in by half a dozen children under the age of ten, and a baby. Kathleen might look fifty, but was probably younger than he was. Given a different life, she might have had the face (and tits) of Diana Dors. Manfully, he tried to force the tea down.

'Do *you* rob dead bodies an' all, mister?' a boy inquired.

Kathleen aimed a playful swipe at her son. 'He means are you on the Bodies like Mr Bleaney was. You know, insurance, the Man from the Pru.'

'That's what *he* said he did,' the boy said with relish: '*I'm a vampire, I eat dead bodies.*' With arms held stiffly out, the boy attacked one of his sisters.

'Mr Beans wasn't very good with children,' Kathleen explained suffering her own jugular to be severed. 'Uncle Burlington's not like that, are you? He works at a library. You know, with nice story books.'

'Mr Beans threw himself off the ferry,' another little girl said. 'Just to get away from her next door, didn't he, mam?'

'That's what some folks say,' Kathleen replied.

'He killed our Trixie,' declared a five year old. 'And she weren't barking *that* much, were she, mam?'

'It was her next door what made him do that,' Kathleen explained.

'Now he's got one of his fancy lasses waiting for him at all hours,' put in the eldest child. 'Young enough to be his daughter. What *can* she see in him?'

'I really must be getting in next door, you know,' said Merryweather. 'Did you say you had a key?'

'Let Uncle Burlington in next door then, you lot,' Kathleen

ordered her brood. The nippers propelled the librarian into a dank yard. 'If you're wondering how I know about your gallivanting,' she called after him. 'Our Stan's a stoker. Nowt he don't know about what's coming and going.'

Unable to penetrate such mysteries of community knowledge, Merryweather let it lie. The smell hit instantly – the outside toilet. An old dolly tub stood by the yard wall. One after the other, the nippers mounted it, and boosting themselves up onto the wall, dropped down into the yard below. 'Find the cubby hole for your foot,' came the advice.

Stiffly, Merryweather stepped up onto the rusty dolly tub. It juddered under his weight. Have to be careful, could easily injure himself. He lifted a foot into the 'cubby hole', a deep dent in the brickwork. After three attempts he was able, sweating and cursing, to lever himself up. Straddling the wall bellywise, he surveyed a vista of rubbish-filled backyards with the odd forgotten, hung out sheet haunting itself on a damp wind.

'Do you really not know any jokes, Uncle Burlington?' the 'vampire' boy demanded from below.

'No,' Merryweather replied breathless. 'But I can pull a face.'

'Go on then.'

'I am.'

'You look like you've sat too long on the toilet.'

Merryweather hoisted his legs round, and lowered himself down as far as he could into sixty-one's back yard. Then, dangling like a cartoon character off the edge of the world, he let go. A rip as his jacket sleeve caught on a rusty nail, and Uncle Burlington landed heavily. 'Vampire boy' had already climbed through Old Ma Glenner's scullery window. He opened the back door from within. 'Right well, thank you,' said Merryweather. After a pause, he handed them a shilling. 'For some sweets.'

'There's lots of us,' Vampire said.

Grudgingly he handed out another shilling.

Using Old Ma Glenner's bin as a mount, the nippers scaled the wall and disappeared.

Sauce bottles stood sentinel on the dining table. They seemed to close ranks as the librarian walked by. He flicked the Vs. Ascending the stairs, the silence of the lodging house felt almost submarine. Alone at last. But no sooner had he got nearly comfortable on the bed, glued ashtray, cigarette, pen and paper to hand, than – voices.

So she was in all the time! Why hadn't she let him in; what crackbrained rule had he broken now? Rage swept through the librarian. Time to have it out.

Halfway down the stairs he realised that he could hear a man *and* a woman. Laughing! Had the traveller in semi-precious stones lodger come back, or even Bleaney, the Sauce Emperor himself? Well, he'd take 'em both on. Without knocking, he shoved open the door of the 'private parlour'. 'I've had about as much as I can...' Miss Glendenning's private parlour was dark. Untenanted. The radiogram was on. Then it went off. Ah. Obviously some connection had come loose. As he trudged back upstairs, a gale of transmitted laughter mocked him.

Back on the bed, he tried to write another letter but – no good. Something else was distracting him. The words spoken by his lady companion seemed to echo in the coffin room: *Aren't you frightened of becoming just like your Mr Bleaney?* As well as this – the stench from next door seemed to have got into his pores. A grim grin, wasn't Sunday his 'tub night'?

Plumbing begrudging each drop, the arthritic taps bled into the verdigris trough with all the flow of an old man. Quicker to bloody well bring up buckets from the kitchen. Five minutes and the bath was barely deep enough to drown one of Teesdale's rats. Patience giving out, Merryweather wedged the door and climbed in. Christ on a bike! Hardly lukewarm. So much for old Ma Glenner's ruddy immersion heater.

Shivering in the tub, inevitably Merryweather's thoughts turned to death. His grandfather had been found dead in a bath almost identical to this one, ironic after all those playful false alarms. The only thing the librarian could remember about him was that his idea of a joke had been to pretend to be dead, and then there he was lying in the bath *really* dead. Only been fifty-three. His father had died even younger. The finger of fate, cold as one of his own in the less-than-luke-warm wash, was already pointing at the librarian. Premature death was as much a Merryweather family tradition as the ironic name itself. He checked his body for tumours, probed his mouth with a tongue, felt a stiffening in the oesophagus, and then jumped when the wireless blared back into life before fading again like a poltergeist. Defeated, he rose from the bath.

Dressing gown on over his pyjamas, British Warm an extra blanket, fag in gob, Merryweather lay in bed trying to reach a decent body temperature. By dint of will he managed a witty letter to his successful friend, one to his sister, and had even written to his 'lady friend' when once again the wireless spluttered into life. This time it was twice as loud. Simply more than flesh and blood could stand.

Sunday fun time with Archie Andrews was in full swing as Merryweather entered old Ma Glenner's 'private parlour'. Well, the creepy cretin could bloody well get knotted. The culprit stood in pride of place – a freestanding, monstrous cabinet complete with wireless, turntable, more knobs than you could shake a stick at and a speaker meshed like a poacher's net. Tempted though he was to lift it bodily and hurl it against the wall, he decided on something more subtle. Didn't want to end up having to pay for a replacement. What he needed to do was get the back off and snip a wire. In search of sharp scissors, he opened the chest of drawers. The top drawer held only balls of wool; the second was stuffed full of nauseating knitted cosies; the bottom drawer – the bottom drawer held a bundle of letters. A bundle on which his own name was topmost.

Three of the two dozen or so letters were his. The handwriting revealed one from his successful friend, one from his mother and the third from his lady friend. So that's what had happened to the habitual punctuality of his correspondents since his arrival chez Glendenning. And he'd been blaming the isolate nature of the town. 'Never underestimate the power of a good woman,' Archie suddenly announced on the wireless to a swarm of odious laughter. That dreadful woman was reading his mail! Another house rule: steam open your guests' letters before handing them out a day or two late with the kippers. This also explained the less than pristine stationery crackle under the cut of his paper knife, one of the librarian's keenest pleasures.

Merryweather wasn't the only victim. Teesdale's correspondence had been intercepted too, business missives judging by the typing. McCoist was yet to receive two personal letters, both in the same female hand. Some of the post bore names the librarian had never heard of. The largest contingent was addressed to Mr Bleaney.

She hadn't even bothered to reseal the former lodger's correspondence, and after only a moment's qualm, Merryweather had brought out the most recent letter. It was a greetings card, postmarked just yesterday. Before he could read the message however, a knock reverberated through the house. The front door. Thrusting his and Mr Bleaney's correspondence into his dressing gown pockets, Merryweather stuffed the rest of the illicit cargo back into the drawer. Three more battering raps chased him out of the 'private parlour' up the stairs and across the landing. What kind of arse knocked like that on a Sunday evening? A third volley, practically lifting the front door from its hinges, caught the librarian fumbling the rescued post into his briefcase. He checked himself. What was *he* acting like a criminal for?

'What the hell do you want?' he demanded, yanking the front door open.

Two men stood on the step, possibly the grimmest pair to be seen outside a Presbyterian Free Kirk or the dock at Nuremberg. One fat, one creepy; Goering and Himmler.

A number of things happened simultaneously. Competing odours of bay rum and bad breath disoriented the librarian as the men stepped towards him. Hands were placed firmly on both his shoulders. His stammer flared so violently that he couldn't properly deny the question: 'Are you, Mr Bleaney?'

The next thing Merryweather knew, handcuffs were on his wrists. 'Just come as you are – dressing gown and all,' one of the men, Goering, said.

A black police car was idling on the road. Mr Bleaney's peasant army of thistles shook their scythes in its headlamps as Merryweather was shunted down the garden path. Just time to hear a child shrill 'Uncle Burlington's being taken away', from a Mealie window, and then, effortless as undertakers, Goering and Himmler were dispatching their prisoner into the back of the Wolseley 19. The young constable behind the wheel was the same young constable to whom the librarian had tried to show a non-existent crime a week ago. The black car roared away.

Dressed in the thick Ulsters, trilbies and terrifyingly impassive facial features of their breed, the detectives sandwiched Merryweather like a pair of anvils. Anvils smelling of bay rum and halitosis. He tried to speak. Explain who he was. Wasn't. His stammer, aggravated by the situation, mashed his words to gibberish. He still hadn't been able to explain that he wasn't Mr Bleaney when the car stopped, and, handcuffs gnawing his wrists like rats, one slipper left in the car, he was being strong-armed into the police station and delivered to a desk sergeant. The same desk sergeant as last week.

A barrage of questions. 'I…' Merryweather stuttered like some kind of tongue-tied simpleton. And then he was being thrust through a door. An echoing, ill-lit passage; a bang on the back to half warn about a steep flight of steps; a shove thrusting him into a cell; a door being locked behind him.

14.

The cell was about the size of Mr Bleaney's room. The bare bulb equally boiling. The bed board even more uncomfortable, as the librarian discovered when his legs suddenly gave way.

In a moment, he heard his mother assure him, a nice police-man will come in and apologise. In a moment a nice policeman will come in and make everything all right again. In a moment a nice, kind policeman will explain how this mistake happened. He waited for the door to open. It didn't. Instead, the bed board and ceramic chamber pot; a white-tiled wall with an impossibly high, barred window; the shallow stone floor; the door without a handle. In a moment the door would open. When would it? In a moment a nice, kind policeman will… a jarring whirr of keys, a jerking open of the handle-less door and a policeman really did come in.

With a gust of relief, Merryweather felt his handcuffs being taken off.

'T- Thank you.' Even now his mother's lessons in politeness delivered behind tall laurels surfaced in his mauled expression of gratitude. Numb, his hands couldn't hold the mug being offered. Rubbing the throbbing hams together, he waited for the apology.

'I'll put it down here then,' said Sergeant Edmundson placing an enamel mug on the stone floor. 'I should drink it down whilst it's hot if I were you.' Merryweather didn't want the tea, he'd even do without the apology, he just wanted out of that cell. 'Hold up, where do you think you're going?'

The librarian's bid for freedom met with a firm shunt from a steak-sized hand that sent him reeling back into captivity. 'Go home,' Merryweather said. Intelligible words at last, but the sergeant was shaking his head.

'If I were you, I'd stop this nonsense, Bleaney.'

'Not… B- Bleaney.' The pins and needles in his hands were excruciating.

Sergeant Edmundson peered at the prisoner. Forty years in this job and he was rarely wrong. Hard to see this queer fish as one of the Thomas gang. Was the stuttering an act? Just hoped he'd have sense when it came to Drax. He'd watched the inspector hone his methods in Ireland. 'Come on, drink up. Not quite the Royal Station Hotel, but you'll have to get used to that.'

A clatter of metal and keys, and the policeman had gone, leaving the handle-less door. Dazed, Merryweather took up his tea. This couldn't be happening. This *was* happening. Back on the bed board he sat numbly nursing the mug, its warmth ebbing like a dead kitten. Foreign literature wasn't much in his line, but he'd read Kafka. What was next – wake up having been turned into a cockroach? He tried to laugh.

Deep breaths, take deep breaths. If he could control his speech, everything would be easily explained. Five minutes passed. Ten. An hour? Deep breaths, not too deep though, better not – what was the medical term? – hyperventilate. Deep breaths, deep… Christ on a bike, he was hyperventilating.

The door opened again. The detectives. A rush of relief. Obviously come to apologise in person. Why were they in shirt sleeves? It wasn't that warm. In fact, it was on the chilly side; was that why he was shaking?

'Right, we can do this the easy or the hard way,' said the obese Goering. 'It's up to you, Bleaney.'

So, the police really did speak like that, Merryweather noted, all at once oddly distant from proceedings. Look, they rolled up their sleeves in a threatening manner too. Yet even visiting this far down in the circles of hell, Merryweather didn't expect Himmler with the bad breath to say: 'Tell us what we want or get eight shades of shit kicked out of you.'

'Mistake,' he managed. 'Been a mistake.'

The detectives exchanged a look. 'That's not a good start, is it Detective-Sergeant?' said Goering.

'Do you think he's going to be a joker, Inspector?' returned Himmler.

Deep breaths. 'Not Bleaney. Got wrong man.'

'I suppose we got the wrong address an' all?'

'Or maybe you was just at Mr Bleaney's by mistake?'

'And just happen to look like him.'

In a desperate attempt to calm himself, the librarian imagined, of all things, a holiday in Frinton. It worked well enough for him to say, 'Only been there for a week. Mr Bleaney – had the room before me.'

Again, the shared look. 'Yes, I thought so, Detective-Sergeant, he thinks we were born yesterday.'

'Have you ever heard a worse defence, Inspector?'

'Must be Irish. Sounds it. Are you Irish, Bleaney?'

'Bleaney O'Blarney.'

When Inspector Goering lunged, Merryweather let out a humiliating whimper, but it was only his dressing gown they wanted. A rifling of pockets. 'Who the fuck's this for then, Muffin the bleeding Mule?' Merryweather looked at the envelope. A fist seemed to ram its way up his arse and grab his sphincter. The name Mr Bleaney swam before his eyes. It was the greetings card. He must have left it in the pocket by mistake. 'From your sister, birthday boy,' Himmler mocked, reading the card. 'Beryl says many happy returns of the day and she's looking forward to your visit at Christmas.'

'Right, shall we make a start,' said Goering. 'You're going to tell us everything you know, Bleaney. Let's start at the beginning. Where did you first meet the Thomas brothers?'

15.

'Who is this Bleaney bloke when he's at home?' the young constable asked after the detectives had been down in the cells for half an hour.

Sergeant Edmundson didn't look up from the folder open on the desk in front of him. 'He was the insurance agent for all the places they turned over.'

'You what, Sarge?'

'His name is at the bottom of the premiums covering the premises what got robbed. Course that could mean nowt but if they're all insurance jobs...'

'Insurance jobs?'

'You know, an arrangement between the villains and the businesses. The villains share the spoils with the business, and the business shares the insurance payout with the villains. No one loses out. They do it in Leeds.'

'So he *might* be one of the Thomas crowd, Sarge?'

The sergeant shunted the folder down. 'What do *you* think, son?'

The constable opened the folder. It was marked, Bleaney. 'So we've had him in before?' A nod from the sergeant. Inside the folder, a photograph. Rather blurred, the subject wore a hat and glasses. 'He don't look much like a hard man, Sarge. When did we first bring him in?'

'Just before you started. As I say, he were the only lead.'

There wasn't much else in the folder. Just a few notes. 'Occupation,' the constable read. 'Life and business assurance salesman. Height, six foot two. Build, lanky. Colour of eyes, blue. Distinguishing marks, none. Well, that's him all right. No previous felonies. How come they let him go, Sarge?'

'Can't have had enough on him.'

The younger man passed the file back. 'Why collar him again then?'

'Still nothing else to go on. Happen they've found something new about him, happen they just need an arrest. Course, he might talk this time whether or no.'

'Keeps on saying he isn't Bleaney.'

'Well, lad, your average criminal isn't exactly famed for his truthfulness. You can never tell how folk will go after a night in the cells, son. And they're really putting the frighteners on him this time. You know, the full panto. What with him not being no hard case. Happen…' The sergeant broke off. A soft exhalation. 'Flamin' Nora.'

Flamin' Nora was about as strong as Sergeant Edmundson went. 'What is it, sarge?'

The senior man's brow furrowed. 'Did he ring any bells when they brought him in just now?'

'Should he? Face like a slapped arse.'

'Well we can't all be Rembrandts, and language lad. Have a think. Ever seen him before?'

'I weren't here when they last had him in.'

'Think back to last Sunday, son.'

'The night we had it all on with the Royal Station Hotel?' A nod from the sergeant slowly lifted the blank look from the constable's face. 'Flippin' heck, sarge, weren't he that fella what come in with the cock-and-bull story? Proper Posh. Summat about Titch Thomas threatening someone.'

'Clive Compo,' said Sergeant Edmundson.

'Aye, Clive.'

The sergeant's finger ran down the piece of foolscap paper on which the few Bleaney notes were written. 'Flamin' Nora Jones.'

'Sarge?'

'One of the robberies was at Clive's Billiard Hall.'

'Flamin' Nora,' echoed the constable when the file had been passed to him for verification. 'Bleaney came in voluntary and we let him go.'

'The inspector won't be happy.'

'What does LBDS mean, Sarge? It's written at the bottom of the file.'

'One of Detective-Sergeant Arbuthnott's acronyms,' replied the sergeant, wondering exactly how to break it to Inspector Drax that they could have had their man a week ago, and in a talkative mood. 'Little Bugger in Deep Shit, if you pardon my French. It's when some ordinary chap gets mixed up with nasty people. Which, it would appear, is a perfect description of our Bleaney's situation.'

16.

'We know you've been on the fiddle,' said Goering. 'Taking some of the customer's premiums.'

'Dipping your hand into the payouts,' said Himmler. 'Only, last time we had you in, you swore on your sister's life you hadn't done nowt.'

Am I going to puke? Merryweather wondered as the detectives loomed over him where he sat on the bed.

'You're looking at two or three years tops for that,' said Himmler.

'Eighteen months if we really sweet-talk the judge,' said Goering.

'But if you bugger us about any more, we'll throw the lot at you.'

'Robbery, violence, member of the Thomas mob, pimping, the works.'

'That's twenty years minimum. You're bald enough now,

birthday boy, what do you think you'll be like in nineteen seventy-four?'

'We know you're not a big cheese. What did they give you to keep stum? Twenty quid? Fifty tops. So let them what did the big stuff do the big porridge. All we want from you is enough to get the Thomas brothers.'

Rummaging in his broken shards of speech, Merryweather somehow managed to piece together, 'Not Bleaney. Nothing to do with anything.'

He didn't see the inspector's huge fist until it was too late. Right at the last moment however, the detective sergeant reached out and caught it. If it was an act, it was sickeningly polished.

'Get up,' Goering roared. Merryweather felt himself being lifted up. A powerful shunt sent him reeling down the cell, and on to the stone-cold floor.

'If I were you, I wouldn't piss the inspector off, birthday boy,' said Himmler. 'It'll just make him tetchy. You have a good think on.'

When the librarian had picked himself up, he was alone with the handle-less door again. The tiled wall. The impossibly high-barred window. Just then, the cell was plunged into darkness.

Ridiculous, absurd, ludicrous in the worst sense! How can an innocent man end up here? To try and calm himself Merryweather turned to literature. But nothing he found there composed him. Oscar Wilde weeping at his arrest; the boy Dickens visiting his father in the Marshalsea; John Clare wondering if the bars of his asylum were the strings of a fiddle; the cockroaches staring at Dostoyevsky from his cabbage soup.

Holding out as long as possible at last he gave in, and fumbled through the darkness for the piss pot. He was still urinating when the light exploded back into life, and the door was thrust open. Merryweather's flow dried instantly. He'd never been able to piss in front of other men let alone a policeman in the scalding brightness of a naked bulb.

Sergeant Edmundson turned away discreetly as the prisoner rearranged himself. 'Take off your dressing gown, son. No need to panic. I just want the cord. In case you're thinking of doing owt daft. Never lost anyone on my shift; and you won't be the first.'

Helpless, the librarian complied. Act of kindness or another threat? He tried to speak, but it was as though he'd swallowed his tongue. Good God, imagine if he really *had* done something wrong.

'How did it start, son?' Sergeant Edmondson asked not unkindly. 'Oh I've heard about your little game. Was it a mistake? Got to the bank late one Friday and couldn't cash in the week's premiums? Bit short at the weekend, so you borrowed a shilling or two. Paid it back. Course you did. Borrowed a few more shillings the next week. Paid them back too. Then you borrowed a couple of quid. How to pay that back? Lucky for you, you got a few new customers that week. What could be easier than just taking their money without bothering to properly insure them? Who's to know? Fingers crossed there's no fires and nobody dies. Might as well let the premiums lapse for a few old customers too, course you'd still take the money. Soon mounts up, don't it? A nice regular earner. But it's not enough, so you have a go at "arranging" the lump sum payments an' all. Some old dear doesn't notice that the payout's five quid shy – what's a fiver when you've got three hundred? Try a tenner next time. Well, the bereaved don't like to make a fuss. But you still need more. What next? Insurance jobs? No, that's not you. You're a little fella. But what if someone else wants to? If I were you, I'd come clean about your part in it otherwise you'll find yourself taking the fall for others.'

'Pen,' gasped Merryweather seized by one of the greatest moments of literary inspiration in his life.

'What?'

He mimed the act of writing. As simple as that!

'Strictly speaking I shouldn't, unless it's an official state-ment.' Sergeant Edmundson havered then handed over the pencil stub from behind his ear and a sheet from his notebook. 'Here.'

Merryweather's hand shook so much that he might have been writing after a spell on the rack. With much face pulling and eye narrowing, the Sergeant deciphered: 'My name is Arthur Merryweather, I am a librarian. Not insurance, not Bleaney.' The sergeant sighed. 'If I show the inspector this, he'll think you're extracting the Michael.' Snatching the sheet back, Merryweather scribbled some more. Again the gurning of deciphering spidery words. 'I work at the University. I only moved here a week ago. I bear a superficial physical resemblance to your Mr Bleaney. Easy to prove. One phonecall.'

The desk sergeant peered at the prisoner. Mistakes happened, been in the force long enough to know that. Even sinners should be given a chance. St Paul himself required an angel to bust him out of gaol. Drax and Arbutnott might not like it, but they'd gone off to their bridge night with the big nobs at the Royal Station Hotel, leaving the prisoner to stew. 'Come on then, lad, look sharp.'

Stumbling back up the gloomy passage, Merryweather's elation was already congealing. Whom to call? His friends lived far away; take them too long to get here. Miss Glenden-ning? Teesdale? He had no one to turn to. No, that wasn't quite right. There was one person. At that moment, he misstepped on the ill-lit stairs. Instinctively reaching out to catch his glasses, he lost his footing. A stone step came up to greet him.

17.

Niamh O'Leary had been in the bath just two minutes when the phone rang. 'Ah bejasus,' she sighed in imitation of her father. Opening the tap with a toe, she submerged beneath the soapy water, but when she came back up for air, the phone was still ringing. It was her father's Knights of St Columba night otherwise he'd have answered it.

Floating in the luxury of the deep bath that she only dared to draw on Knights of St Columba evenings, Niamh let the phone ring and returned her thoughts to Thomas Hardy, and Arthur Merryweather. She'd been reading the Dorset poet because of what her boss had said about him. Perhaps depressing wasn't the right word. Morbid? Too pejorative. Some of his poems were lovely. The nature and fiddle playing. Wessex sounded like Ireland without the priests. Shot through with melancholia, that was the best description. As well as being shot through with melancholia, Thomas Hardy was an atheist, you couldn't deny that. Was Arthur an atheist, or just shot through with melancholia? What was his poetry like? Wonderfully deep and sad no doubt. Yet her new boss was also the funniest person she'd ever met. Wasn't as old as he looked either. So what if Ernie had already got some of the unqualified staff to call him Uncle Tortoise; hadn't she always liked Uncle Remus's tortoise almost as much as Brer Rabbit? Still the phone rang. Here I am, she said to herself, thinking about Thomas Hardy, also about a living poet, whom I know personally, whilst letting the phone ring its head off. It made her feel bohemian as though the bath was not at the top of a substantial house on Thinness Road, but in a left bank Parisian garret.

But bathdreams cannot outlast its bubbles, and dentist's daughters really *have* to answer phones. People with toothache can't be left waiting. With a regretful grunt, she rose from the bath in great gouts of steaming water.

'Hello, 6781, how may I help you?' she said in the telephone voice befitting a dentist's daughter. 'Oh, it's you, what do you want?' Niamh, not one for long, loose telephone chattering at the best of times, allowed Ernie just a few seconds. 'Yes, all right, but you could have told me this tomorrow.' Whether Ernie had only called to tell her that the New Dawn Cycling Club's first outing of the year was taking place on Wednesday, or whether he had had a more tender purpose Niamh didn't consider. Upstairs, a tub with the last of her Turkish bath salts was rapidly cooling. Also it was draughty in the hallway, and that pool of water forming at her feet would be the first thing her father noticed coming home. Why had he kept ringing like that anyway? He was growing bold. Last week he'd tried to kiss her. What if her father had answered the phone? He couldn't stand Ernie, and that was without even knowing he was a communist. 'I'll have to go, the bath's running.'

No sooner had Niamh replaced the receiver than the telephone started again. She plucked it up. 'Hello, 6781?' she said, just managing to keep her telephone voice intact. After all, *this* time it might be a patient. It wasn't a patient. It wasn't Ernie. 'What do you want?' she asked, surprised by how her breath caught. It was the last person she could have expected. Once again, that odd, unsettling yet invigorating sense of excitement.

18.

'What the hell were you playing at?' Inspector Drax demanded. 'Letting him make a phonecall.'

'Kept maintaining his innocence, Sir.' Sergeant Edmundson replied. 'Continual assertion of mistaken identity. Thought we should at least give him a fair chance.'

'A fair chance? We're not here to give crooks a fair fucking chance. Don't you know that by now?'

'Just thought we should do things by the book, sir.'

'So you let her down into the cells to see him?'

The old hands peered at each other over the inspector's desk. 'You could have been someone, Edmundson,' said Drax. 'Maybe made inspector, but you've always been too fond of the bloody book. Well, you just better hope you haven't buggered this up. The chief constable and his brother weren't very happy when I had to tell them I was leaving the bridge table because of some uniform pissing on our first proper lead for a crime spree that's put us on the map for all the wrong reasons.' Drax glanced through the smoked-glass window to where Niamh O'Leary sat in the waiting room nursing a slipper. 'Get rid.'

'The young lady vouches for him, Sir.'

'She'll just be some bloody Thomas tart.'

'Says he's a librarian. Says she is too. Says he's not Bleaney.'

'Have you just come off the flamin' ark? These types of lasses say owt for their fellas. Tell you what, mind, Tom,' said Drax ogling Niamh O'Leary through the smoked glass. 'Sometimes I think we've got it all wrong.'

'Sir?' Edmundson stiffened, you had to be doubly on guard when the inspector called you by your first name.

'Molls. Hoodlum's lasses. Your criminal pulls the lasses. Look at her pretty as a picture and him a toad in a coal scuttle. Any road, go and tell her to sling her hook. Understand?'

'She didn't seem to be lying, Inspector Drax.'

'Don't make me have to tell you twice.'

The sergeant went back out to his custody desk, and took another deep breath. 'Look, love,' he said to Niamh. 'If you get yourself off nice and quiet like we'll say no more.'

With an Irish father, Niamh had none of her boss's respect for the forces of the crown. 'I'm telling you he's Arthur Merryweather,' she retorted, coming over to the custody counter. 'And he's only been in this town for a week.'

'How long did you say you knew him again, Miss?'

'A week.'

The desk sergeant and his constable exchanged glances. 'What you mean is, Miss,' said Edmundson. 'You don't know him at all.'

'He came with references. They were checked. Everyone knows him. He's a famous poet.' The last bit was only a white lie. Hoping her blush didn't betray her, Niamh glanced down at the folder open on the counter.

Drax's silhouette flared and shrank in the smoked glass behind them as he paced his office floor. 'Do you realise how serious perverting the course of justice is?' Edmundson tried to point out as gravely as he could.

'That's not him,' said Niamh.

'I'm sorry, Miss?'

She pointed at the folder. 'For a start his eyes aren't blue.'

The young constable snatched up the photo from the folder. It was black and white. 'How can you tell?'

Niamh too had the librarian's art of upside-down reading. 'You've written it yourselves. Colour of eyes, blue. Arthur Merryweather's eyes are brown, the man you want has blue eyes.'

19.

'They didn't apologise,' Niamh repeated, as they walked through the police station car park. 'Treated you like a common criminal and didn't even say sorry.'

The chimes of a distant clock sounded; he counted them. Could it really only be midnight? Nearer at hand, in the square, other spires chimed. He counted again – and got thirteen. He looked down bemusedly at his slippers. One his own, one Niamh's father's. 'Thanks for bringing the slipper.'

'Well, when you said you'd lost one on the phone. Cigarette, Arthur?'

'Rather.'

Niamh didn't usually smoke on the street; neither did she normally walk unchaperoned with a man in dressing gown and slippers after midnight, having just sprung him from a police cell. Again that strange excitement of being amongst poets, only partially diluted by how she was going to explain her lateness to her father. Not to mention taking one of his slippers. She lit two cigarettes, their fingers touching as she passed him one.

'So sorry for having got you mixed up in all this, Niamh,' Merryweather said, thrilling at the touch despite everything. 'Don't know anyone else here. I suppose one had better take the dressing gown off, it may look eccentric.'

Calmer now, his stammer had been dreadful when she first arrived at the police station. No wonder he hadn't been able to make himself understood. Of course Niamh had glimpsed it at the library, flitting across the glades of his speech, but this had been a forest fire. 'I must say, you're taking it all so bravely,' she said.

Bravely? He was still shaking. Yet, was that admiration he could detect in his assistant's voice? He wasn't used to being cast in the heroic role. 'Oh,' he heard himself lie. 'It was nothing really.'

'Not many people would see it like that.'

'Well, you know.'

'Who is this Mr Bleaney anyway; why did they think he was you?'

Walking across the midnight square, Merryweather explained about his predecessor in the frowsy rented room, the robberies the detective seemed to think he was linked with, the Thomas gang, the talk of fiddling insurance accounts, their passing resemblance. Cream of wheat telephone boxes glinting under spire and dome, he told her all he knew about the former lodger.

'You'll have to change boarding houses,' she said, thinking how wonderfully, bafflingly unworldly poets were, whilst praying not to encounter Fr. Carrick or any of her father's friends, unlikely as that might be.

'The police told me to stay at sixty-one Corporation Road until they gave me notice. They may wish to speak to me again. You know, I got the impression they still think I'm Mr Bleaney.' Reaching the train station, all the buses had gone. Not a sign of life. 'How *does* one go about getting a taxi in this town, Niamh?'

'One doesn't, not at this time.'

Absurd how despite everything Merryweather felt his spirits rise. Was he actually enjoying himself? 'Come on, I'll walk you home,' he said. 'Your father might be anxious.'

'Anxious isn't the word for it,' she didn't say. Instead, 'How did you know our phone number?'

'There was a directory.' Merryweather recalled how he'd read her records at work to find out that she was twenty-eight years old, unmarried and lived at a high number on the Thinness Road with her father, a dentist. Just as well he had.

'But there are four O'Learys in the book, how did you know which was us?' she stopped herself from asking.

'By the way, I read that book you loaned me,' said Merryweather. 'Gerard Manley Hopkins.'

'And I've been reading Thomas Hardy,' she replied, as she did so something inside of her danced. Was this the right kind of excitement?

Thinness Road was the longest one in town. For Merryweather it could have been thrice the distance, as an animated discussion about Gerard Manley Hopkins carried them down its length. Naturally, he was lying out of his arse about liking the Jesuit, but what did that matter? It pleased her. With each eulogiac opinion exchanged, each lamppost passed, his euphoria grew. When he quoted those verses from *Bisney Poplar*, that odd elegy to Hopkins' favourite trees being cut down, which somehow he'd learnt by heart, her eyes sparkled, and for a moment he *really* did feel as though he loved the Jesuit poet too. I've been mistakenly arrested by the police, he marvelled, threatened and three-quarters terrorised, and I feel light as Mary Fucking Poppins.

'You'll think I'm foolish,' she said, 'but I sometimes dream that Hopkins' Bisney poplars grow over our house.'

'That's not foolish at all,' he only half-fibbed. Before fully fibbing, 'once I dreamt I met Thomas Hardy on a train.'

Twice he felt his elbow touch hers. Once something softer. After which he soared into the stars and she kept her distance. Just because he liked Gerard Manley Hopkins didn't mean she didn't have to be careful. A man was a man, as Fr. Carrick often warned her. After all, Arthur was also a poet. Not all poets were priests. Especially after midnight.

All too soon the townhouse with its plate advertising dental services. A light on inside. Her father waiting up. Niamh steeled herself. 'Thank you,' she said with a formality he hadn't seen since she thought he was an intruder. Only a week ago? 'You can go now.'

'Oughtn't I to explain to your father?'

Niamh had briefly considered telling her father the truth. 'No.'

'What about his slipper?'

'Just keep it.'

Merryweather understood the seeming terseness. He already knew enough about domestic arrangements in the Thinness Road surgery to realise she had a lot of explaining to do. Deeply moved, he walked away. He made it to a tree some fifty yards distant before turning. She was still standing uncertainly at the front step. At last she knocked. A cone of light fell from the opening door, and like a character in a sci-fi film, or Catholic theology, she was assumed within. He hugged the tree. Fuck the *Bisney Poplars* this was Merryweather's maple. A holy spot, the tree where he'd watched Niamh O'Leary assumed into her house. Balls, balls, balls, and yet, *not* balls.

His way home was paved not by outrage at the police, not even by the fear of meeting the Thomas gang, nor the blisters growing from the disintegrating slippers, but by the touch of their fingers as she'd handed him the cigarette. The kiss of their elbows. The something softer. The unmistakable hint of admiration. He'd always secretly feared he was a romantic. So be it. He was in love with Niamh O'Leary. Thunderbolt job, as Teesdale had said in bibulous prophecy. Of course he didn't stand a gnat piss's chance, but even Icarus was allowed an hour of flight before plummeting into the unwrinkled Dardanelle Sea. Merryweather put his dressing gown back on and pulled it tight against the high winds of these giddying new altitudes.

Looking up from the still distant surface of the unwrinkled Dardanelle Sea, Merryweather realised he'd reached his lodgings. It was two o'clock.

How the buggery to get in? He couldn't knock or go through the Mealies' again. What about just kicking the bastard door down? But it didn't have to come to that. Given a despairing jab, the front door swung open.

He so nearly made it to his bedroom. In fact, his hand was actually on the doorknob when: 'You've got a brass neck, lad.' The librarian turned to see his landlady watching him from the darkened landing. She was wearing a grotesque confection of nightwear. 'Swanning back here like this,' she continued. 'Oh aye, I know where you've been. This house has always been respectable until you –'

'Yes, I was arrested,' Merryweather interrupted. Well, he'd intended to have this conversation tomorrow anyway, might as well get it out the way with. 'You see they thought I was Mr Bleaney.'

Old Ma Glenner's hair rollers nodded like a brood of vipers as she padded towards him. 'What did you say?'

'I think you heard, Miss Glendenning. It was a case of mistaken identity. The police are trying to find Mr Bleaney, and – '

'How dare you!'

'So, I'd very much appreciate it if you'd come down with me to the police station tomorrow, and tell them that I'm not Mr Bleaney.'

'Not Mr Bleaney? I'll say you're not Mr Bleaney. You're not half the man Mr Bleaney was.' The name of the former lodger wailed on the landing like an air raid siren. Merryweather couldn't suppress a giggle. 'You're not right in the head,' the landlady said staring at the dressing gown and slippers. 'What did they have you in for – Peeping Tom? Ought to be ashamed of yourself.'

Somehow the conversation wasn't going to plan. 'Miss Glendenning,' he tried again. 'The police wish to trace Mr Bleaney. They thought I was he. Now I don't know what he's involved in, I don't particularly want to know, I just want you to accompany me to the station and vouch…'

Merryweather broke off. The landlady was sobbing. Not histrionically, nor operatically, just clear tears like drops from a leaking ceiling. The librarian felt he knew enough of the north face of life to recognise genuine desolation. 'There, there,' he said instinctively.

A mistake. Like a crocodile smelling blood, she darted towards him. In horror he watched her slippers, all fluffy wuffy and pom-pommed, come in to canoodle his own. With a cry, she fell into his arms. Lacking the balls to simply thrust her aside, he rode the awkward embrace. In between the whooping cough-like gulps of her sobbing, he could hear all the other night sounds of the boarding house. The snoring of his fellow lodgers, the shallow growl of the immersion, the clanking of the plumbing above his own room. 'And after I sewed your jacket for you,' she whimpered.

Eventually Merryweather managed to extricate himself, and get into his room. Fighting against the impulse to go to the window, he naturally lost and saw the girl standing beneath the hawthorn. Flinging caution to the wind, he threw his door open, took the stairs two at a time and lurched into the garden. She was gone.

When he finally fell asleep, he dreamt that instead of the hawthorn the maple grew in the tussocky garden, arching protective arms over the inmates of the lodging house, McCoist, Teesdale, the man in precious stones, the mystery girl, the ghost of Mr Bleaney, the cracked landlady, and even the librarian himself.

20.

The gruel of dawn light dribbling through the threadbare floral curtains splattered on Merryweather's unshaven cheeks and gradually woke him. The first thing he remembered was floating through the midnight streets with his assistant librarian. Even the recollection of the cop shop couldn't diminish the magic. Nor old Ma Glenner's grief. None of it mattered. He lay there in stunned rapture, like some idiot from a Shakespeare play who finds himself, after a must-be-fatal shipwreck, lying on the shingle of an enchanted isle.

Quietly as possible, he rose. At the memory of Niamh's touch, the lack of sleep seemed to fall from his back. Sod kippers and sauce – breakfast at the Royal Station Hotel. Best avoid a repeat of last night's scene with the landlady; besides, he felt like celebrating! He'd take old Ma Glenners to the police station after work, and get the whole thing cleared up properly then. Shaving in cold water – the landlady's ears being preternaturally attuned to the least protest of the immersion heater – Merryweather realised that he had a humdinger of a black eye. When had he got it, falling on the steps or when he was shunted across the cell? Despite his unaccustomed happiness, it gave him the look of a malcontent panda. Dressed and at the front door, he was quietly letting himself out when he saw a note tonguing the letter box. The words *Mr Bleaney* caught his eye. Good god, was there to be no end?

With a quick glance over his shoulder, he slipped the letter into his briefcase. The police might want a look at that, and all Mr Bleaney's other letters in there too. Of course they already had the birthday card from his sister in Stoke. (Think of that: either yesterday, or perhaps today, was the disgraced insurance agent's birthday!)

At this hour the trolley was quiet, a smattering of anaemic clerks and scowling labourers. Spreading out his trusty newspaper more from habit than necessity, he took out the note. *Don't you want me no more, Mr Bleaney?* it asked in round girlish letters largely untroubled by the Butler Education Act. *You promised but were are you? And I wait practicle every night.* The hieroglyphic of a kiss' x, took up the rest of the space.

The scent of an ill-starred love story reached his nostrils. This could only have been written by the hawthorn girl. Well, he'd have to show the touching piece of illiteracy to the authorities, as well as all the other letters he still had. Yet, wouldn't it be a ticklish business explaining to the police how he came by them? No, no, better to get rid of the lot without even reading them himself. Breakfasting safely in the Royal Station Hotel (how lovely to have a change from kippers), the resolution not to read his predecessor's post lasted until Merryweather was on his second pot of tea. There were about a dozen letters. Most were from his insurance company. They told the story the desk sergeant had outlined. Beginning with a request for clarification over a payout discrepancy and culminating in a demand for a full explanation about a recent widow, who despite keeping up the weekly payments faithfully, had found after the tragic death of her husband that he wasn't insured. The sergeant had known what he was talking about. Two of the letters came from a Methodist society assuring Mr Bleaney that he was still on their prayer map. One was from a boarding-house proprietress wondering why he hadn't been in touch to confirm his usual fortnight, and hoping he would be back again with them this summer. It was franked Frinton-on-Sea.

Was this all the former lodger's life had amounted to? The letter from the hawthorn girl was the only hopeful thing – yet what true hope can a middle-aged man find with a girl half his age?

Like a withering wind from the Essex East Anglian coast, the emptiness of his predecessor's life harried Merryweather as he headed for the university, gusting as he passed through the enchanted gates and stepped down the chestnut avenue. He paused on the library steps. The angel seemed to lean down and say: *And what about you; aren't you frightened of becoming just like your Mr Bleaney?* Shoulders stooped, the librarian passed through the vestibule flicking the Vs at the beetle-browed philanthropist before he could get *his* sneering ha'p'orth in. Then – he swore ripely, and not under his breath either. Someone was in the library. How had they got in? Typical! He'd been looking forward to half an hour alone. The moment he saw the transgressor however, face slowly peeping round a tall stack of breast resting books, the Bleaney bleakness dropped from his withers like water from an otter's pelt. 'Hello,

Arthur,' said Niamh. 'How are you this morning? Let me have a look at that eye. It looks nasty. Did they hit you?'

'They may have done,' lied Arthur unaccustomed to the role of hero, but enjoying it.

PART TWO

21.

Spring arrived at bloody last. April lit the chestnut avenue with candles; May clothed the library in her promised bridal blossom; a hot June gathered its bouquet of stinking fish and cast it over the city – if Arthur had thought the stench had been bad before! Standing at his office window, he shook his head in a pantomime grimace at the girl on the bike below. He could see Niamh's responding laughter and furious nod as, lifting a hand from the handlebars, she beckoned. 'Take that ghastly bone shaker away,' he shouted, lifting one of the great sash windows.

'No excuse this time,' she called back up. 'Dad's oiled it for you.' She rang the bell.

The winding stair sounded its habitual chromatic fanfare as the head librarian descended. The three or four students in the vestibule involved in the usual earnest conversation about bugger-all didn't even glance up as he hastened by; the beauty of academic librarianship – complete fucking anonymity. He'd even been able to move that annoying beetle-browed bust so that it couldn't spy on his every coming and going. Passing under the art deco angel's still watchful eye, (there were plans afoot with porter Harry Oxley to topple that tosser as well) Arthur headed for the still tinkling bell. 'Bicycle clips to boot,' Niamh greeted him, holding out a pair of metal omegas.

'I'll end up under a baker's van.'

'Nonsense. You can ride in the middle of the group.'

The head librarian grimaced, genuinely this time. 'Group.'

It was the weekly Wednesday afternoon New Dawn Cycling Club outing, and this time Arthur couldn't see how he might get out of it. Big gesture from Niamh's father to lend him his bike. Had he finally forgiven him the 'stolen slipper' incident? The scent of wisteria filled the air. Niamh had already changed into the crimplene slacks she always sported on cycling days. Like a eunuch permitted to the Sultan's harem, Arthur felt a rush of pointless lust. 'We're going to Thinness today,' she grinned. 'You'll love it. There's an inland lighthouse.'

'An inland lighthouse? That sounds marginally interesting.' Nautical eccentricities aside, Arthur couldn't think of anything more interesting than spending a whole afternoon with Niamh. Unfortunately, Ernie, that bloody 'Kirk Douglas' of the Sociology department, would be there taking centre stage as usual. Watching Ernie all over Niamh had about as much appeal as lancing a haemorrhoid with a rusty fork.

Luckily a head popped through the fire door, open in honour of flaming June, and saved him. 'Quick, Mr M,' gasped Harry breathlessly. 'We've got him for sure this time.'

With a wry smile at Niamh and a helpless lift of the hands, Arthur followed the porter into the library. He was pretty sure that they *hadn't* 'got him for sure this time', that this was just another false alarm in a string of false alarms, but it was sufficient to get him off the hook that afternoon. By the time he'd cleared it up, Ernie and the rest of his commie chums would be halfway to their defunct lighthouse.

The events leading to the porter's 'we've got him for sure this time' had begun back in April, only a week or so after Arthur had started at the library. William Wordsworth had been the first to disappear. Quickly followed by Keats and Byron. By the time the copies of T.S. Eliot had been taken from the shelf, the library had to face up to the fact that there was a poetry thief at large. A thief with shocking taste, as Merryweather had quipped on the disappearance of Robert Bridges' complete works. The thefts had continued despite the porter's dogged but fruitless vigilance, and all his *we've got him for sure this times*. Just last week, the poetry thief had struck again, nicking Milton's *Paradise Lost*.

Arthur followed the porter rather circumspectly across the well of light. The last suspect had turned out to be a visiting lecturer from Scarborough, something the librarian had only found out *after* he'd been goaded into attempting a citizen's arrest. Harry gave the agreed hand signal to 'look natural' so as not to alert the potential thief. 'Is this really necessary?' Arthur murmured, still able to smell the wisteria framing the girl on the bike.

Feeling uncomfortably like a minor character in an Ealing Comedy, Arthur tagged behind the porter as he ascended the gallery to take up their usual position overlooking the literature section. 'Now you're not telling me that *he's* a student,' Harry announced in a stage whisper that could have been heard at the far side of the library. Gripping the railing tightly, Arthur peered down at the suspect on the ground floor. True, the man browsing in the poetry section was far too smartly dressed for a student. Also he was old, easily as ancient as Merryweather himself. 'Been loitering there all morning,' the porter breathed, eyes gleaming with the hunt. 'Look out, he's reaching for a book. He's got it. Now he's off. Quick, Mr M. Go, go, go!'

By the time they'd reached ground level there was no sign of the poetry thief. Just a female student with an unnecessary woollen hat and an armful of books. Almost knocking her down, Arthur and Harry rushed through the literature section, and rounded the corner of history. The black-suited back of the crook was just disappearing. They headed him off at the loans desk where he was handing over a volume of A.E. Houseman along with his ticket. Harry's suspect turned out to be a miner from Selby with an interest in minor poets of the early twentieth century, and a fully paid-up subscription for the library. Feeling sufficiently ridiculous, Arthur apologised and stalked away. But the female student with her armful of books and woolly hat, to whom he wished to apologise, had gone. So had the New Dawn Cycling Club.

Back in his office, the head librarian lolled almost pleasurably on the chaise longue. If only that bastard Ernie would fall under a baker's van. Rousing himself eventually, he attended to the post. A quick peek at his personal mail first. Since uncovering Old Ma Glenner's penchant for reading her lodgers' letters, he'd advised his correspondents to direct their post to the university. One from his mother, one from his famous friend and one by a hand he didn't recognise. It was from the editor of a prestigious magazine. Short and to the point it informed him they were publishing the poems he'd recently sent.

The news took Arthur to the window. It was still open. As though perfectly calm, he lit a fag with a steady hand. The scent of wisteria mingled with his smoke. A bee was busy on the wall. Sparrows chirped. The gracious little world of lawns and willows and learning seemed to blow in like a breeze. Somewhere cricket was being played. For the life of his Park Drive he did not move. He was a poet. His feelings about this office when he'd first arrived were right; he *had* been able to write a line or two of verse here. Through the window, the world kept on turning as it always did; for him, everything had changed. A sudden yell of triumph sent the sparrows darting from the foliage. Before Arthur could stop himself, he'd thrown his head back and given another holler. The metal stairs played out their fanfare far quicker than usual as he recklessly hurried down. He was a bloody poet!

The dentist's newly oiled bicycle was deep in the wisteria. Taking the clips from the cross bar, he battened down his trousers, and, in shirtsleeves and without a penny in his pocket, set off. He was a fucking poet and he had to tell Niamh!

Been a while since he rode a bike but after a few wobbles he was making his way down the enchanted avenue. The New Dawn Cycling Club was going to Thinness. How to get there? Thinness Road of course! He burst through the open gates.

In no time at all the 'Merryweather's maple' hove into view. Arthur waved. No sign of the dentist, that rather forbidding figure with whom he'd actually had tea in the Thinness Road house; Arthur reciprocating at the Royal Station Hotel, conversation languishing somewhere between modern dentistry techniques and T.S. Eliot's use of ether as a metaphor. 'Look where you're going!' a lorry driver shouted as the bike careered in front of his wagon.

'Road hog!' the head librarian laughed back, and then shouted. 'I'm a fucking poet!'

He was sweating heavily by the time tethered ponies and scruffy fields announced the countryside, or at least the end of the town, but he wasn't flagging. Why, he could cycle to the moon, or at least the sodding Soviet Union. With a whinnying hurrah he began to sing *The Red Flag.* The bicycle really *was* well oiled. His mind too span on freshly lubricated cogs. This elation wasn't just due to the fact that his poems were to appear in the country's top publication. No, there was something else. Now he had an actual chance of getting to pull Niamh's knickers down. Crudely put perhaps, but in essence true. He'd lived long enough to know that outside fairy tales, Beast didn't have a flying fart of a chance with Beauty, especially with bastard prince charmings like Ernie sniffing about the whole time, but what was impossible for other ugly-ites, *poets* somehow pulled off. Cyrano de Bergerac might have had a hooter to shame a trombone, but he wrote his way to the heart of Roxane. Having accepted that he and his assistant could only ever be friends, now, at once – bugger it all, Arthur had caught the whiff of a very different future!

Loud peeping from another motor vehicle. Wobbling even more crazily, Arthur flicked the Vs with some panache. What he was trying to articulate to himself was: 1) Niamh idolised poets in the same way that others looked up to stars of the silver screen. 2) He was now a poet. 3) Niamh *might* idolise him. Well, the idolatry wasn't necessary; he just wanted the password to lift that golden crucifix aside.

Bowling through the Queen Anne's lace and the blossom-frothed hedgerows, each rising skylark was a Sidney Bechet solo lifting from a throbbing trumpet. Wild hopes blazed with June. Beast was on the way to conquer Beauty! Arthur narrowly avoided a head-on collision with a dairy horse and cart. 'Watch where you're going, you bloody four eyes nutter!'

A crossroads. Arthur didn't even slow. The fingerpost warning him that he was still some miles from the coast flashed by unheeded. He couldn't stop now. When she heard, she might even kiss him there and then. Hedge followed hedge, village green gave way to village green, and with the spinning of his wheels, span ever more fantastical movie reels of the moment he told Niamh. 'Oh, Arthur forgive me. I lost my head when you told me. I think I'd better wipe that lipstick away.'

At last, lathered, light-headed, aching of arse, wrist and limbs, but still pulsating, Arthur reached Thinness. A newly built junior school greeted the traveller. To the head librarian's eyes, the school had the look of a unit on a light industrial park, but then so did everywhere these days. The children waved through the railings. He waved back. A linear high street, echoes of the Vikings, drew him into the little resort town. Comatose with Wednesday's half-day closing, bakeries, butchers, teashops and greengrocers slumbered with less than half an eye open. Above them all rose a tall white column, the landlocked lighthouse one supposed. Around the base of the lighthouse lounged the New Dawn Cycling Club. Loose limbed and nauseatingly athletic, they were passing around large bottles of sarsaparilla. 'Arthur,' said Niamh, rising. 'You've made it.'

But before the librarian could even catch his breath, let alone mention his elevation to Mount Parnassus, fucking Ernie was wheeling both his bike and Niamh's over. 'Right,' said the tosser, looking even more like bloody Kirk Douglas. 'Time for the ritual dipping.' And without acknowledging the new arrival, pedalled off on his dropped handlebars racing bike.

With a semi apologetic smile Niamh followed. Merryweather threw himself to the ground. It had been a little further to Thinness than he had anticipated.

'Have you ever read Engels' *The Part Played by Labour in the Transition of Ape to Man?*' an elderly bolshie, superannuary of the Philosophy department asked Arthur as the rest of the group took up their bikes.

'No.'

By the time Arthur had dragged himself to his feet and caught up, the others stood undressed on the beach. In his bathing trunks, Kirk Douglas had become Johnny Weissmuller's Tarzan. When he saw Niamh's white swimming costume the head librarian dropped his bike. Attempting to pick it up, he entangled the others leaning against the esplanade railings. Three then four dominoed to the ground. 'Come on, new chap,' the elderly bolshie cajoled, stripped likewise but in a less appealing one piece. 'Club rules – total immersion.'

'I don't have my c-costume.'

'Got your smalls haven't you?' And the retired philosophy lecturer whooped into the scalding fizz of the waves with the others.

Arthur limped off. Now wasn't the time to tell her. Better have a drink. Solo celebration to begin with. He looked at his watch. Naturally, he'd missed last orders. Despite his good news, he felt a familiar, senseless rage. What sort of a bloody excuse for a country was this where pubs closed just when people were thirsty? The puritan heritage, one supposed. A twinge in his lower back. Gordon Bennett, he hadn't done himself an injury had he?

The seafront was as sleepy as the little town. Young mothers pushing prams for the most part, with a few couples at the other end of life sharing benches, thermos flasks and (more than likely) silent despair as they waited for the inevitable wave of cancer or coronary disease to sweep them apart. The usual refugees from the workday world loomed large. Nervous and starey eyed – singed moths in a world full of flames. The lazy, the feckless, those recovering from surgery or bad nerves, losels, loblolly men, clerks caught with their fingers in the tills, safe crackers, Mr Bleaney?

For Pete's sake! Why think about the disgraced insurance agent on this day of all days? Well, that wasn't entirely fair since one of the poems to be published was actually about the former lodger. Down on the beach, a fat man in a knotted handkerchief sat alone in a deckchair like some National Assistance Board Canute. Close by, a dog defecated. Perhaps the law had caught up with the real Mr Bleaney by now. Since his own arrest, Arthur hadn't heard anything more from the police, even though he hadn't managed to get the landlady down to the police station to vouch for him. They'd obviously forgotten all about him. Probably no need even to stay at sixty-one Corporation Road anymore. With every passing day, the night of the arrest seemed more remote. Well, let sleeping dogs lie. If it wasn't for the hawthorn girl continuing her frequent if not constant vigils, he could forget all about the unfortunate occurrence.

Shouts from the sea. Ernie romping like a sodding Grecian God. Was there a pier? Yes. The librarian headed for it. Sometimes the licensed premises on piers had special arrangements.

One gained entrance via a surprisingly grand brick folly of twin turrets. Queasily he picked his way over the pier's wooden slabs. Some seventy odd feet below, the saltwater's jellyfish slap.

'Have a go, boss?' A squat individual demanded from the recesses of a hook-the-duck, one of a handful of attractions open.

'No, thank you.'

'Don't you want to win your sweetheart a prize?'

'Bugger off.'

'Give yourself a thrill, chum,' the proprietor of the Ali Baba's Magic Carpet Helter Skelter challenged.

Arthur glanced at the flimsy tower leaning perilously out to sea, and walked on. Under the torn awnings of a coconut shy some jittery clerk was trying to win his girl a poisonous-looking coconut. Arthur watched him spend penny after penny without success. 'It don't matter, Dennis,' his pallid girl said as the boyfriend finally shuffled away. Like love, the librarian reflected, failure wears a thousand faces.

'Think you can do better, long lad?' a voice inquired. Arthur saw a woman – he'd thought her a man – sitting in an immense array of balls. Fag in gob and a growth on her neck getting on in size for one of her own missiles, she looked like some grotesque booby on an over-productive nest.

'All right,' said Arthur inexplicably touched by the scene. Three wooden balls had been handed over before he realised he'd come out without any money. How embarrassing. In desperation he checked his trouser pockets. His luck really *must* be changing, half a crown lay folded in his handkerchief. He handed it over and got – short changed. After a bitter argument, the woman grudgingly yielded up the proper amount. Of course, *he* didn't get the coconut either. Indeed, had to pay an extra shilling for the third ball which flew wide and into the sea. There must be a poem somewhere in all this, he thought. A coconut shy as a metaphor for the failing reach of human hopes. God, that sounded a load of shit. Were the poems they were going to publish a load of shit? Not if they meant he could get to pull down Niamh's crimplene slacks. My God, Arthur reflected, I think I might even mean that. The sacred *is* the profane. But how could he get her away from Ernie and tell her about his good fortune? Where could he take her? A café would be good. A pub better. If somehow he could get a port and lemon inside her first.

The doors of the Pier Pub were closed, and, what's more, didn't look as though they'd been opened since the war. The dusty windows were blind with flyblown bills. One advertised an act called 'Gormless Gordon' who was guaranteed to 'rickle your tibs' and pull your 'bunny fone', as well as being, good God, *Thinness' answer to Archie Andrews*. Forget poetry, someday someone *had* to write a monograph on failure. One could call it Gormless Gordons. A whole chapter of course would be devoted to librarians. But not poets. Ah, *not* poets.

A young couple were snogging at the end of the pier. A sign of things to come for him? Christ, imagine snogging Niamh like that. Lip to lip, tit to tit, hands following those sculpted contours. Why not? Why settle for the pig's trotters of life when a prime cut was on offer?

Eyes narrowing, Arthur stared out over the sea. It stretched as blue and empty as ever; the horizon framed its usual unsolvable geometry. What was it that he couldn't see? Holland? The low countries? Maybe Scandinavia this far north. What was it that he could hear? Niamh and Ernie. Having splintered off from the main group, they were directly below. Typical of that bugger to take the gloss off Arthur's special day. In the weeks since his arrest, whenever he had managed to wangle some time alone with Niamh, that ruddy square head would show up more often than not. Although he knew that he wasn't going to see anything welcome now,

Arthur, pressing gingerly against the rickety railings, leant out.

He saw Niamh first. Spangled with surf and sun, her bridal bathing costume taut – part cabbage white butterfly, part Venus rising from the sea at Cythera. Arthur gulped. Easy to allow Ovid and other classical authors their punitive metamorphoses for mortals caught spying on goddesses. Even if he was going to be turned into a toad, Arthur couldn't have looked away. Sunlight sparking the water around her ankles, she stood, arms outstretched, her very own railway advertisement, *Come to Sunny Thinness*. My God, put that up in a station and the bastards would pile here in their droves. Ernie wasn't worried about divine punishment, his eyes were all over her. Hands would be given half a chance. Who said anything about Neptune being at Cythera anyway? Let alone Kirk fucking Douglas. For the first time since knowing her, Arthur was relieved by Niamh's rather baffling Catholicism. Catching the salty sun, the crucifix glinted its *noli me tangere*. And to be fair, she *was* fighting off the woodentop with genuine commitment. Pushing him away so firmly in fact that he fell.

Arthur stalked back down the pier. He'd get the train home. Now definitely wasn't the right time to tell her. Also one had rather overdone it on the old pennyfarthing.

'I've brought you something.'

Looking up from where he'd taken refuge at the base of the landlocked lighthouse, Arthur saw the same face that had just been smiling down at him in his daydream. The real Niamh was holding ice creams. Before he could get up, she'd leant her bike against his and joined him.

Still wet, the salty tips of her hair crackled. In her glow the litter of dog turds drying in the sun simply ceased to be. After the bathing costume, Arthur could only trust himself to look directly in her eyes. That didn't save him either. He crossed his legs. The ice cream was proving treacherous too, bleeding white streamers down his fingers; ice-cream cones were always a disconcerting tightrope between childhood and dotage. 'Look, you go off with the others,' he said. 'Don't let me stop your fun.'

On cue, the ring of a bike bell and Ernie was freewheeling over. 'So this is where you skulked off to, Merryweather. Didn't fancy a dip? Saw you up on the pier. Looked like you were going to end it all.' Ernie's too-loud laugh was not reciprocated by Niamh whose glare seemed to say quite plainly *don't be such a bollocking cretin*. 'Well, bring trunks next time, Merry-weather, there's a good chap,' said Ernie visibly chastened. 'Or I could lend you a pair of mine if you like. Although they're likely to be too big.'

'Too small surely,' returned Arthur, unable to stop himself, ludicrous though he knew he must sound.

An infuriating grin. 'If you say so. Anyway, come on Niamh. *Avanti popolo.*'

'You go without me, Ernie,' Niamh replied. 'Arthur and I have to pop into the local branch library. On business – inter-library loans.'

The head librarian experienced such childish delight that he knew already he would worry over it later, poet or not. Was his moment nigh?

When Ernie had gone, Niamh and Arthur got up. At least he tried to. Niamh had to assist. Despite his glee, the librarian grimaced. The bike seat still seemed wedged halfway up his arse. Stumbling, he only just avoided the dog dirt. 'Does your religion allow you to lie?' he asked. 'About the branch library, I mean.'

'I wasn't lying,' returned Niamh. 'How long is it since you've been on a bike?'

'Oh, about two hundred years.'

After a quick look in the window of the branch library,

closed of course, Niamh said, 'Come on, Arthur, I want to show you something.'

If only one could be entirely sure of not having trodden in the dog shit at the base of the redundant lighthouse, this would quite possibly be the happiest moment of his life. 'Where are we going?'

'My childhood. It's where we always went whenever we came to the seaside. The owner was a Catholic.'

Frankly, the O'Leary family's favourite tearoom was ghastly. Tablecloths splattered with grease, cracked vases troubled with wilted weeds, a Glencoe scale massacre of flies. The ghosts of fried breakfasts haunted the walls. Enough spilt sugar to keep Daddy dentist in tooth decay for the rest of his natural. Arthur's heart sang. 'Tea for two please.'

'We close at four,' the proprietress said without rising from her stool, the spitting image of the coconut shy lady, save for the lump. And the balls.

'It's not even three-thirty yet,' Arthur pointed out.

'Just two cups of tea?'

'Well, we'll have high tea I think.'

'I'm not putting the frying pan on at nearly four o'clock.'

'Well, afternoon tea then.'

'*Two* afternoon teas?'

'Yes, two afternoon teas.'

The woman shuffled off to the kitchen. 'This used to be a lovely place, honestly,' Niamh whispered. 'Different owner.'

'Maybe they've nationalised it,' he just managed to stop himself from saying as he tried to manoeuvre his burning arse into a comfortable position. He'd learnt the hard way not to annoy Niamh with jibes about socialism. 'Oh, it's still lovely.'

'No, it isn't.'

'Well, it's the only place that's open.'

'Are you in pain, Arthur?'

'It's no laughing matter.'

'You'll have to bike out with us more often.'

'How do you know I'm not a capitalist infiltrator spying on your little ring?' That kind of joshing was fine. In fact she liked it. 'Message to the secret service in London,' he pretended to telephone. 'Communism is being built with bicycle wheels in Thinness.' Laughter. Oh, he could talk to her like this until the cows came home; could talk about a whole world of things – when she asked whether he and the porter had caught the poetry thief, Arthur's retelling of it brought belly laughter. It was only when he thought about his feelings that he became a gibbering dolt. But remember, he was one of the poets now.

Clearing his throat and fixing a wry grin (he'd decided on a kind of playfully nonchalant announcement), Arthur was just about to share his news when the tea room hag returned. 'These want finishing up,' she said, banging down a tin of homemade cakes that had seen better days.

Arthur lifted their bicycles into the guard's van. The train was departing in three minutes. Leaving the tearoom they'd had to pedal fast to the station. He hadn't told her yet. Each time he'd been on the verge of the revelation that bloody woman in the café had interrupted. Then there'd been the fact that he hadn't had enough money to pay for the tea, let alone their train tickets. Hard to play the debonair hero when you're freeloading off your girl. 'No hurry, cocker,' said an unshaven British rail guard sauntering down the platform, obligatory cup of tea stuck to his mouth.

'Beg pardon?'

'We don't leave until quarter past five.'

'Quarter past five? We're supposed to leave at twenty past four.'

The unshaven cheeks were scratched with a dirty forefinger. 'No, we aren't.'

'What do you mean, "no, we aren't"? It's written up here.'

The head librarian jabbed a finger at the timetable pasted on the wall.

'Is everything all right?' Niamh called through the open window of a carriage in which Arthur had chivalrously installed her.

'Perfectly,' he called back.

'Wrong timetable, mush,' the guard explained. 'We're on the summer one now. Twenty past four don't run in summer.'

'So that's the idea, eh. Have fewer trains just when people want them?'

'No need to get shirty, chum.'

'I'm not getting shirty, I'm merely inquiring why the hell –'

'Arthur.'

A tug on his arm made him look away from this infuriating bastion of the proletariat. Niamh had come over. 'Sorry,' he grovelled to the whiskery British Rail functionary. 'Not your fault, obviously. Happy to wait.'

As it happened the delay simply added icing to an already buggeringly brilliant cake. They went for a walk along the beach, all theirs now. Shoes and socks cast off, they paddled. Then rockpooled. Arthur was just about to announce his humble deification when Niamh dipped a hand into the pool. The water rode up past her elbow, sending goosebumps up the rest of her arm. All at once he was seized with madness. Not only did he want to share his news, he wanted to take that hand. To boot, he wanted to kiss her. Why all the fannying around? Just snog her now. Wasn't that how poets behaved? Before he could act however, she was bringing out a crab from under a rock. It was large. The pinchers waved. Arthur blenched. He wasn't a fan of flailing crustaceans.

On the pier, the coconut shy and the rest of the attractions had closed. 'Niamh,' he said as they stood searching for Scandinavia. 'I almost forgot tell you. I'm having some poems published. Oh, it isn't a big deal. Rather a small affair actually, but...'

The four-fifths empty train cradled them back through the fields. They were alone in the compartment. In the world. The smoke of their cigarettes mingled. 'Fancy that,' Niamh was saying. 'A published poet. It must be wonderful to have a gift like yours.'

'Yes, and I've something else to tell you. I'm completely and utterly in love with you,' Arthur almost said. Instead, 'Oh, I'm no Gerard Manley Hopkins, you know.'

'When did you realise you had a vocation to be a poet?'

How typical of Niamh to use theological imagery; from her, there could be no higher compliment. Arthur felt another dangerous prompting to take her hand. 'When I realised I couldn't get people to read my novels.'

'Really? Well, your mother must be so proud.'

'Oh, she'd far rather I was a municipal accountant like my father.' What the hell did he say that for? And that other bloodless guff about failing as a novelist. The truth couldn't be allowed to fuck up the perfect moment. Instead of uttering inanities – take her ruddy hand. He reached out but at the last moment, as though by its own accord, his grip diverted itself to a copy of the local newspaper left by an earlier traveller. Blindly he turned to the cricket scores, and pretended to read. Safely screened, a fierce struggle raged through his breast, a wild wrestling bout between man and mouse Merryweather, between wild hopes and the equally wild terror of rejection, between the thirty-odd years of emotional permafrost and the recent thaw of knowing Niamh. 'I see they still haven't caught anyone,' he remarked in a curiously flat voice, turning the page and seeing the headline midway down. *'Police still can't crack the safe crackers.'*

'I don't think they ever will,' she replied.

'No, I don't suppose they will.'

Arthur's eyes darted behind his screen. Was that disappointment in her voice? Was she *waiting* for him to act? 'Says the chief constable ought to resign,' he continued wretchedly.

'Been saying that a while.'

Oh, what was the use of being a poet if you didn't have any balls? Enraged by his timidity, the head librarian might have punched a fist through the carriage window, though he sat there docile as a gelding pretending to read the paper. When they passed through a tunnel, he dared a glance at her reflection in the window. She was staring straight at him. Or rather, would be if the newspaper wasn't in the way. That decided him. The moment had come. But even as he was lowering his screen and reaching out, she was too… 'May I borrow the paper for a moment, Arthur?'

'Of course.'

Now it was her turn to disappear behind print. Arthur sat there helplessly, a woodlouse turned on its back. Just when he felt he couldn't stand another second, Niamh reappeared. 'I thought of you when I saw this in last night's paper,' she said, holding the newspaper out, thumb marking a paragraph.

'Two bedrooms,' he read. 'An ideal self-contained flat overlooking the park, all modern conveniences…'

'Why don't you go and have a look, Arthur?'

'Beg pardon?'

'Why don't you go and take a look at that nice-sounding flat they're advertising? The lease is ready now.' For a few giddying, intoxicating moments, Arthur thought he'd entered one of his own, least credible fantasies in which Niamh, so impressed by his achievement, was asking him to provide a pied-à-terre for their amorous liaisons. 'I mean living alone would suit you better. The way you're so fond of your own company. It even says self-contained. That's what made me think of you. And the police can't want you to stay on in Corporation Road any more, can they?'

'No, they can't,' said Arthur, understanding, and weeping within.

Still, a flat to oneself seemed to come with a myriad of marvellous possibilities; well, one or two anyway.

Both bikes and daughter delivered safely back to the dentist, Arthur and Niamh parted in the gorgeous June evening light. 'I've had a super day,' he said. Again, he willed his own hand to lift and take hers; but some hidden puppeteer had commandeered the strings.

'So have I.'

'So sorry, you had to come back on the train with me.'

'Not at all.'

'And pay for everything. I'll pay you back though.'

'I've said there's no need, Arthur.'

'And I'll have to get into more training on the old bicycle.'

'It might help.'

Sage and onion stuffing! Arthur admonished himself in despair. Got to do better than this. 'I say, Niamh,' he blurted. 'Would you come with me, help me flat hunt?' Not exactly a verse from the karma sutra, but at least he'd said something. 'You know, when I go to inspect that flat.'

A pause, long enough for him to fear he'd contravened some obscure Catholic bylaw on cohabitation. But then, 'all right. How about tomorrow dinnertime?'

'Tomorrow dinnertime,' he agreed lapsing gratefully into local parlance for the midday meal.

'Would you like me to pick out a few more properties?'

'Good thinking,' he stammered, not quite able to take in the enormity of what she was saying.

'If I were you I shouldn't stay where you are a day longer than you need to.'

'Quite.'

'By the way, I knew,' she said when he'd turned to go. 'The moment I saw you.'

Arthur's heart clawed at his ribs like a crab. 'Knew what, Niamh?'

'I knew you were a poet.'

All at once, the puppeteer had been overthrown – he was reaching out to her. Her hand was reaching out too. Now the hands were shaking. Then just as his other hand was edging over to tenderly take her cheek – 'I'll see you tomorrow then, Arthur,' she said stepping back.

'Yes, indeed. Tomorrow.'

Arthur floated down Thinness Road. Tomorrow dinnertime he was going flat hunting with Niamh O'Leary! It might not sound much to normal people, to the likes of Ernie, nor Arthur's own chief correspondent the successful novelist, but for him it was like a day ticket to Shangri-bloody-la. Probably for the best that he hadn't tried to make a pass. He must have been out of his mind at that rockpool. Someone like Niamh had to be wooed, earned, won.

A swift one under the chandeliers at the Royal Station Hotel in celebration and Arthur was just walking across the station to the trolleys when something brought him up sharp. A pen had been to work on the *Come to Sunny Prestatyn* bill poster. The girl had been given boss eyes and snaggle teeth. Huge tits too. A fissured cunt gave access to a fairly tuberous cock and balls. She'd been too good for this world. The knife that had gouged out the pearl of her mouth, leaving a gaping shell between moustached lips, had hacked out an autograph at the bottom of the destruction, *Titch Thomas*.

Good lord, was he still at large?

The station clock announced seven thirty. He'd missed the meal chez Mad Ma Glenners. The boarding house rose in his mind like a kraken of the deep, boiling a wake of sauce bottles, insomniac telephone, salesman's broken dreams, and the girl under the hawthorn. Aside from being able to do it with

141

Niamh, the idea of flat hunting was a capital one. He'd been bonkers to stay at Old Ma Glenner's all this time. Why not just take the first flat he saw?

Instead of heading for 'home', Arthur bought himself fish and chips (by God you wouldn't get a cod like that in Oxford!) and retreated to his lair in the library to eat them out of the paper. It wasn't the first time he'd 'worked late'; in fact evening vigils in the rococo office were becoming something of a habit. Usually he warned his landlady in advance. Well, no need now. Soon he would never have to set eyes on her again. Realising this, he saluted the angel above the library door.

Despite the half day habit of the rest of Haddock town and its environs, Wednesday was late opening at the library. Although they weren't due to shut for another hour Arthur allowed the unqualified staff to go home. He and his number two (properly called under-librarian, although undertaker would be a better description) could manage the handful of conscientious scholars remaining. Safely ensconced in his office, Arthur dragged the chaise longue to the window. Groaning with pleasure, he'd only just eased his aching body into the rich give of the upholstery, and begun to take in the *dies mirabilis,* when footsteps sounded on the stair. That slow plod of death could only presage the under-librarian. What the bloody hell did that officious Jeremiah want? Arthur rolled off the chaise longue. Landing heavily, he hauled his aching carcass over to the desk so one could be discovered suitably busy. The strictly unexcitable under-librarian practically fell into the office and breathlessly poured out his news. Apparently there'd been a stock taking and a loan cross-referencing and another stock taking, and the upshot was, the poet thief had struck again. Today. 'Thomas Hardy this time,' said the under-librarian with cold glee.

Following his number two downstairs, Arthur saw the absence immediately. Wheeling over the ladder, he climbed gingerly up. All five copies of Hardy's complete poetry had been nicked, along with the new critical editions specially ordered in. Really, it was past ridiculous the way this man was working his way through the nation's literature like a wood-boring beetle. At the last staff meeting, the under-librarian had strongly urged that the police be involved. Arthur had demurred, but now? *Something* was going to have to be done.

Having chivvied out the five industrious students remaining, and sent the under-librarian packing, Arthur locked up, and at an hour when other men his age would have long since headed home to pipe and slippers, wife and kiddies, evening paper or screwdriver (yes, the whole box of nasties by his age) he took to his winding stairs.

The faithful in-tray was squatting on his desk. Half-a-dozen matters or so required more or less immediate attention. The spare parts they'd sent for the radiators in the Physics section had been the wrong gauge, and so forth. Increasingly one found a kind of reckless comfort in such tongue-pulling tasks. At last, all completed, the librarian was about to retire to the chaise longue again when he saw the note.

Having been pushed under the door, it was half hidden under the mat. The famously ominous, missed letter of Hardy's *Tess of the d'Urberville's* flashed through his mind. He dismissed it. Ludicrous. It would just be some student request. Hobbling over, he picked it up. Written on lined paper, the cheapest of stationery no doubt sourced from one of Mr Paper Products' *Woolworth's*, the note bore no address, neither of sender nor recipient. No name either. Must be from a student, but even so the handwriting was shockingly bad, and as for the grammar and spelling. A looping, girlish, elementary school pen had scrawled: *Sorry for all them books, I am not really a theef. I would not of took them if I could of done without poetry.*

Arthur had poured and drunk a glass of Glenlivet before he accepted the connection. This note and the one delivered to Mr Bleaney all those weeks ago, which now lay on his desk before him, had been written by the same person. An identical, feral syntax; the same tortuous yet curiously touching idiom; each vowel a balloon barely held by a string. The hand of a hairdresser's apprentice or shoe-shop girl. The poetry thief was the girl from under the hawthorn tree.

A second dram strengthened this baffling link. He'd barely noticed her at the time, but now he thought (drank) about it, hadn't he seen that student with the unnecessary woollen hat before? That girl he and the porter had practically knocked down in pursuit of the Selby miner. The girl with the pile of books. Yes, he *had* seen her before. Well, one sees so many students. Yet he hadn't seen her at the university. Somewhere closer to home. He'd seen her *sans* woollen hat, standing under the hawthorn tree. A third glass considered the armful of books she'd dropped. Not only had they been red, the same colour as the Hardy collections, but Arthur couldn't be entirely sure that he hadn't spotted a glint of gilt – the embossed head of that familiar and well-beloved Dorset misery guts.

Just that afternoon the hawthorn girl had stolen Thomas Hardy from right under his nose. 'Bleaney's bint' was the poetry thief.

22.

The front door of sixty-one Corporation Road was locked by the time Arthur returned. A bearded head appeared at an upstairs window after the librarian had spent five minutes shying pebbles at it. 'You bloody missed tea again, Merryweather,' McCoist snarled, letting him in with supreme bad grace. 'She wouldnae serve it until it was dried oot.'

Trudging up the stairs after the irate fellow lodger, Arthur had only just collapsed, exhausted, on his bed when he heard heavily slippered feet padding down the landing. 'You in, Mr

Merryweather?' the landlady demanded. The door handle turned; the bolts held. 'I know you're in there, I heard you come in.' Again and again the door handle turned. Thankfully Merryweather had put in an extra pair of top notch Chubb bolts. At last, the slippers padded back up the landing.

The librarian had only just started a letter when, 'Open up, old man,' came a whisper. Once again the bolts counteracted the hand on the other side of the door. Teesdale's this time. 'Look here, I'm worried about you. Unhealthy the way you coop yourself up the whole time. Not thinking of doing anything stupid in there are you?' Once more Arthur didn't reply. 'You won't believe what I've got to tell you. Couldn't believe it myself when I heard. Of course it changes everything.' The librarian's golden rule for living with Teesdale was never, no matter the bait, believe that he had anything remotely true or interesting to say. 'I've got some whisky. '

Arthur's reply was a pretend snore.

'It's just that this is how it began with Bleaney,' Teesdale continued. 'Suddenly went all quiet. Clammed up. The next thing I know, I'm having to cut him down from his door hook.'

At last the man in fur gave up.

God, it was hot in the coffin room. As the year lengthened, the sun had crept further round the house until Mr Bleaney's box baked all afternoon in the full glare. It was all he could do to keep up his correspondence. Arthur's letter to his successful friend was a description of that afternoon's New Dawn Cycling club outing. Ernie was writ large, as was the elderly bolshie, but not Niamh; he'd never introduced her into their correspondence. *Any* of his correspondence. He wanted to keep her out of the glare of any banter; undefiled, without finger marks. *Had* he known about her, his friend would have just issued advice that could only have ended in disaster and humiliation. The postscript was given over to his good news.

145

A laconic, yet eternally effervescent *they tell me I'm having a few poems printed*. His friend would understand the understatement.

The second letter of the evening was brief and easily executed, a promise to his mother that he would visit home this weekend. He'd tell her about the poems face to face. The third epistle presented more of a challenge. How to inform his lady friend of his good news without her immediately dropping everything and coming over. Mind you, she'd find out herself anyway sooner or later. Impossible to keep anything from that woman.

Arthur was just screwing up his third attempt to pass on the momentous news to the wearer of the electric-green dress, when his mind jagged on the book thief again. What ought one to do? Impossible to tell the police without re-embroiling himself in the whole Bleaney business. Yet how could he simply ignore it?

The heat in the box room was becoming unbearable. Stripped to his singlet, Arthur lay there feeling like one of old Ma Glenner's sausages sizzling on a frying pan. With a wail of springs, he crawled out of bed, and agile as someone recovering from heart surgery, hauled himself to the window. God he'd be stiff in the morning.

A peek through the curtains. The girl wasn't there. Most nights, when she showed, she came around midnight. He opened the window. A welcome cool stole over him along with the stink from the Mealie's backyard bog. Unkempt when Arthur first moved here, number sixty-one's front garden had flared into a waist high pampas. The hawthorn's summer green burnt like a bible bush.

Leaving the window open, better the stink of a piggery than to sweat like one, he lay on the bed watching the young summer light's lingering death. Glenlivet in the crook of his arm, ashtray on chest, *Lyflat* memo book on his heart, pen in sword hand, he was a stone statue sculpted on a medieval tomb with his badges of office. But tonight his sleeplessness had a grace of its own – he could think of Niamh!

The librarian had wandered deep into the garden of Niamh when he heard voices. They were coming from the garden outside. One was his landlady, the other was one he'd only ever heard on the telephone – Bleaney's bint, the poetry thief.

He hauled himself back to the window, and peered through a sliver in the curtains. The well-known girl was back in her place. Yes, that was the face under the woollen hat. Standing under the hawthorn during the wide fortnight of the bush's bloom, she'd looked like a figure in a fountain, now, peering out from the tangle of leaves she was one of those green men that medieval craftsman hid in the corniced corners of churches. Beside her, on the ground, stood a large, heavy-looking suitcase. She was talking to the landlady, who stood, arms akimbo, on the garden path.

23.

As Merryweather had lain on his bed thinking of Niamh, Mavis Glendenning had come to decision. Time to deal with that girl. Past time. Creeping down the stairs, she'd opened the front door to find the brazen tart standing under the hawthorn.

The landlady's first surprise came when the girl didn't bolt. The gormless cow stood gaping in the moonlight as Mavis walked up the path. She wasn't any prettier close up – no surprise there. 'He were going to chop that tree down,' the landlady began. 'He never liked it.' The girl looked up at the hawthorn. 'There's a dog buried under it,' Mavis added. 'Just where you're stood.'

The girl looked down. 'You what?'

Common as muck, just as the landlady had thought. Yet, staring at the girl, something very strange happened. For the first time on seeing that hussy in the bushes, she didn't want to tear her face off. 'He's not here no more,' Mavis said, more gently than she had planned. 'He's gone.'

'I know,' the girl said.

'So what the hell are you doing here night after night?'

'I thought he come back a couple of months back.'

'What you talking about?'

'That new one in his room. I thought it were him. Same bald head. So I followed him one morning. *He* works in a library.'

Slow witted as well. Probably dropped on the head as a baby. Mavis was going to have to spell it out. 'Look, lass, Mr Bleaney's slung his hook and he's not coming back, so there an't no point hanging about here no more.' What the hell had he seen in this? Stupid, moon faced, hardly any tits. Well, tonight she was going to get rid of her even if it meant slapping her all the way to the docks. Yet as Mavis moved in for the kill, that odd feeling bordering on gentleness hampered her once more. 'What does your mam say about all this?' she asked.

'An't got one.'

'No dad neither, I'd wager. Your type never do.' Mavis couldn't resist that. 'How old are you?'

'Nineteen.'

'Listen, lass, don't you think it's time you stopped coming here bothering all my nice respectable gentlemen?'

'Can't.'

'Why not?'

The girl's eyes climbed up to Mr Bleaney's room where the curtains flickered slightly as though in a breeze. 'He said.'

'What did he say?'

'Said I'm to wait for him. Said he'll come back.'

'He was lying, you stupid little bitch!'

'No he weren't.'

Heedless of the cat messes and dog do, Mavis' anger waded

her through the grass to where the girl stood over the dog grave. Moths fluttered between them. Neither flinched. So, there was steel as well. Mavis could barely trust her voice, but in for a penny in for a pound. 'Where did you meet him?'

'Down the docks.'

The landlady rode a wave of sickness. 'You on the game?'

'What do you take me for? It were at the all night cafe. I work there. Dad would come in and chat.'

'Dad?'

'That's what the other girls called him. Cos he were like one. I think he were lonely. We made friends.'

'Men don't make friends with tarts.'

'Yes, they do.' A flare of courage: 'Anyway, I'm not a tart. And Dad were different.'

'If you call him that again I'll bloody break every bone in your body.'

Mavis glared at the halfwit to make sure her threat had sunk in, but the stupid bitch was just staring up at Mr Bleaney's old window as if he was there now, stood at the curtains, peeping out like he used to do for hours. 'He were always saying that if he could come into a bit of luck he'd start a new life as far from here as he could get,' the girl explained. 'So one night I said, that sounds nice I wish I could, and he said well why not?'

'What are you talking about, you daft bitch?'

'So I said, what, you'd take me with you? He said, why not? I said, don't be daft you wouldn't. He said, yes I would. Then he said, if I come into a bit of luck we could go as far from here as you can get, and you could go to college instead of serving teas and coffees. I said, what me at college? Yes, he said, people have to go to college otherwise they end up nowhere. If I could only come into a bit of luck, he said, we could both start a new life as far from here as you can get, and you could go to college, I know just the place.'

'*You* at college?' the landlady sneered.

Nodding, the girl pointed at the heavy suitcase. 'I've made a start.'

Mavis bent down and tore open the luggage. It was full of books. 'Where did you get these from, you stupid cow? I bet you can't even read.'

'Yes I can. Anyway, he said he'd learn me to do it better. And you know what? Dad *did* come into a bit of luck – '

The slap was resounding. Mavis paused a moment. No, it didn't make her feel any better. Neither did she feel better when she lifted the girl up by the roots of her hair and snarled: 'If you don't clear off, lass, and stay cleared off, I'll break your bloody neck and dump you in the river. You've been warned.'

Mr Bleaney's curtains twitched as Arthur stole back to bed. He'd heard every word. Seen it all too. Having warned the poetry thief off, old Ma Glenners was kneeling under the tree, hugging herself, weeping. Lying there, Arthur listened to his landlady's sobs. Allow the mud flats with its docks and terraces to be an Egdon Heath of dark barrows and cob-walled hamlets, and you had yourself a right little three-cornered Thomas Hardy poem here. One of the really nasty ones from *Time's Laughingstocks*. Tragedies are best left on paper. Just as well he was getting away from here.

24.

'Well?' Niamh smiled as the librarians stood in the new flat at dinnertime the next day.

'As billed,' Arthur smiled. 'An ideal self-contained flat overlooking the park.'

'With all modern conveniences?'

'Indeed. And now I'd like to take you into that bedroom and remove every stitch of your clothing,' he didn't quite add.

He signed the lease there and then, thrilling that the landlord might think that he and Niamh were married, or even better, were going to be living there in glorious sin. He agreed to move in on the coming Sunday. The key was in his hand, then his pocket. His famous friend wasn't the only one to play the impulsive bohemian. Walking back to university, or hobbling rather since he was still buggeratingly stiff from yesterday's exertions, he decided that his instinct not to mention the library thief was right. He couldn't quite trust Niamh's Catholic morality. She might think he ought to report it, and the last thing he wanted was to draw the attention of the police. Also, one of his own tenets of faith, next only in Godliness to *thou shalt not get involved*, stated quite categorically – *it'll all blow over*. Besides, other fish to fry. He was a poet, and he was going to act like one. That watchdog crucifix had to be pacified, its wearer wooed and won. The only thing was to work out exactly how and when. And then find the balls to do it.

As chance would have it Harry Oxley provided him with the perfect opportunity that afternoon. 'Who are you taking then, Mr M?' the porter asked bringing up to Arthur's office an impressive envelope delivered by internal post.

'Beg pardon?'

'Well, if I'm not wrong, this is your invitation to the Swank's Soiree. Also known as the Big Knob's Ball.'

Arthur took the envelope and opened it. 'You're not wrong, Harry.' The thick cut, embossed card was an invitation to the annual midsummer gathering of the University Top Table Club. It was next Wednesday night. Late for an invitation. Arthur must have been an afterthought, a stand in. So bloody what? He'd just been handed a ticket for winning a certain dentist's daughter.

'Nice posh do that one,' the porter grinned. 'Strawberries and cream. String quartet. Champers. Only for top brass.' There was a wink. 'Who you going to take?'

Little more than a decisive quarter of an hour later as he waited for Niamh to answer his official summons and come to his office, Arthur felt less like a bold poet than A. A. Milne's Piglet. Twice he had to stop himself from downing a quick neck of scotch. What if she turned him down? What if she was already going? No, Ernie wasn't quite in the Top Table Club league. What if she thought it was too elitist? Too Protestant?

In the end the suave speech he had rehearsed flew out the window the moment she arrived. Instead he heard himself stumble through a cack-handed, half invitation whilst thrusting out the gold embossed card. 'You probably won't want to go, but if you can put up with it, you're more than welcome. I mean, you'll be representing the library.'

'The Top Table Club?' said Niamh. 'I'd love to.' A blush at the quickness of her acceptance. 'I mean, to represent the library.' She fingered the invitation. 'But I'll have to be home for ten.'

When she'd gone, Arthur stood there motionless. The date was set. The Rubicon located across which the poet must wade. Zero hour – 'guests to gather on the Vice-Chancellor's lawn for champagne cup at seven o'clock'. His own zero hour – kiss her by ten o'clock or have perished in the attempt. For the first, and perhaps last time in his life, the head librarian danced a hornpipe only stopping when a flailing hand sent the lamp tottering across the carpet.

Next Wednesday evening! Well, until then plenty to keep him busy. The lease to the flat started on Sunday night. He already had the key. Tonight would be his final evening at the boarding house. His plan was to spend Friday night at the Royal Station Hotel, go home to his mother on Saturday, and then return after the weekend to his new pied à terre. A fully furnished pied à terre! A poet's bolthole. Just the place to bring a girl back to after a 'swank's soirée'!

The last supper at old Ma Glenner's was a muted affair. The landlady seemed to be punishing him for missing yesterday's tea; his fellow lodgers were lost in their own worries. The toad in the hole being uncharacteristically bland, Arthur even found himself reaching for the Lea and Perrins. 'What's the matter?' the landlady had snapped. 'Now, all of a sudden he *wants* sauce.'

Later, as the radiogram blared, the librarian put cotton wool in his ears. And kept the door double bolted. One more night to survive, he wanted nothing to do with any of the dramas going on either outside or within. Let a hundred girls congregate under the thorn bush with the whole ruddy British Library in a bag, and he'd have nothing to do with them.

The final night in Mr Bleaney's bed? Restful and refreshing! Just one stupid nightmare in which *he* was the one waiting under the hawthorn staring up at the room of doom. He rose early. Leaving a note of explanation for Old Ma Glenners and a month's rent (more than bloody generous), he stole from the house, all his wordly chattels in the Antler suitcase, and shook the dust from his feet, or would have done if he could have shaken a foot after Thinness. This stiff in his thirties, what was waiting for him in later life – crutches at forty-five? 'Off on your hols, Burlington?' Kathleen asked at the trolley stop.

'Yes,' said Arthur, adding after a moment's pause, 'Frinton-on-Sea for a fortnight.'

She peered at him oddly. Well, let them gape; he was finished trying to understand.

At work Arthur convened an emergency staff meeting. Well one had to be *seen* to do something about the book thefts. His remedy was to move the poetry section to the bay closest to the loans desk where it could be continually under watch. Meeting concluded, writing the minutes and reading half a dozen Hardy poems took him within sniffing distance of dinnertime and the train home, when a hefty foot on the metal stairs caused the ceiling to shake. Harry Oxley's step was unmistakable. 'Going somewhere nice?' the porter asked, jackdaw eye noticing the suitcase.

'The laundrette,' replied the head librarian. 'I'm rather busy, Harry. What do you want?'

'Just to tell you we really have got him this time. Come on before he gets away.' Reluctantly, stiffly, quarter-curious, the librarian followed the porter down the stairs. 'This one's getting on for your age,' the porter said. 'Shifty isn't the word.'

Even as they were making their way round the gallery to their lookout post, Arthur heard a familiar voice down below asking one of the unqualifieds where he could find his old 'mucker' Mr Merryweather. 'Bloody hell.'

'Know him, do you, Mr M?'

A quick peep confirmed the identity of the voice. 'I'll see to this, Harry. And by the way, he's older than me.'

Working his way reluctantly to the ground floor, the librarian wondered what the bollocking hell that terrible twerp Teesdale was doing here. 'You've gone and done it now, Merryweather,' the salesman greeted him.

'Ah.'

'Come on, I'm taking you to the hospital.'

'What on earth are you talking about?'

'It's old Ma Glenners. Been taken badly. The doctors don't expect her to last long. Apparently she won't rest until she's seen you.'

'Are you joking?'

'Who on earth would make a joke like that? It was your note that did it. Took one look and fell to the ground like a nine pin. Good job this address was in her rates book.'

Sunny as the day was, the hospital blazed with electric lights. Getting off the bus, the high building rose before the fellow lodgers like an ocean-going cruise liner just about to weigh anchor. Except who would envy these passengers? Even with all those chandeliers? 'That's next on my list,' Teesdale said, staring after a car as they crossed the road. He was carrying a bulging 'samples' bag over his shoulder. 'My own wheels by the time I'm forty.'

As soon as Arthur entered through the double doors, the reek of disinfectant hooked the back of his throat. His last visit to hospital had been to see his father, the day he first saw what cancer looked like. Until then an oesophagus had just sounded like something marginally interesting you'd find in the British Museum. And hospitals had still masqueraded as places of healing. 'We're at the far end,' declared Teesdale.

They joined the silent ranks of visitors trudging the endless corridor like a football crowd after a heavy defeat. Only the fast-stepping, white-coated doctors lifted their gaze to look the great furlongs of illness in the eye; only the flat-footed nurses chattered, swallows nesting in the rafters of an abattoir. Ball, balls, balls, and yet. A little girl skipped two or three steps before her mother clapped flat this butterfly of life. Arthur passed ward door after ward door on the windowless corridor, each containing its own festering secret. The important thing was not to look. But when one of the doors opened directly in front of him to allow an egress of doctors, he was forced to stop. Before he could turn away – an abyss of white heads on white pillows plunging to indistinct windows. A geriatric ward. The future. 'We're here,' declared Teesdale reaching the end of the corridor fully five minutes after beginning it.

They weren't sodding well there. A porter directed them back the way they'd come. 'You want the top floor.'

Chest heaving, invisible crabs nipping at his calves, Arthur followed Teesdale up the stairs. The salesman's samples bag had come open and what looked like a small furry creature seemed to be peering at Merryweather. Both men, equally breathless, rested halfway up in a stairwell. 'If I were you I'd start drinking milk,' panted Teesdale.

'What the hell do you mean by that?'

'Build you up. Or you might be the next one we have to come visiting.'

'Can't you close that bag properly? You look like a cat butcher.'

Sod's law proclaimed an emergency in the ward – visitors had to wait. As some poor bastard met their doom at the hands of strangers behind white curtains, Teesdale bought himself a cup of tea at the Women's Institute hatch. There was nothing of any interest in the rubble of paperbacks. They sat, two amongst twenty or thirty, as odd a couple as any.

'Do you know what breadfruit is?' the man in fur said.

'Breadfruit?'

'Breadfruit.' Teesdale sampled the exotic word like a toothsome pear.

'No idea. Something tropical. Why?'

'Oh just something I've always wanted to know.'

Arthur gazed at the other visitors. Women mainly. Of course the men were in the ward. Men always die first. Mother nature's revenge. Who were they all? Wives, daughters, sisters, cousins, and if they were exceptionally unlucky, mothers and grandmothers. Lovers, childhood sweethearts, middle-aged flings, neighbours, colleagues. In short, a berth for each human animal on this ark of misery. Some, like Arthur himself, would only be vaguely connected to it all. Agnostic even in the most committed of congregations. Yet if he wasn't kindred to death now, he soon would be. In hospitals, as in life generally, all reprieves are temporary.

'When I die,' Teesdale was saying. 'I don't want any of this.' One hand caressing a piece of fur, the other wafted over the hospital expansively. 'No, I intend to go out like a light.'

'How exactly will you manage that?'

'Friend of mine snuffed it on the job. You know, between

the sheets. And that sounds pretty bloody perfect to me. By God yes, that's the ticket.'

A stampede of activity. White-coated doctors sprinting grim faced into the ward. Arthur sucked in his cheeks. Maybe the poor bastard snuffing it was old Ma Glenners. Why on earth did she want to see him anyway? Poor woman obviously can't have anyone else. Christ! Imagine it. After years of setting traps for the cast of odd bods and arch failures blown into her boarding house web, she'd come to this. A solitary death barely attended by two casual lodgers, the consummate detail in a masterpiece of meaninglessness. This was more than just Sod's law; God must be in on it. 'Being knocked down might not be too bad,' Teesdale wittered on. 'Or being struck by lightning.'

'What, and fry in your own fat?'

'Is that what happens?'

'Agony apparently.' Arthur fumbled for his fags. Really he didn't feel up to a deathbed scene. What could one say? *Cheer up we'll all snuff it sooner or later.* True enough, but small comfort. One's own death wasn't exactly a hundred miles away. In fact, easy to see it in the distance like a bank of dark clouds. Might even break over him in this hospital. This very ward. Even now he could be harbouring the fatal seed. The possible ways of dying vied in the librarian's head like one of Kathleen's kids' skipping rope chants: *heart, liver, oesophagus, brain, which little nasty will quench life's flame?* And who would there be to dread a deathbed scene with *him*?

Teesdale was right, better to die when you weren't expecting it, preferably when you were fucking. Like a rabbit being taken by a fox.

'You've been very clever, Merryweather,' said Teesdale suddenly clapping him heartily on the back. Arthur sighed. 'Getting yourself an office in the university. Yes, they told me you had your own room. Sets a tone when it comes to flogging your encyclopaedias. A touch of class. I've underestimated you. And what a chap of your means requires is something to reflect it.' He dug into his 'samples' bag and brought out a brochure and four or five fur coat half-sleeves. 'Now, something like this will set your lady apart from the crowd, and tell the world – '

'Not here, Teesdale, for godsake.'

The white-coated doctors drifted out of the ward. Not so bloody chatty now. Were such seasoned tillers in the fields of death still capable of being awed by an individual's suffering; or was their habitual imperturbability just an act, a funeral director's mask? The visitors eyed each other like stock penned in a shambles, one of them, probably, had just been widowed. 'I lied, you know,' Teesdale said. 'Before. That stuff about a car. I'm already forty.'

Arthur got up. He couldn't bear it in here another moment.

Blundering from his chair, he reached the vague clarity of a window, and cooled his forehead against the glass. Why not just bugger off? No, deathbed requests can't be ignored. He went over to the tea hatch. Thrupence a cup? Daylight bloody robbery. At last, something tangible he could complain about. After a fractious interchange with the tea lady, he bought two cups and sat back down again. Teesdale snatched the refreshment handed him. 'Of course you'll have to stay now, Merryweather.'

'Beg pardon?'

'Well someone's going to have to look after her if she gets out. McCoist's hopeless. He was the one who found her. Gone completely to pieces. And since it's your fault. First Bleaney clears off, and then you. I can't do it. I'm not going to be around for much longer myself. Put it this way, I'm on the cusp of big things. There's a new breed of rabbit being developed with a pelt that would pass for ermine eight times out of ten.'

All at once Arthur wanted to wail. Teesdale, Bleaney, McCoist, Glendenning, no finer examples of the unique British ken for tragicomedy. Until recently he'd have placed himself firmly in that cast. But then the poems. A distant squeaking slowly took shape – a trolley. The patient was elderly. Bird boned, bewilder-eyed, Silas Marner shock of hair, ward clothes washed to rags: a refugee from the inevitable famine lovingly prepared for all of us. The bible had missed a trick; one of the four riders of the apocalypse ought to arrive on a hospital trolley. The librarian was still staring after the decrepit harbinger of the End of Everything when a nurse opened the cardiac ward door and kicked a wedge in. The visitors rose. 'I'll go and get another chair,' said Teesdale.

The asbestos ward ceiling was low. Just let one of Gerard Manley Hopkins' bloody kestrels try and hover in here, mused the librarian walking between columns of beds. Would she be able to speak properly? Would her face be twisted? Would she weep? Or would she be sitting up like four-penny rabbit scoffing chocs? He'd been duped by Teesdale's dramatisations before.

He found her lying staring at the ceiling, the only visible sign of distress her utter stillness. Without her teeth she was already a cadaver. Leaning into her eye line, she didn't seem to notice him. He cleared his throat. She didn't seem to hear. Where the hell was that twat Teesdale? And then – a finger moved, the flutter of a broken butterfly. Beckoning or just smoothing the sheet in the way the dying do? 'I'll go and get Teesdale.' This act of cowardice took Arthur halfway down the ward before he returned shamefacedly. He'd contrived to miss his own father's death by leaving the bedside on some similarly fictitious pretext. Seeing him at last, the landlady's dry lips moved. Stirring with words, or just caught in the breath of the ill wind, which had blown her here? No, being fucking clever about it wasn't going to help. 'Hello,' he whispered. 'Miss

entrance. 'The police have been in looking for you, Mr M,' the porter announced.

A punch to the head librarian's midriff. 'Beg pardon?'

'This bobby popped in looking for you. Gone now. He wanted to see about the book thefts. The under-librarian sent for him.'

'Oh, I see.'

'The bobby liked your idea to move the poetry. So we've done that. And,' he added with relish, 'we have to up our vigilance.'

Just as well Arthur *hadn't* told Niamh about the hawthorn girl. She might have blurted out anything. A few routine tasks took the head librarian to closing time. A deep peace came over him as he heard the last person leave. With a thrill that he couldn't quite smother, he brought out the proofs for his poems, which had arrived in the second post, and set to correcting them. A pleasing-enough activity on its own, but when overlaid with flat-related fantasies! O, to wake up beside Niamh in that high-ceilinged bedroom; O, to breakfast with her in that aqueous light pooling through the park trees; O, to prove that wankers like Shelley weren't the only ones to skirmish in the battles of Venus; O, to read this very magazine with its pages spread on her naked buttocks. See, Arthur grinned to himself, I am a romantic.

Proofs corrected, Arthur went through some of the dustier box files he hadn't got round to yet. They contained enough eye-wateringly boring memoranda to blind one at ten paces. Passing down into the library, he headed for Niamh's periodical section. He hung around there for a while before drifting off to the other places she frequented, breathing in the air she breathed, touching the same books until, feeling uncomfortably like a cross between a ghost and a peeping Tom, he deliberately went to the sciences section where she never went. Here he tried and failed to read Isaac Newton's *Philosphiae Naturalis*

Principia Mathematica. Throwing the book aside, in a fit of futile machismo he fought his vertigo and tried a circuit round the gallery. Halfway round, just where the railing was the flimsiest, he lost his nerve, and retreated. Safely downstairs again, he browsed through the local interest section until the clock told him he might as well go to the hotel.

Why not have fish and chips again? This time a haddock. Once he'd finished his haddock, instead of going into town, he wandered back to the library. Why not spend the night there? He let himself in through the side door.

The air coming through the open window of his office was warm and scented. A dust sheet from the storeroom sufficed as a blanket on his chaise longue bed. Lying there on the grand couch of his future, only once did he picture his landlady fading in the restless twilight of the hospital night, staring at the low sky of that ceiling and murmuring, 'Mind or find Mr Bleaney.' She'd never know that her beloved lodger was the inspiration for the best poem Arthur had ever written. This brought a melancholy that wasn't entirely displeasing. Tomorrow he was going home to see mother. Sunday, he was moving into his flat. Then there was the Top Table Club do. He fell asleep at last to the gentle play of bats about the wisteria.

25.

The next morning his train home got away on time. Three quarters empty to boot. Luxuriating in sole occupation of his compartment, he watched the now familiar streets slide by. The windscreen of each parked car caught the sun. Then there was the level crossing. After which, the river. It was low tide and gulls thronged the mud. Opening the window to its widest extent, Arthur breathed in the mixture of hot, buttoned carriage cloth rising from the seats and fish from the docks, and waited for the wider world. It arrived in the shape of short-shadowed cattle, the white flare of a cricket match, a pair of power station chimneys rising like the spires of a great gothic, nationalised cathedral, and the unique oddity of a hothouse.

By the time the furnaces of Sheffield roared into sight, he'd written a whole new verse of poetry. And it wasn't utter crap! Well, too early to tell. Like taking an enema, one didn't know if a poem had worked properly until at least twenty-four hours after the first gripe in the gut. He closed up his notebook and thrust it in a breast pocket. He'd know better later. The train passed into a tunnel. The sudden reflection in the carriage window was half reassuring, half disturbing; anyway it brought him back down to earth. That querulous, bespectacled giraffe was him.

By early afternoon he was approaching the laurel-lined street of his Coventry childhood. Arthur still had his own key, but decided not to use it. Mother would think he was a burglar. His first knock received no answer. His second echoed unheeded down the tiled hall. His third was loud enough to have raised his dead father. He knew she was growing a little deaf but surely things hadn't got this bad? Then at last. 'Who is it?' a timid voice.

'Me, mother.'

Locks being fumbled free, and at last the door opening underneath its stained-glass fanlight. 'Arthur, you've arrived. I was beginning to worry.'

How had she become so old in the few months since he saw her last? This strange change in his mother took ten minutes and two cups of tea to disperse. Didn't quite. A salad lunch and then they fell into old patterns, he listening to records whilst she dusted. She'd always dusted on Saturday afternoons. And would if the Queen herself came visiting, as Arthur had quipped a number of times in the past. 'That was a pretty one,' she called from the hall as one jazz number ended.

'Riverside Blues,' he called back, supine on the sofa. Already the next track was starting. The strains of a trumpet blowing from the far side of nineteen twenties Windy City.

'That one's a bit thrashy,' she called, in the lounge now.

Stubbing out another fag, he grinned. She'd never been interested in jazz. What *was* she interested in, that British variant on Tantalus' stone, dusting? 'Don't forget the piano keys, and under the metronome, mother.'

'Long noses,' she said, a childhood admonishment.

'Find the thorns in roses,' he finished.

Arthur stretched luxuriantly. His records littered the living room. Good to be home again. Why, he might be eighteen once more and on the threshold of things. Facile delusion. His life was halfway over, *more* than if his span replicated his father's. Yet – he was a poet, and there was Niamh. The exciting life he'd once planned might be about to happen after all; perhaps like the year itself, his spring was simply late, and he was about to enjoy a flaming June. Well, he'd enjoy giving his mother the good news about his poems. The tune ended, and in the crackling silence of the eager needle's tread, he heard his mother grunt as she reached up to dust the pelmet curtain. 'Time you got someone in,' he said as he'd been saying for years now. 'You know, to do the housework.'

'What and have some stranger all over the house?' his mother replied, as she'd been replying for years now.

He didn't turn the disc but lay there listening to the room's own spinning recording. The strike of his father's match on the hearth, arpeggios of cups on saucers during the rare (and ghastly) visits of relatives, the sudden wingbeat of a turning page as he sat on the thick rug reading his way through childhood, his sister's comb running through her doll's hair. Christ, but the bible had it true; one's days *are* the wind that passeth through the perishing grass. What to do in the face of such relentless emptiness but to fill it with what came to hand:

books, poetry, love, marriage? Hitherto, his creed had been to avoid the marriage game at all costs. Hitherto. Well, perhaps he'd been wrong. Just because his parents' marriage had been a loveless cage, did that mean his would? Good Lord, he was getting before himself. Hadn't even kissed her yet. 'You all right, mother?' he called when he hadn't been able to hear her for a while. 'You haven't been assaulted by the vase again?' Curious, no answer. Getting up, he went to the piano room where he'd last been able to hear her working.

For a brief, absurd moment he thought she was praying, and then he saw that the piano stool was open and she was merely kneeling down going through some old sheet music. One song brought a smile to her tired face. Sitting down at the piano, she opened the sheet and fingered into life the first, frank submissive chord. A few notes followed before the finger's froze. 'Oh, hello, dear.' A doe's surprise. 'I was just looking for that first piano study book, you know for little Robert and Sue.' Sullen Sue and Monster Robert, Arthur's nephew and niece. Before she could rise, he'd sat down beside her. 'I haven't played any of these for years,' she admitted, 'I don't know why I keep them. Except – the covers are pretty.'

'I'll do the left hand,' he said.

And for the first time since he was thirteen, mother and son played a duet. Sang too. It was one of those (to Arthur) ludicrous ballads from before the Great War, full of hyperbolic woodbine and hearts. Was this honeysuckle litany of endlessly hyphenated endearments how his mother's generation had thought of love? As they played, he pictured her as a girl before she'd met his father, or in the parlance of the song – an artless maiden emerging from a bower. Despite himself, as another cloying, half clownish chorus pedalled round on its pennyfarthing again, he pictured Niamh strolling along the same fragrant, Edwardian lanes in the hat of the era, corseted, and sporting those charming, high-laced boots. Finishing with a flourish, they both laughed. She reached out and touched him, a gesture buried deep in his childhood. Smiles were swapped. A tear on her cheek surprised her. 'Mother, I've fallen in love,' he wished he'd said, could never say. Instead, 'I'm having some poems published.'

Later as Arthur helped her in the garden, there was another revelation. 'Funny thing is, I was sort of arrested.'

'Beg pardon, dear?' she said from the roses.

Relief. She hadn't heard. Why mention it? In this hushed world behind the laurels, being arrested was akin to the Victorian son's profession of atheism or marriage to a musical hall girl. 'I'm saying the roses are looking nice.'

'I was worried that they had blight.'

Worry, his mother's middle name. Glancing back at the house, Arthur half smiled at the resolutely closed windows; even on the hottest days she kept everything shut against the burglar forever lurking in the laurels. What the hell would she do with a girl beneath a hawthorn tree? 'Are you limping, dear?' she asked.

'I went for a bicycle ride the other day and I'm still a little stiff.'

'Is it safe, riding a bicycle these days?'

'Oh, perfectly.'

'Your sister Maimie's husband's given up bicycling. Too much motor traffic. I don't like to think of you on a bicycle, Arthur. You hear of people being paralysed from the neck down.'

Once again the revelation came tumbling out unbidden. This time she heard. 'Beg pardon?'

A half smile. 'Well, as I say, I was sort of arrested.' The smile retreated even further when he saw his mother's face as she dropped the secateurs.

Tea was required. He sat with his mother under the

laburnum with her bewilderment and a pot of Ringtons. She even smoked one of his cigarettes, each birdlike inhalation tightening her skin against her skull. Yes, she was growing old, and he – increasingly twattish. What a great idea to give the world's worst worrier something to really get her teeth into. 'They thought I was someone else. They've apologised.' One supposed Niamh would categorise such lies as venial sins.

'What did you do?'

'Nothing.'

'You must have. The police don't just go around arresting anyone. I've been wondering why you hadn't been home.'

'I haven't been home because I've fallen in love.' Again, the words remained unspoken. Arthur cursed the sentimental sheet music. Its candour was catching. If he couldn't share his tale of love, he had to share something.

'Maimie thinks you're in love.'

'Beg pardon?'

'You're normally so good at visiting home so your sister said there must be a romance. He's gone and fallen for one of his assistant librarians, she said. Are you all right, Arthur? You look rather peaky.' A long silence. 'There's nothing the matter with loving someone, you know,' his mother said, getting up at last.

That evening over dinner, they talked about Arthur's success. 'Your father would have been so pleased.'

'Would he?'

'He didn't say much but he was always very proud of you. And what are your poems about?'

'Oh, train journeys and rooms.'

'Not people?'

'Occasionally.'

She went to bed early. For a long time he stood by the fire

watching his shadow flicker against the wall. Picking up the vase, he stared at it. One could still see the crack where his mother had mended it after father had hurled it against the wall in one of his tempers. 'Niamh's not going to like those poems of yours, you know,' his father said, stepping out of the drifting silence.

'Oh, piss off,' Arthur grinned.

'Wanking and the despair of commercial salesman are not her kind of thing.'

'To say the least,' Arthur agreed.

'No one normal will think you're a good poet.'

'I suppose they won't.'

'Why the hell wash your dirty linen in public like this?'

'It is rather repulsive, isn't it?'

'We've all got stained smalls. Trick is to soak them in secret.'

'Yes, I suppose.'

'You're like me, you know. We're a right bloody pair of odds and sods. Girl like that won't go near a chap like you. I speak from experience.'

Just in time, the librarian stopped himself from hurling his mother's favourite vase at his father's shadow.

26.

After Sunday lunch with his mother, sister, Sullen Sue, Monster Robert, and their 'did I ever tell you that the future is fibreglass?' father (Maimie's husband held a position in a manufacturing concern), Arthur was rather glad to get away. In fact, he found himself at the train station this side of two o'clock. He was idling on the platform thinking of the flat when the tannoy announced the lengthy delay of his train. A moment later, it announced that the 13.49 to Stoke would depart in two minutes. Stoke. Why did that ring a bell? Of course, it was where his predecessor spent Christmas with his sister. A number of things occurred to the librarian simultaneously. Firstly, thanks to British Rail he had an hour to kill, secondly he'd always enjoyed the Stoke-based novels of Arnold 'The Potteries' Bennett, thirdly, the Stoke train was standing, open-doored at the next platform, fourthly, since he seemed to have shared everything else with his predecessor, why not one last thing – Christmas?

Nearly being in love is making me spontaneous, Arthur decided, finding himself boarding the train. The train crawled through an unlovely smokescape of towering chimneys and squatting kilns. It was a longer journey than anticipated. Eventually alighting at Stoke, he set about immediately looking for the return service. Bloody hell! Two hours until then. He grinned grimly at the twisted sentimentality which had lured him here – to do what exactly? See the place through which the disgraced insurance agent passed every Christmas? Take a quick stroll in the town? Find Mr Bleaney's sister?

The grin became a laugh. How could he hope to find his sister when the only clue he had about her whereabouts was that birthday card with a Stoke postmark? Yet if one really did wish to dig around then the name Bleaney was unusual enough to be of assistance. There was another clue too. During his arrest, when the detectives read the card to him, they'd said the sister was called Beryl. Couldn't be too many Beryl Bleaneys in the world, let alone Stoke. A sense of the ridiculous persuaded the librarian over to a phone box where he snatched up the local phone directory. Strange, he mused, my hand is shaking with anticipation. Oh, she wouldn't have a phone, hardly anyone did, and even if she did then she wouldn't be Beryl Bleaney but Beryl Derricot, he giggled to himself thumbing through the directory, or Beryl Clayhangar (append the correct potteries' name!). Arthur's eye came to rest on Miss B. Bleaney. It was complete with address. He placed his overnight bag in left luggage. Curiosity killed the cat, and no doubt would take a pot shot at the pratt too. Still, a quick gander at the Bleaney Bethlehem stable might be rather worth the risk. After all, it was a kind of obligation – the poem.

Straddling an exhausted clay pit, Nelson Street had the appearance of a township huddling in the crater of a volcano. A potteries Pompeii. Shadowed on all sides by the potbellied chimneys of the ware makers, as Bennett used to call them, dusk seemed already to be dropping on Beryl Bleaney's terrace. Noisome and dank on a beautiful afternoon in June, what must it be like in December?

Despite the mucky air and glutinous soil, each house was a burning beacon of cleanliness. Here, respectability had to be won daily. The doorsteps he passed on the way to number forty-two were all freshly scrubbed; their brass work bullied to a shine. Hanging like shrouds, the net curtains seemed so starched that they'd stand up of their own accord. Aspidistras, sleek with decades of sponging and tea leaves, peeked from the window ledges like the carnivorous triffids in that book everyone was reading. And by the look of the gleaming house front of forty-two Nelson Street, Beryl Bleaney (spinster of this Parish?) was keeping her end up in the good fight. One supposed this was what that new-fangled sociology studied, why people living in shit holes kill themselves trying to make them look like *shining* shit holes. Lighting a fag, the librarian walked straight past number forty-two. What the hell was he doing here? What could he hope to achieve? What if Bleaney himself was behind that closed door?

'What do you want?' a woman said, the immaculate front door opening when Arthur had forced himself back and knocked.

Taking the precaution of fully displaying his brown eyes against any momentary shock of likeness, Arthur noticed the look of surprise flare and then die on her face as she nearly recognised him, as it were. Yes, this was the right place. 'Hello,' he began. 'I'm Mr McCoist.' Well one couldn't use one's own name. 'I've come about your brother.'

The woman, a caricature of the kiss-me-quick seaside mother in law – a fat-faced, narrow-eyed harridan, capable of a knock-out punch – stared at him coldly. 'Haven't got one.'

'Sorry, I thought this was number forty-two.'

'So it is.'

'I'm looking for Beryl Bleaney. It's about her brother.'

The door was slammed in his face.

Well, that was that. Arthur was walking away when the door opened once more. A different person stood there. Not the harridan, but a frightened mouse. Slight, tremulous, she seemed barely capable of looking him in the eye. 'I think you'd better come in,' she whispered, glancing at the net curtains twitching in the houses opposite.

Arthur followed her into a short, lightless hall from which stairs lifted into darkness. The mouse, of an age to be elder sister to his infamous predecessor, led him into a front parlour of ornaments, framed bible samplers, and a strident though untrustworthy clock. A perfectly preserved relic of the Edwardian era, and the epicentre of all that respectability. 'Oh,' she half-whimpered as she sat down. He followed her lead. 'You're not the police, are you?' the woman asked in such a trembling whisper that Arthur had to strain every ear muscle to hear her over the clock, which continued to count an eternity of uneventful afternoons.

'No, I'm not the police.'

'Are you from the insurance company?'

Police. Insurance company. A strange thrill at how deeply he'd been thrust into the plot. Even now maybe Mr Bleaney was listening at the door or, thinking Arthur was a detective, was making good his escape over a maze of backyards. 'No, I live, *lived* in the same boarding house as your brother – '

'But I sent you those twenty pounds,' Mousey put in. 'Postal order. What you said he owed you when you wrote.'

'Beg pardon?'

'You are Mr Teesdale, aren't you?'

'No, my name's Arthur Merryweather.'

'Oh.'

Bugger. Too late to remember he was masquerading as McCoist. So, Arthur mused, Teesdale had already been sniffing around. 'I'm sorry for bothering you like this,' he said whilst thinking, what the jiminy fuckit am I doing here?

'Does my brother owe you money as well, Mr Merry-weather?'

'No.'

Then with a sudden hunger: 'Are you his friend?'

Before Arthur could answer, a summoning voice (the harridan's?) from the deep depths of the little house. 'Beryl.'

Scurrying away obediently, the mouse left Arthur alone in the museum. Under the watchful eye of the clock, he surveyed the knick-knacks crowding each level space. China dogs, cats, shepherdesses, plough-boys, heavy horses, flower girls, delivery boys and apple cheeked chimney sweeps. The whole sick-making milieu invented to pretend that British history wasn't a hideous parade of scrofula, suffering and child exploitation. As well as ornaments there were photographs, the usual fare, which the librarian recalled from childhood visits to relatives' front parlours – nervous, wasp-waisted brides and pretend debonair grooms, family groups with half-terrorised kids and soppy stern fools in old style hats and coats, girls in what would pass for being dolled up in an Arnold Bennett Sunday school, knickerbockered boys, and young men in khaki. A kettle's shrill pipit could be heard from the scullery. The soldiers were Great War in the main, their bones no doubt long since ground to fertiliser in Flanders, but one young man stared out in the familiar attire of a midlands regiment from the last conflict. Arthur picked up the frame. A stab of recognition. This young soldier could only be Mr Bleaney. Strike a light, there *was* a similarity.

The door opened, Arthur thrust the framed photograph back.

It was the harridan. She bore a tea tray. With the unassailable pedantry of a tyrant, she laid the crocks (one ought to use the Arnold Bennett terminology) on a low table according to some precise coordinates. 'I won't have you upsetting her,' she hissed just as the mouse was coming in with a cake and a pale face. 'And he's not having this house, if that's your game. Now, I'll be mother.'

As the pouring tea played its sad flute, Arthur planned his retreat. 'You see,' he tried to explain. 'Someone asked me to – '

'I always said he'd come to no good,' the harridan interrupted. 'Didn't I, Beryl?'

'You did,' whispered the mouse.

The harridan shivered long sufferingly. 'We've had the police and all sorts. You wouldn't believe it. Can't think what the neighbours have been saying. Mind you, not the first time he had his finger in the till, was it Beryl?'

'No.'

'That's why he left Stoke. Had ever such a good position here, but got caught fiddling the stamp money. They let him go rather than prosecute and lose their good name. Didn't they, Beryl?'

'Yes.'

The harridan paused to assault a massive slice of cake; Arthur seized the opportunity to get his word in edgeways. 'I don't really know him (fucking understatement), but someone asked me to find him. His landlady, I think they were close. You see, she's very ill.'

'You're barking up the wrong tree,' the harridan continued. 'Except for Christmas we haven't seen hide nor hair of him for years. Christmas is enough, let me tell you. Picky so and so, isn't he, Beryl? Always has to do things his own way. Pudding too hot, turkey too cold, why can't we do such and such in such and such a way. Where are the sauces?'

Again Arthur kicked a foot in the door as the harridan bit into her cake. 'That's why I'm here, I think she might like to see him before she – '

'How do we know where he is?' the harridan demanded, mouth full. 'I've told you, we don't see him except for Christmas. And that's the way we like it, don't we, Beryl?'

'Yes.'

'Prison's the best place for him, isn't it, Beryl?' The mouse hesitated. Sharper – 'Isn't it, Beryl?'

'Yes.'

Arthur was relieved when he was told that the ladies had to get ready for afternoon chapel. 'Does brother still go once a week of a Sunday morning?' Mouse whispered as she showed him to the door. For a moment he thought she was referring to some kind of hideous constipation. 'Chapel, I mean,' Mouse clarified.

'Yes, he did.'

The lie brought a profound relief to Beryl Bleaney. Perhaps it was this that gave her the nerve to murmur as Arthur stepped outside, 'it wasn't him, you know. The stamp money. His friend was the thief. Let my brother take the blame. Same friend got his promotion too. And Ethel Rupp. Ethel and my brother had been engaged since the war. Secretly of course – father would never have stood for it.'

Back on the train, Arthur was unable to get a compartment to himself; targeted sneezing at least maintained the empty seats on his either side. In time with the quadruple rhythm of the tracks, phrases played in his mind over and over again, *Are you his friend?/are you his friend?/ Come to no good/come to no good/ Christmas enough/Christmas enough*. Heavens, the book of failure must run to countless volumes. More than enough to fill the whole library and gallery too. Poor old Mr Bleaney. Poor old Miss Bleaney. Who was the harridan anyway? Well, it was nothing to him now.

To escape the Bleaney bleakdom, Arthur brought out Friday's poem. He hadn't been wrong. No pile of crap; a masterpiece. He *was* a poet.

Changing at Sheffield he bought a pie. It was awful. Wandering to the end of the platform, he watched the furnaces play at dragons, and felt another poem coming on. Could an awful pie bought on Sheffield station masquerade as the meaning of life? Could his poems, starting with the one about Mr Bleaney, soon to be published, eventually win him fame, fortune and Niamh O'Leary?

He caught the connection home, no problem getting a compartment of one's own in trains *going* to the terminal town. Just short of fishville however, they stopped at a harsh named halt on the raw bank of the river, and showed no sign of starting again. On enquiring how long the holdup might be, the conductor informed Arthur the signal was down and how the bleeding heck did he know when it would come back up? 'Well, could one get out and walk from here?' the librarian asked in exasperation.

The nationalised employee seemed to enjoy his. 'Ah, but then one would be trespassing on publicly owned land, wouldn't one.'

So near, yet so far, the flat remained tantalisingly out of reach. Just to play with him, the plebeian British Rail Gods sent the train jolting forward for a hopeful few seconds before shunting it to a screeching and unequivocal halt in a siding. Yanking down a window, Arthur thrust his head out.

Inscrutable as the Ganges, the river flowed by. The smell of herring hung like a drag net. He could hear another train coming up on the line behind them. A grinding of points as an express train crawled towards them. The reason for the stoppage. Arthur gazed at the favoured coaches of the Haddockton-upon-Mud bound express, which had precedence over the stopping service. Slowly it inched past. In the last carriage sat a man. Arthur let out a resounding belly laugh. And then another. The resemblance between himself and the other traveller was marked. In fact, should it have been remotely possible, Arthur would have thought he was witnessing the return of the disgraced insurance agent.

As the express pulled away, the librarian was helpless with laughter.

27.

It wasn't him, Arthur realised as he got off the train at the station. Of course it wasn't. What had his lady friend once said? That he was fixated on Mr Bleaney. Well now was the time to cut himself loose. He'd left Bleaney's room, let him leave Bleaney behind too. With mounting excitement, Arthur headed to the flat. Now the key was in his hand, now it was in the door, now the door was opening, now he was home.

He wasted no time in locating the kettle, and was soon sitting on the horsehair sofa drinking a first cup of tea. A toast to domestic freedom. Horsehair perfectly comfortable; the evening light, filtering through the mature park trees, positively Parnassian. Were they poplars? Christ but that would be the final touch. Worth remembering if he required a pretext to get Niamh over the threshold. Not only did she like nature and so forth, but her favourite poem was the Hopkins one about chopping poplars down. A nasty moment when some teenage voices came burgling in through the open window, but the hectoring tone of a park keeper turfing out the youths reassured the librarian. Dead on ten o'clock, the comforting sound of the park gates being slammed shut and locked. And then, blessedly oblivious of all human concerns, owls hooting.

Altogether a fine neighbourhood. A good fish and chip shop, a newsagent with the national newspapers and several pubs within easy walking distance. Not that he felt like a drink. Good god, was that the miracle of love? As mother had said, there's nothing the matter with loving someone.

His mother's pronouncement returned to him later as he lay on his gloriously comfortable new bed. *There's nothing the matter with loving someone.* Didn't sound as though that had been the case in the Bleaney household when his engagement with Ethel Rupp had had to be kept secret. A fleeting thought; *could* that character on the train have been the fugitive insurance agent? No, it *couldn't* have been. After all, even with his specs on Arthur wasn't exactly blessed with twenty-twenty vision. Old Ma Glenners herself had come to accept that the prodigal was never coming back. Poor cow. By now she might be pushing up the daisies. *Sic transit gloria mundi,* as Niamh might say.

No snoring, no attempts on his door, no wireless, no girl looking up from outside, Arthur slept like a king. The sleeping giants of the park's mature trees seemed to cradle the flat in their arms. Maybe one day he'd do the same with Niamh. All was right with the world. And how fucking often can one make that boast?

Naturally fate was hiding a fish up its sleeve, and it wasted no time slapping it across the head librarian's cheek. Next morning he'd been at his office desk for only half an hour when he heard a strange step on the metal stairs. A few seconds later, the door was thrust open by a woman in an electric green dress. 'Arthur!' his lady friend cried. 'Congratulations! I heard about the poems and simply had to come in person.'

Standing up, Arthur clenched his buttocks so violently he almost put his back out. Of course she'd find out, might as well try and keep a secret from the Gestapo. She knew every editor in the village of academic literature. 'How do,' he just managed to say in the local vernacular.

'I'm relieved to see that you're still the same old miserable bugger,' she laughed. 'I've been worrying myself sick that poetic success would spoil you. Extravagantly marvellous office. Positively Rococo.'

The fond future Arthur had imagined with Niamh flickered. His mind span with how to get his friend away. And quick. Somehow he managed to get her out of the office and down the stairs. Whisking her through the side door, they emerged amongst the wisteria. He chivvied her up the chestnut avenue. 'What's the hurry, Arthur?'

'I want to show you something,' he lied, and headed for town.

'I came yesterday,' she explained. 'But couldn't find you.'

'I was at mother's.'

'You must have caught an early train this morning to get back on time.'

'Yes,' he said guardedly. Clearly, she didn't know about the flat yet. Best keep it that way if humanly possible.

'I had to stay at this rather grim hotel. By the way, Arthur, I met your chum.'

A clamping of buttocks threatened Arthur's back again. 'Beg pardon?'

'Your donkey. Teesdale. Well, when you weren't at your digs he looked after me as I waited. He's exactly as you described him. Actually, he was rather sweet, he almost sold me a fur coat. Told me something about you that I couldn't possibly believe.'

'Indeed.'

'He said that you were going to look after your Old Ma Glenners when she gets out of hospital.'

Arthur took her to the Royal Station Hotel. The bar wasn't yet open. He had to settle for a cup of tea.

'This is where I stayed last night,' she said. 'A distinctly rude youth on reception. Now what's the big mystery; what are you so desperate to show me?'

'Well, this,' he improvised, and, cigarette in hand, picked out the high chandeliers and the four differently coloured, low seats. 'I wanted to bring you here because it's a rather special place. It's where I write my poems.'

Swallowing the bait, she went into ecstasies about his creative processes; asked endless questions and wrote down his replies. 'And do you *always* sit on the brown chair?'

Arthur was working out a fool-proof method of limiting her visit when she finally put her notebook down and said, 'actually, I thought I saw you last night. It was all rather odd and embarrassing.'

'Beg pardon?'

'Well, they were just walking down the street from your lodgings, and – '

'Who was?'

'The man I thought was you, and a girl. I even called over to him.'

'What did you say?'

'Hello Arthur, you terrible bugger. You know me. Well, of course he didn't reply.'

'What were they doing?'

'Walking. He was carrying a suitcase. When he turned, I saw that it wasn't you after all. He was about your age and she was no more than a girl. She looked so happy. Father and daughter, I thought. What's the matter, Arthur? You look as though you've seen a ghost.'

The conversation drifted up into the chandeliers with their cigarette smoke. The next thing Arthur became aware of was his lady friend saying, 'actually I've finished my lecturers for summer, so I was thinking, why don't I stay here for a few days?'

Horrible though it might be, it had to be done. Shaking off the revelation of Mr Bleaney honouring his promise to the poetry thief (what sodding well else could his lady friend's sighting presage?), Arthur pulled himself together and did what he ought to have done weeks ago. He told her all about Niamh. Everything. Everything that had happened; everything he hoped would happen. When it came down to it, he valued his friend too much not to tell her the truth, unpalatable as it was. She slapped him, then apologised, and slapped him again. There wasn't a second apology.

All afternoon the head librarian was on tenterhooks in case his lady friend came back. He even sent Niamh on a spurious errand to the library in town to get her out the way should such a probability occur. Fortunately, closing time came and no friend. Was he really going to get off this lightly? As for his lady friend, well, if he'd said it once he'd said it a thousand times, she really was better off without him.

Standing at his office window, Arthur smiled mistrustfully at the universe. The *old* Arthur would have turned his ankle on today's banana skin. Niamh would have been certain to come up to his office at the same time as his visitor. Or the dentist would have been sniffing about the Royal Station Hotel. Had something changed in the mechanics of existence? Was he becoming that rarest and most favoured of beings – a lucky bastard? A thrush was even singing somewhere. The sky was bluer than it had any right to be.

Back in the flat that evening, the new, fortuitous Arthur fried himself the sprats he'd bought on the way home, then sat back on the horsehair sofa, the proofs of his poems spread out before him. They were to form the main thrust of

Wednesday evening's campaign. The goal – a kiss at the Top Table Club 'do' and then, by hook or by crook, persuade her back to the flat where the forces of the poems would be ready to go into battle on his behalf. One's poems were to be the bridgehead over her maidenhead. So to speak. Well, literally, in a perfect world. Once she'd actually seen him in print, read him, the moment to strike home would have arrived.

Almost solemnly, he lit a fag. Maidenhead? My God, did he know what he was doing? Was this simply another implausible castle in the air, or a slap across the cheek in the waiting? Or might it actually come to be? Well, he'd soon see. No self-respecting troubadour could jib at the prospect of a slap or a crushing humiliation.

Arthur was leafing through his poems and snuggling into a cosy and unfamiliar fantasy of everything going absolutely swimmingly when suddenly: 'Bloody, frigging, fucking hell!' He'd just realised that in the rush to leave, he'd left something rather important behind at sixty-one Corporation Road. Something he had to retrieve.

The trolley bore a decidedly reluctant passenger along its prescribed line to old Ma Glenner's. If it had been anything but a manuscript, wild horses couldn't have dragged Arthur back. He probably would have been prepared to leave a twenty pound note, or a little toe. By some staggering act of clotdom, he'd left behind the work that he had gleaned from the moon-scorched months of insomnia. The manuscript had been kept hidden in the bedpost, close at hand for when the night troll should strike. It was the distinct suspicion that at least *some* of it was wasn't utter bollocks, which drove him back despite all his reservations.

The librarian alighted at the boarding house stop, and for old time's sake trod directly in a pile of dog dirt. Cleaning the sole of his shoe as best he could, he tossed the soiled handkerchief into the infamous front garden; it landed on one of the young thistles that covered the ground like spiny star fish – there let it lie at rest. The front door was unlocked. Lucky bastardom still favouring him? Of course, Old Ma Glenners was in hospital. Perhaps there was a chance of getting in and out unseen.

Without its presiding spirit, already the house seemed to be ailing. A cobweb hung above the phone. A fug of unwashed crocks and food scraps crept from the kitchen. Before retrieving the manuscript, Arthur decided to check his mail, just in case some correspondence had strayed into her snare before the stroke. The 'private parlour' felt particularly forlorn. The pom-pom of an abandoned slipper peered out from beneath the sofa. The lone, flounced paper of a chocolate truffle lay abandoned on a cushion. The scene almost had the poignancy of a Victorian painting. *Her Last Sunday Funtime.* His own note explaining his departure was prominent on, of all places, the radiogram.

There were no letters for him in the chest. Teesdale's bundle was larger than ever. After a brief tussle with his conscience, Arthur drew out the man in fur's mail to find a score or so of outstanding bills. Correspondence course invoices in the main: *Breast the Ribbon in the Race of Life in just 10 weeks £1. 10s and 6d,* and so forth. Amongst the red payment reminders, a lone personal letter. Less than a moment's qualm before Arthur opened it. *Dear Mr Teesdale,* the letter was written in a curiously old fashioned copperplate style and had been sent by Hardwood, Fergusson and Co, Furriers, *with sales figures continuing to disappoint and an increase in unfortunate incidents of the type we have previously discussed, the company has no choice but to terminate your position as our representative on the river forthwith.*

Good God, it was all so relentless. Ought one to leave it for Teesdale to discover, or allow him a few days' more blissful ignorance?

Unwilling to face yet more unforgiving failure, Arthur ignored McCoist's letters (still all written in the same feminine hand) and was giving the drawers a final root around when he saw the red ribbon tied round a bundle of postcards. A quick investigation revealed that each card showed a different view of the same place, and bore the same signature. Frinton-on-Sea; Mr Bleaney. These weren't postcards for the former lodger, but *from* him. And the postmarks showed they'd been sent since he left fish town, the last two from just before the landlady was taken ill.

Tottering over to the settee, Arthur sat heavily. Every time he thought he'd pulled himself free from the mystery man, a tentacle reached out.

At last, shoving the haul of postcards in a pocket, he went upstairs. Unscrewing the bed knob, Arthur hoiked out his rolled manuscript. A rush of relief to have it back in hand. Was this how fathers felt when a lost child came safely home? He scanned the verses quickly. Well, one of them almost passed muster. No modesty, a couple of lines were nipple-bitingly brilliant. And it was days since he wrote them! 'What do you think you're doing?'

Arthur turned at the peremptory voice from the landing. It wasn't one he'd heard here before. 'Beg pardon?'

'I asked you what the hell are you doing in my room?' A face craned round the door jamb. Unfamiliar, with bouffant hair and more teeth than he had any right to.

'I'm Arthur Merryweather and I –' Arthur tried to explain.

'So you're the joker that snaffled Bleaney's room?' bouffant interrupted.

Was this the man in semi-precious stones – who else could it be? 'Ah,' said Arthur.

'Saw your note. You can't change your mind, you know. It's the best room in the house. I've had dibs on it for yonks, and now that I'm going to be around for a while, I'm bloody well having it.'

'Fine,' Arthur replied. Then, just as he was leaving, on the spur of a foolish moment: 'How's tricks with the tiaras?'

'What?'

'How are your crown jewels?'

'Do you want a punch in the mush, fathead?' the man in semi-precious stones growled.

'Sorry, I thought – Miss Glendenning said you dealt in semi-precious jewels.'

'No, that line's about as lively as a funeral in a nursing home. Changed trades, haven't I? Look, this is what I travel in now.' A salesman's suitcase was hefted onto the bed. An opening zip revealed a cargo of ladies unmentionables. A wink. A music hall French accent. 'Lingerie à la nuit. Got yourself a sweetheart have you, *mon-soor*?' Goaded by some primitive bravado, Arthur nodded weakly. 'Treat her then.' The man delved into the lemon, rose and blue layers of sheer bri-nylon nighties, baby doll shorties, lacy nightwear, and plucked out a frilly mystery of womanhood. 'Treat yourself at the same time.' The tone of voice was part dirty weekend nudge nudge, part command.

Twenty minutes later Arthur sat on the trolley, his purchase hidden rather insecurely under his jacket, along with the rolled manuscript and red-ribboned bundle of postcards. The first rubbish bin he came to, he'd dump the naughty night gear. If Niamh got wind of such a confection, she'd send him to the Catholic version of Coventry. And that was the last place he wanted to visit. Do the same with the postcards. The connection with Bleaney was now severed for good, why keep any mementoes? All he wanted to think about was the romantic rendezvous at the Top Table Do.

28.

The big evening came round. Arthur could hear the string quartet playing in the distance as he passed down the chestnut avenue. He was to meet Niamh by the wisteria at the side door of the library. Naturally he'd offered to pick her up from Thinness Road, but nothing doing. Sometimes she showed a maddening disposition to independence that he could only compare to his own. He was quarter of an hour early and feeling distinctly skittish. His dinner suit might have cost an arm and a leg to hire, but it felt on the tight side, especially – for pity's sake – around the crotch.

He was just wondering if he had time to pop inside and use the gents – or a convenient bush – when he heard footsteps on the avenue. Glimpsing Niamh in snatches through foliage, the head librarian feared that when seen whole, the sight might rob him of the power of speech.

It very nearly did. Strawberry blonde hair sculpted in a wave, wasp-waisted, saffron evening gown, corsetry emphasising breasts despite best work of crucifix, calves flowing out from the upended funnel of the dress, white gloves, shining black handbag, and shining 'Cinderella at the ball' shoes – it was enough to rip the lips from his face.

Following the sound of music and chattering voices, they crossed a couple of lawns. 'I love Mozart,' she said.

'Schubert, surely?' he replied.

'It's Mozart.'

'Schubert.'

They glared at each other. Clearly, she was nervous too. This is going to be a cock-up of gargantuan proportions, his father warned from the shadows of a weeping willow. The couple turned a corner, passed through a door in a tall wall, threaded their way through a fragrant rose garden and then there was the Vice-Chancellor's lawn. At the sight of the musicians and the hundred or so people gathered, Niamh blenched. 'Are you all right?' Arthur asked.

'You don't think this dress is too showy?'

Arthur took the licence to look her length. 'No,' he said, only getting the word out with difficulty. 'It's perfect.'

It was clearly a bigger matter than the head librarian had realised. He'd been right to stump up for a dinner suit. One could tell at a glance that a good half of those gathered were utter tossers. Adipose alderman types or mutton dressed as lambs. The Vice-Chancellor's Aide, whom Arthur hadn't seen since his first day, proved himself an arch prick. Fixing himself onto Niamh, he proceeded to bludgeon her with one self-regarding story after another. If the bastard wasn't directly staring at her breasts, then he was squinting at her shiny shoes to try and get a shufty up at her knickers. Coming back from the gents, Arthur found himself buttonholed by some blood-less bore. 'What do you think of installing a wicket gate in the library?' Heart thrashing against his ribs like a bat, Arthur glanced furtively around the lawns for an appropriate bower in which to secure his first kiss. 'Or would that be an affront to its democracy?' bore went on. At least Ernie wasn't here.

The buffet was served outside. Enough ham, tongue, beef and salmon to feed the whole bloody university. Not to mention the garden green salad and mountains of buttered teacakes. Now that meat had come off the ration, people ate like crazed gluttons. Aide to Vice-Chancellor and bore stuffed their faces, and if the mutton dressed as lambs crammed any more pork products in their gobs, they'd grow curly tails. Neither librarian ate much, and Arthur was too wound up to do his usual trick of filling his pockets for later. His assistant refused each arrival of the drinks waiter. Not wanting to be seen as a dipso, he had to confine himself to a single flute.

Increasingly stiff, Niamh held her head unnaturally still, as though mistrusting the robustness of her hair wave. Perched high above her forehead, guarding a little surf of curls, the set wave bore some resemblance, her boss decided, to Britannia's helmet as she sat on Albion's shore, trident to the fore. He felt a frisson at the thought. Yet despite all his assistant's attempts, as bloodless bore went on relentlessly, Arthur watched more and more wisps of strawberry blond hair pull free and dangle at her neck until Britannia had become the tinker's daughter. He got even more of a frisson at that thought. 'And so how do you find your new boss?' the Vice-Chancellor's Aide was asking.

'Oh, he seems to be doing a very good job,' Niamh replied.

The Aide to the Vice-Chancellor clapped Arthur on the back. 'Hear that, Merriman?'

Actually it was the Aide to the Vice-Chancellor who threw Arthur a lifeline. The back slap had upturned the head librarian's orange juice all over Niamh's gown.

What seemed a disaster showed itself in a new light as the head librarian took his assistant to the kitchen. At last they were alone. Not a bower strictly speaking, but beggars can't be choosers. This, if ever, was the moment. 'What have you put the light off for, Arthur?'

'Have you managed to get the stain out?' he asked through suddenly cloying lips.

'Put the light back on, how can I see to get the stain out?'

'It'll all come out in the wash.'

'What are you doing? Arthur, give over. Put that light back on now.'

No, the kitchen was no bower. The stain proving incalcitrant, the head librarian was sent to the library to collect the cardigan Niamh kept there for late closing days. Before he knew it they were walking away from the lawns, cardigan covering not only the damp stain but all his high hopes. Told you, his father commiserated from the shadows.

Niamh gazed at Arthur through the corner of her eye, and wondered why he'd been acting so strangely all evening.

Arthur gazed at Niamh through the corner of his eye, and wondered how he ever thought he could get anywhere near her. 'Niamh?'

'Arthur?'

Reaching the library they both stopped. The scent of wisteria drugged the air. 'Niamh, I… Niamh, I want you to come back to the flat with me.' Yes, he decided, I *must* have said those words because of the way she's looking at me. The rest of the words tumbled out. 'You see, I've got poplars growing there… and… and the proofs of poems have come. I'd like you to be the first person to read them. Well, they're about someone who's become rather special to me. You're the only one who'll understand.'

If this works, Arthur promised God as he let Niamh into the flat, I'll do anything you want. Even if you don't exist, I'll pretend you do. I'll find Mr bloody Bleaney and give him a hundred quid in ready money. 'I'll put the kettle on,' he said.

Arthur's head swirled. The poems had done the trick and got her here. What he'd said about her being the only one who'll understand had been a stroke of genius. She'd even blushed. Now – the bridgehead. He looked through a slit in the door. Yes, she was sitting on the horse-hair sofa. Yes, she was picking up the poems. Yes, she was reading them.

Was the smell of yesterday evening's sprats lingering? Ought one to open a window? Too late to worry about details like that. The tea things clattered as Arthur brought the tray into the lounge. Niamh was too deep in the poems to notice. Just managing to set the tray down without mass spillage, Arthur asked the question every poet dreads and yet cannot live without. 'So, what do you think?'

'Oh, it's all very clever.'

'Clever?' Not quite the response he'd been looking for. Neither was her tone, nor the tight lip.

Niamh couldn't hide her disappointment. Quickly she scanned the poems again. No, not a word about her. 'Yes, it's all very clever.'

'Clever?'

'But I feel sorry for your Mr Bleaney. The way you stand in judgement over him.' Niamh tried to stop herself, but couldn't. 'It must be very cold up there on your great height, Arthur.'

'I know, they're a load of crap,' Arthur burst, blood trumpeting into his ears. He cast the poems aside. They scattered like pigeons. His meticulously prepared speeches became simply, 'Oh, I'm no poet. If I was, you'd be what I wrote about.'

Grammatically cretinous as it might be, unwittingly Arthur had played the trump card. 'Really?' she asked, equally out of her depth.

'I'd write a whole book about just how lovely you are. Eyes, hair, the lot.'

The words were far from poetic, they even tripped over themselves in a sudden bout of stammering, yet they carried him to within an inch of her on the horsehair sofa. Carried him so close that he could see an unexpected line on her forehead; could taste the scent only ever glimpsed from a respectable distance. Then his lips, somehow warm with her breath, were murmuring her name. Now both lips were so close that you couldn't get a page of poetry between them.

Bang! A heavy object hit the flat window. A tangle of shouting rose from the park. Stumbling away from the horsehair sofa, Arthur went to the window. Someone was standing at the railings under the poplars. The librarian opened the window. 'I know it's you,' Teesdale cried, straddling the stocks of the railings. 'Encyclopaedia Britannica my arse. *You're* the bloody interloper. Never mind pretending to be a librarian either. *You're* in fur as well. *You're* the bastard who's got me

PART THREE

29.

As June gave way to July, the pleasant weather fell arse over tit into an all-out heat wave. Despite Teesdale's claim, Old Ma Glenners *hadn't* died. She lingered another fortnight. Arthur only decided to go to her funeral at the last moment when he saw the service at the crematorium listed in the paper – yes he'd succumbed to the habit of reading the local rag. At elevenses he left the library. The wisteria was no longer in blue bloom.

Christ on a bike, the heat. Walking smartly down Cemetery Road the head librarian felt as though he'd wandered into the pages of a Graham Greene novel and become some whiskery gringo foolishly challenging the midday Mexican sun. Blinded by sweat, a bread van passing him too near the kerb could have been the flaring wings of a landing vulture.

In the cemetery, the sun glazed the rows of gravestones into a single blinding wall. Even the flowers of that morning's funerals had wilted. With its furnace chimneys and municipal brickwork, the crematorium rose before the librarian like a cross between a giant public convenience and a power station. A choke of cloying smoke from the last funeral reached him.

McCoist was the only other mourner in the crem's 'chapel of rest'. The Scotsman wept throughout, a disconcerting creaking like a gate in a night wind. Oh, if only Niamh was with him. Truth be told, since the night of the High Table Do and the 'almost kiss' in the flat, things had been a touch strained between them. A touch? She'd done everything she could to avoid him. Twice she'd rejected his advances out of hand. His bold invitation to dinner at the Royal Station Hotel had met with a single, terse shake of the head. A rather tamer, 'I don't suppose you'd care to' kind of inquiry into whether she'd like to go to the literature society lecture on the life of Tristram Shandy author, Laurence Sterne, received the same treatment. A third invitation to a funeral, right at the last moment, somehow hadn't seemed viable. 'A woman whose life was dedicated to hospitality,' Arthur heard the minister say as he tuned back into the service. 'Well known for her solicitous care of generations of lodgers…' Clearly never met the woman. What next? *Justly lauded for her devotion to the privacy of her tenants and Archie Andrews.*

A Church of Scotland affair, the service must have been organised by McCoist. Good God, could the seaside trade man really have cherished feelings for the late landlady?

Matters concluded swiftly. Before the final words, a noise at the back. Arthur turned. Quarter expecting to see Mr Bleaney, it was Kathleen with her string of kiddies. The minister began *The Lord is My Shepherd*. McCoist's tenor was plaintive and unexpectedly sweet. The curtains parted and the conveyor belt jerked Old Ma Glenners on her final, short journey to the fiery furnace. As quickly as was seemly, Arthur made his way past the head-in-hands McCoist, and the kneeling line of Kathleen's tribe. He stepped outside, eager to retain his liberty, and staggered under the sun's sledge hammer. Didn't befall many British people to be laid to rest with the mercury rising in the eighties. Laid to rest? Burnt to a crisp more like.

At least the chapel had been cool, now once again Arthur was trespassing across one of Graham Greene's Latin American plazas. The Catholic writer was one of Niamh's favourite novelists, and he'd hoped to use him to bridge the newly

192

swollen river flowing between them. Hadn't done any good. 'Oh,' she'd said when he'd half managed to engineer a conversation about the author's view of damnation just yesterday. 'I don't think it's right for anyone to gloat over some-one else's perdition.'

The cemetery arch was in view when Arthur heard shouting. Someone was waving at him from the crematorium. He looked over his shoulder. Whoever it was, they were coming after him. The librarian swore, and hurried on. No good, the figure bounded over like an hirsute bloodhound. McCoist. The fancy goods salesman brought the librarian to bay under the cemetery arch. Chest heaving, gulping desperately for breath, glistening with sweat, the Scotsman couldn't talk. Instead he gestured in a threatening manner. Bloody hell, Arthur wondered, is he going to hit me? Behind the Scot, the last wisps of Old Ma Glenners could be seen rising from the crem chimney. 'This is yours,' McCoist managed at last. The Scotsman was holding something out. 'Right at the end, she asked me to give it to you.'

Numbly Arthur accepted the small object. His erstwhile fellow lodger stumbled away weeping. The librarian stared at what he'd been given. It was the glued ashtray saucer. 'Wait!' he cried. The Scotsman did not wait.

Here it all was again. The ceramic seaside scene. Sky, sea, esplanade, pier and gulls caught in a painted circle. Arthur hurled it away with all his might. Veering to the left, the souvenir seemed to be trying to come back to him like a boomerang. And perhaps it would have returned, right into his hand, but for the grave it struck. The glazed glory of Mr Bleaney's Frinton smashed into a thousand scintillations.

Back on Cemetery Road, he mulled over recent events. Amongst all the mushrooming bad news, one welcome truffle could be dug out. That morning he'd received a letter from another magazine requesting six of his poems. Six! They'd be fucking lucky. Like reading Catholic authors however, it did his cause with Niamh no good. 'Another judgement on some poor man's shortcomings?' she'd replied to his news.

Reaching the library, Arthur still hadn't managed to work out why she was acting like this. Was it the 'almost kiss'? Or had his poems repulsed her? Had he had bad breath, or was it simply because he was ugly? After all, perhaps he'd misread the fairytales. Being a poet wasn't enough to hoodwink a princess into kissing the toad.

By the time he'd arrived back at his office, he'd made a plan. Of sorts. In this far, he was bloody well going to plough on. What did he have to lose? After all, it might just be her natural reticence. In Victorian novels, your heroine wasn't worth a candle until she turned a suitor down at least three times. Not forgetting the *Noli me Tangere* religion. 'Niamh,' he said when he'd finally got the courage to summon her on the pretext of the library subscribing to some new periodical. She could hardly refuse a work matter. 'Will you come to Thinness with me this Saturday?' he asked, his mouth dry as the dog turds littering Corporation Road. 'I mean your father too,' he added quickly losing his nerve at the words of rejection forming at her mouth. 'The three of us. I'd love him to explain some more about the lighthouse. Well, he seemed to know a lot about its history last time we talked.'

If she was some Sultan's daughter the invitation couldn't have been less fucking presumptuous. Nevertheless, she seemed to think about it forever, and Arthur had sunk into despair long before he heard, 'I'll let you know.'

She let him know the next day at which he rose into the rafters of joy. 'Dad says, all right.'

Oh, with the dentist in tow there'd be no chance to scale the giddy heights of that near kiss, but at least some of the golden steps leading up to that delightful tower might be re-laid. Surely a man of the dentist's age would have to relieve himself a number of times in the day? Half his age, Arthur's own bladder was beginning to be distinctly querulous when sufficiently goaded by too much tea. During those toilet breaks what might be achieved?

At one minute to nine o'clock the following Saturday morning, the head librarian was approaching the dentist's surgery. He paused for a moment under the Merryweather maple. Today could be the beginning of everything. Yes, Arthur reflected, I really *am* a fucking romantic. Move over Percy Bysshe Shelley, and make way for Arthur 'jam jar specs' Merryweather. (What kind of a bloody middle name was Bysshe anyway?)

Naturally, fate had other plans. King Sod announced his return to power in grand style. That Saturday was the annual Catholic Church Thinness walk. The barely tolerable 'threesome' became a 'three hundredsome'.

So that's why she'd agreed. In company with all the Catholics of the area, Arthur spent the greater part of the broiling afternoon bearing one arm of an immense banner dedicated to the Virgin Mary. Up and down the seafront he paraded behind a battalion of priests, lace, statues, and elevated crucifixes. Frequently blinded by his own stinging sweat, he continually stumbled under the weight of the banner. His jokes didn't seem to go down too well either. 'Now I know how Simon of Cyrene felt,' he quipped.

'And why would that be?' demanded a rather stolid priest by the name of Fr. Carrick, no less a figure than Niamh's confessor.

To compound matters, the scorcher had brought half of Fishtown to Thinness. Flat caps, knotted hankie hats, teddy boy quiffs, head scarves, and, more widely than he had hitherto seen, uncovered female hair, and flesh too – the water positively rippled with limbs. Any cat calls from the general population of fun seekers directed at the faithful were dealt with by a group of burly Catholics patrolling the edges of the procession whose kicks gave a whole new meaning to the term 'left footers'. Afterwards, at least half of the parade went to the pub, apparently owned by an Irishman, who was allowing a lock in. Arthur's hopes at rehydration were dashed by the dentist. 'Ah, no. I think we'll have tea with the fathers.'

'But most of the bloody fathers are going to get pissed as well,' the librarian somehow managed not to remonstrate. Instead he bleakly followed the dry brigade into their desert.

The tables had been specially roped off at the O'Leary's family tearoom. Turned out it was still a Catholic establishment. The current owner being a niece of the original. Arthur found himself at a table with Niamh, the dentist and Fr. Carrick. No sooner had they sat down than Niamh went to powder her nose, and the dentist crossed to the till to talk to the proprietress. 'Are you a married man, Arthur?' Fr. Carrick asked without ceremony.

'Beg pardon?'

'Now, I understand you and Niamh are great friends.'

'Well, yes.'

'So,' Fr. Carrick gave what could have been a smile or a growl, 'I'm asking, are you married?'

'No, I'm not married.'

'Have you ever been married?'

'No, never.'

A look exchanged between priest and dentist showed Arthur that this moment had been planned. 'I'm sorry I had to ask you that,' the priest said. 'In my experience it's best to clear the decks from the start. Don't you agree?'

'Well, yes,' replied Arthur not knowing what the hell the cleric was on about.

'Now, you know of course that people marrying Catholics are expected to become Catholics themselves?' Fr. Carrick continued.

'So I gather.'

'It goes without saying that any issue must be brought up in the faith too.'

'Issue?'

'Children.' There was a deep pause into which the conversation fell and couldn't quite climb out. 'Well, now we've made ourselves crystal clear, I understand you favour poetry, Arthur. What would your opinion be of a fellow like William Butler Yeats?'

30.

Fr. Carrick's use of the word 'married' must have burrowed its way into Arthur's ear like a jungle jigger because all next day, it wriggled in his head. Lounging on the horsehair sofa in his flat or strolling through the adjacent park – married, married, *married*. It might die for a while only to intensify again until the sharp, serrated hook of sound deafened him to all else. Married, married, *married*. No, Arthur wasn't married; had always meant to remain *un*married. Being *married* meant death by a thousand cuts. Rooms to be painted, pictures to be hung, cardigans to be worn, screw drivers to be wielded, toxic in-laws, festering arguments, and then children to drain what little was left in the tits of free time. They didn't call it wedlock for nothing.

Have you ever been married? The priest had asked. Well, that explained Niamh's standoffishness. Fr. Carrick was behind the 'frozen fortnight'. The conversation in the tearoom made it all clear. Niamh must have told the priest about the 'almost kiss' on the night of the Top Table do. Add the late hour, the venue and the proximity of a bedroom, and there was more than enough to make the Catholic carnal Geiger counter bleep its head off. Once the possibility of impurity had been detected, Fr. Carrick would have instigated the usual 'no joy protocol', and Niamh would have been ordered to back off until the interloper had either been castrated or converted. No pleasure without a ring, no delight without a priest's fat fingers ready to tie the knot, and above all not even a sniff of sex without 'issue'.

A stark choice faced the head librarian. Now that he had jumped through the priest's first hoop, if he wanted Niamh, they would have to get married.

Married. But one wouldn't just be marrying Niamh. The dentist and Fr. Bloody Carrick would walk up the aisle behind the bride as surely as her train. Just say that he and Niamh didn't end up suffering (and administering) the usual slow strangulation of wedded bliss, and somehow stumbled on happiness, there'd be all the thousand and one clown saints of Catholicism hanging in the pantry (let alone the bedroom) like carnivorous bats. All the million and one medieval rules hammered to the wall with the holy pictures. Not forgetting, the *issue*.

Married. How had one pretty face dislodged a lifetime's commitment to singletude?

Now it was Arthur's turn to back away. He avoided his assistant's periodicals section, stopped the habit of sending for her at the drop of a hat. As he fell away, Niamh grew noticeably more receptive. After the tearoom chat, Fr. Carrick must have given her the go ahead. Twice she mounted the winding stairs on a spurious pretext of her own. The head librarian was courteous, but definitely distant. At her bringing up Thomas Hardy as a topic for conversation, he said, 'well, he was a committed atheist you know.'

As though to make up for his recent neglect, Arthur set to re-woo his real wife, somewhat deserted of late – solitude. Lovely to see his young assistant during the day and chat sometimes and maybe laugh, and perhaps even shed a dream or two, but at night what he really wanted was a coal fire, a tumbler of Glenlivet, a reading lamp and a good book. How could he have ever thought that it wasn't best to be alone?

To celebrate his narrow escape, Arthur decided to spend the weekend with his successful friend. How right he'd been, never to have mentioned Niamh. A *long* weekend, he thought. 'Oh, by the way,' he heard himself telling his under-librarian. 'I'll be in London this Friday. Apparently the bods at the British Library want me to discuss cataloguing ideas.'

Friday came. He caught the morning express. With a spring in his step, Arthur strode almost waggishly out of Kings Cross Station, and hit London town. For the first time as a proper published poet, he headed for the Soho coffee bar, habitat of writers and jazz. The capital was suffocatingly hot. The tube a torture. At the coffee bar, the espresso was as good as ever, but the jazz band had been replaced with a hyperactive quartet, who produced a kind of whining drone. 'Skiffle, mate,' a shoddy youth shouted in Arthur's ear by way of explanation. 'You know, for all the cool cats.' So much for the Soho coffee bar being a writers' hangout. Second espresso only half drunk, he left without writing a word.

Following old paths, Arthur wandered to Russell Square. Although he sat long in the shade of the plane trees, idly dreaming of poetic fame, T.S. Eliot didn't leave his office at Faber and Faber. Nor did Auden or any of his bum chums enter it. For a moment Arthur thought he saw Johnny Betjeman, but it was only some character in a trench coat going through a litter bin. Braving the tube again, the librarian found that the newsagents sold only nationals, not a sniff of the fishtown bugle. He also found himself thinking about Niamh.

By early evening, even the pleasures of the Charing Cross Road bookshops had been exhausted. In Foyles he'd only bought that copy of *Charlotte's Web* – because Niamh would have liked it.

Niamh, Niamh, Niamh! Stop bloody thinking about Niamh, he ordered himself. Easier said than done. All day she'd been with him. What would she think of skiffle? Would she like espresso? Chocolate ice cream? How would she look in Bobby Socks?

In the end, the need to hear her voice, slowly building, brought him to a halt at the next phone box.

Sheer bloody madness of course, and as he queued he changed his mind three times, but all the same somehow he found himself dialling the number. 'Hello 6781. The O'Leary surgery.' It was a man, not the dentist. Good God, was it — 'How may I help you?' Fr. Carrick asked.

The clerical tone brought the librarian back to himself. 'May I speak to Stanley please?' he asked, adopting a voice, which he realised too late was ridiculous.

'Stanley who?'

'Stanley Smallman.'

'There's no Stanley Smallman here,' said the priest. 'What did you want him for?'

Before he could be drawn deeper in the farce of his own making and reveal himself by the lurking stammer, Arthur hung up.

A taxi took him to his friend's flat. The street front alone showed that their lives were on different trajectories. Not only the enviable address, but an undeniable grandeur. Beside it, Arthur's place, poplars not withstanding, was a bedsit.

A note poked out from the flowerpot on the front step. His friend had been delayed in the country with his wife and young daughter; Arthur was to make himself at home; the friend would try and get back to London by Saturday night. In a gesture typical of his successful friend's magnanimous trust in life, the key was placed in the same flowerpot. Arthur had soon let himself in and got the kettle on. A strange humming was located to what one supposed must be referred to as the kitchenette. Since Arthur's last visit, a Frigidaire refrigerator had been added to the mod cons. Peckish, he opened it and found – a brace of kippers.

The panful of smoked herrings and pot of tea were soon dispatched. The smell left behind was almost welcome. His friend had a good supply of malt whisky, and jazz records. The librarian helped himself to both. The well-remembered riffs lifted him straight back to Oxford. Right from the first week he'd envied his friend. No shoe gazing for him, he always knew what wine and when, which tie and why, what woman and how. It hadn't been merely women; *everything* was attracted to him. He was one of those who get to peel down the knickers of life. Whereas Arthur... Whereas Arthur what? Whereas Arthur was an antisocial baldy, a half toad, half Pinocchio hiding in a library at the ends of the earth. Whereas Arthur had just turned his back on a woman whom he might have been able to love, or, equally importantly, who might have been able to love him.

Making a bed of blankets and pillows on the sofa, the head librarian turned his attention to *Charlotte's Web*. On the face of it a talking spider and a stupid piglet trying to save its bacon sounded about as appealing as finding blood in your own faeces, yet Arthur turned page after page transfixed. Then he realised why. He was imagining Niamh as all the female characters. Spider included. Imagining Niamh curled up beside him reading the same book. Imagining Niamh reading it to him. He took out his *Lyflat* memo book. Agreed, he wasn't cut out for the love game, but was it too late for his poetry? Oh, he was no Byron or shoulder-haired Tennyson, but couldn't his brief encounter with love allow him at least to be the kind of writer that feels the wind on his face? He stared at the blank page. Forget the fields of John Clare or Wordsworth's fells, it replied, yours is a country of airless bed-sits and train compartments. *Your muse is the likes of Mr Bleaney*.

Must have been getting on for midnight and the procession of champered-up Bullingdon Club arses passing outside was reaching its odious apogee when Arthur, rummaging in his briefcase, found the Frinton postcards. He'd forgotten all about them. No, he hadn't. He'd squirrelled them away for the perfect moment to read them. For the life of a Park Drive he simply stared. Upwards of a dozen photographs of sea, sand and esplanade. Breath running curiously short, Arthur turned them over. What he was looking at now were words actually written by his enigmatic predecessor. Was this how a biographer felt on chancing upon a cache of unpublished letters. Or a sceptical medium when the glass really does begin to spell out a name. *So word by word, and line by line, the dead man touch'd me from the past* as Tennyson had written.

Prompted by some dark, residual superstition, the librarian sat up and looked over his shoulder. No, of course the doppelganger wasn't standing there – just his own shadow on the wall. A pause; a deep breath; glasses taken off to postpone the moment; glasses put back on; and then he was reading, *Dear Mavie, cor, I don't half miss your kippers…'*

He also missed the chops 'done special' in Lea and Perrins, and the sausages and mash too; missed the bubble and squeak 'all cooked to a T in lovely HP', and the 'liver and onions ditto'. Missed the shepherd's pie 'all juicy with Hendo's', and the Irish stew 'perked up proper' by Yorkshire relish. Clearly the man had also missed his vocation – he ought to have been a sauce salesman. Each card featured a fondly recalled product of the sixty-one Corporation Road kitchen. By way of variety, he likewise longed for her plum duffs and spotted dick, and her special way with a teapot – 'Just to think of drinking a cup with you now, fresh poured, makes me spit feathers'. Not a word however, about what had made him banish himself east of this saucy Eden.

Was Mr Bleaney mad? This conviction strengthened when

Arthur encountered the words *Say hello to the old room for me, Mavie, where so many happy hours was spent by yours truly.* Mad? He was a basket case.

Yet was Arthur so different? What else was he doing all alone in the small hours, lying on his back stubbing out fags on the ashtray lining his curiously clunking heart, and brooding on the many plinthed Parthenon of failure? There was the lotus position, the missionary position and this one – the Bleaney position. Good God, was he going to have to *find* him after all? Was this the only way of laying the ghost to rest? After all, his old faith was useless against Bleaney. Don't get involved? He had no choice. It'll all blow over? It bloody well hadn't. More than that – he knew where he was.

31.

In the morning, a shit, a shave, and, of all the new fangled, Frenchie things, a shower, saw Arthur leave the almost-pent-house and head for Fenchurch Street Station. 'Is this the Essex coast service?' he asked a guard.

'Was the last time I looked at it,' came the cockney retort.

London was not long behind when a row of huge trees flashed at the window. Poplars! One couldn't mistake the sheer scale. Great galleons sailing England's shallow sounds of corn and cow, and so fucking forth. Made the trees in the park look like saplings. No wonder Gerard Manley Hopkins went on about them so much. Had Mr Bleaney ever noticed them on his many journeys down to the Essex East Anglian coast? Mad he might be, but at least he'd been capable of enthusiasm for something real, even if it was only for a shithole in Essex. And not forgetting of course, his faithfulness to the hawthorn young woman.

The first alarm bells of the day rang when the stop at a station began to feel too long. Looking out of the window, Arthur saw the front carriages disappearing round a curve whilst his own carriage remained stubbornly stationary. Craning right out, he realised that what was left of the Essex coast service no longer had an engine. 'You want the front coaches for Frinton,' the guard explained when Arthur ran him to ground guzzling tea in the van. The same man from Fenchurch Street Station. 'Train divides here, see? You're in the Clacton half, cock.'

'But you never told me anything about that.'

'Didn't ask.'

'Yes, I did.'

'You asked if it was the right train for the Essex coast. Last time I looked Clacton was on the Essex coast. '

As the librarian walked back up the platform, another engine was being shunted from a siding and coupled to the remaining carriages. Arthur watched the Clacton half piss off up the line. The guard waved. Arthur forked him. The next Frinton half wasn't due for an hour and three quarters.

Sitting under a toxic-looking hanging basket, Arthur took out his notebook. His pen, forbidden to write about Niamh, could only grub out facile rhymes such as 'all cooked to a T in lovely HP'. A wasp began to buzz around him. Getting up, he walked away. It followed him. He sat down. It appeared again. Enraged by the insect's feckless stupidity, the librarian slaughtered it with a rolled-up newspaper. 'What harm did it do you?' the station master accused, watering the hanging baskets. Getting up to avoid the dripping water, Arthur lit a fag and wryly considered his quest to Bleaneyland. Did he really think he had any chance of finding him? And if he did, what on earth would he say to him? What did he *really* know about his predecessor anyway?

Arthur paced the platform. From what he'd gleaned from Old Ma Glenners, Mr Bleaney had been at number sixty-one for at least five years. Good God! Half a decade cast away on the shingle shore of that rented room. Picturing the room now, Arthur encountered first the splintered wood where the high hook hung in the door, damage which, Teesdale had seemed to corroborate, had indeed been caused by a botched suicide bid. No way of proving it of course, but easy to picture the ligature of a dressing gown cord, the brief dance on the edge of the chair, and then the hook ripping out of the wood. Saved not by human hand nor kindness, but by a hook unable to bear the load. As cack-handed a suicide attempt as could be sensibly imagined. From the missing hook, Arthur's memory moved to the marks decorating the wood around the bedroom door handle like scratches inside the coffin lid of a premature burial. Clearly the disgraced insurance agent had reached the point where he no longer cared enough about his personal appearance to trim his nails.

The librarian felt a tightening of his underpants. Normally fastidious in these matters, he was still wearing yesterday's pair. Was this the beginning of *his* slide into shabbiness? What next, hair flourishing in the ears and nose; werewolf eyebrows? He pulled his thoughts from himself and returned to the abandoned room. The windowsill. What could that elaborate Venn diagram of ring marks pocking the rotting wood be but evidence of Mr Bleaney's slow plod into decrepitude – the placing of a nightly tooth glass for his falsies?

Toothless he might have been, but at least his predecessor had broken out and sowed his wild oats with aplomb – *You've really brought me out of myself, Mavie*. He'd had his annus mirabilis of shared antimacassars and radiograms, Thinness jollies, and nights at the Royal Station Hotel. Then of course – Bleaney's bint. To quote Teesdale, 'By God, this is living.'

What about his crimes? Well, who could blame anyone for resisting a fate that sentenced them to five years in that room? A miserly destiny had left Mr Bleaney 'spitting feathers', so Mr Bleaney had forced destiny to provide him with a cup of tea. Who wouldn't do the same? When one considered the question, rammed the thermometer up the human bum, the only crime is being born, all the rest is self-defence. Reaching the end of the platform, Arthur stood there for a long time. 'Your train's coming now, chum,' the stationmaster announced eventually.

'What's Frinton like?' the librarian replied with a strange hunger.

The station master considered Arthur narrowly. '*You'll* like it.'

Ours was the marsh country, Dickens had written of the coast not far from here in *Great Expectations*, his pen sketching a ghostly flatland under brooding chiaroscuro skies, lonely with churchyards, sluice gates and escaped convicts hiding in eel-livid dykes. Looking through the train window now, Arthur saw a plateau of 'villas', golf courses and retirement bungalows strung on an arterial road. Under the march of electricity pylons, the housing thickened to a prosperous resort. Only Dickens' unforgiving sky remained. And the fugitive. Somewhere, hugging himself in the bitter ditch of a lodging house, shivered Mr Bleaney as renegade as any Dickensian convict. Unless of course he was happy as a sand boy joyfully rogering his girl.

A sally bash band welcomed the traveller to Frinton with *Onward Christian Soldiers*. Well, what else? Ears ringing, he surrendered his ticket, and hurried into the town. Even if it was opening time, no point looking for a pub, a quick traverse of the 'Bond Street of East Anglia' yielded five separate groups handing out tracts about the evils of drink. 'No one knows when the Lord is coming,' a hare-eyed pantry boy challenged Arthur outside a milliners.

'Indeed,' the librarian returned.

A mistake. One should never look these people in the eye. 'It could be tonight,' said the pantry boy, fixing on the librarian like a pallid lamprey. 'Or tomorrow.'

'Or the next day.' Sometimes one couldn't help oneself. It took Arthur fully ten minutes to get clear of the pantry boy, who, as he testified, had once himself risked losing thrones and dominions by being tight on bitter shandy.

Passing over an immaculately cut greensward, Arthur found himself – in Mr Bleaney's saucer souvenir. The same too blue layers of sky and sea, identical ribs of esplanade and pier, that golden scimitar of sand. Even the gulls could be falling fag ash. Only there wasn't a pier. *That* existed only on the ash tray.

The seafront bristled with double-breasted blazers, hat feathers, walking sticks and beneficiaries of colonial service pensions. Invalid chairs choked the esplanade, grim rickshaws with a one-way fare to Death Avenue via Decrepit Crescent. As though the town council laid on a pied piper out of the rates, there were no children. In comparison with most of his fellow strollers, Arthur might still be in short trousers. With only one in thirty faces below pensionable age, he really would have a sporting chance of spotting his predecessor's relatively unworn visage. What was he looking for? A tall figure. On the lanky side. Baldhead and glasses. Well, someone like himself save for the 'bint' in tow.

After pacing the long length of the esplanade a few times, Arthur felt unaccountably weary, but a seat on one of the many benches couldn't be had for love nor money, the old boys and girls guarded them as jealously as hyenas a waterhole. He perched on the edge of the esplanade, feet dangling over the beach. As well as the children, the teddy boys must have been rounded up too. And the Catholics. In fact the entire working class, who usually swarmed at the seaside, were completely missing. One suspected McCoist wouldn't find many outlets for his wares here. Only a limited market for saucy postcards amongst the horde of evangelical grave dodgers buoyed in the choppy sea of life by sensible investments. What was this – was Arthur actually missing the presence of the great unwashed?

Buying an ice cream, he pressed on with new resolve. Trudging over wet sands, circumventing a 'sand-castle pulpit' from which a preacher sermonised the genteel hordes, the head librarian continued his search for the man whose shadow fate had thrown over him. No joy on the beach, he returned to the esplanade. Hungry, practically ravenous, what wouldn't he give for a Thinness board tied to a lamppost with the simple offer, *frying now.* Instead, high-poled orders hectored: *Abstain from the consumption of Fish and Chips on public thoroughfares. Refrain from Expectorating. All medicine balls will be confiscated.*

The centrepiece of all this horror was a lecture hall, which boasted, on the hour every other hour, *Reminiscences of a Brigadier of a Sambo Regiment.* Imagine being in the audience! The lecture was in progress now. Was this the kind of thing Mr Bleaney would be interested in? Arthur peered through a window to see a rubicund cunt with a hamster moustache droning at an audience of crones, a naked tribesman projected onto a sheet behind him. So, this is what Mr Bleaney deserted his prison cell for? *This* was his fortnight of freedom? 'Hello?' A severe jolly hockey sticks type demanded from the lecture hall door. 'Come for the talk? Frightfully interesting. Room for a little one at the back.'

In a reckless moment of abandonment, Arthur allowed himself to be bullied towards the open door before rallying. 'Do you happen to know someone called Mr Bleaney?'

'Who?'

'Mr Bleaney,' he blurted. 'I'm looking for him. He's – my brother.'

Jolly hockey sticks peered narrowly at the librarian before shaking her head as though to an obscene proposal. 'There are no Bleaneys here.'

Arthur walked quickly away. Oh, he was never going to be able to find him. To do so, he'd require the services of a character from one of Niamh's other favourite authors, G.K. Chesterton's

Father Brown. The librarian frowned and then smiled. Wasn't Father Brown, Chesterton's ingenious priest detective, from East Anglian Essex too? The smile became a giggle. Yes, he sodding well was. Another thing – and the laughing stopped – why was he still thinking about Niamh?

Well, he was no Fr. Brown but he had one or two leads. Securing directions to the Methodist chapel however was no simple matter. 'Depends which one you want,' the man he asked replied, glass eye fixing on the librarian. 'Wesleyan, Primitive, Salem or just the normal variety?'

'Oh, any.'

A rather disconcerting history of the schisms of Methodism followed before Arthur was at last pointed to a redbrick edifice just round the corner.

After weeks of sunshine, the weather was on the turn. Over the shoulder of the Methodist church one could see a cloud bank hulking in from the offing like a sperm whale. Arthur loitered around the chapel for a time and had just turned away when the door opened. A strait-laced individual, who looked as though he'd had his last bit of fun one half afternoon between the wars, poked his head out. Already hurrying away, the librarian stopped himself, took a deep breath, and returned. 'I'm looking for someone,' he said. 'Mr Fun' said nothing. 'You may know him,' Arthur added, feeling his stammer bridling. 'Someone by the name of Bleaney. He's my brother. Twins actually.'

At last, after an eternity, 'Mr Fun' shook his head. 'Never heard of him.'

Arthur turned on his heel.

After an outrageously over-priced late lunch, the rain caught the librarian on the esplanade. Shoulders rounded, he made for one of the green shelters on the front. Typical, just when you're forgetting how cretinous the British climate is, it reminds you. Well, the souvenir ashtray had been well and truly dropped in the lavatory. The whole ceramic scene had been washed away. The fag ash gulls rinsed clear. And with them, his hopes of finding his fabled predecessor.

He needed more to go on otherwise it was like finding a needle in a haystack or at least finding a fully functioning bladder in Frinton-on-Sea. Drops drumming the roof, he fumbled out the postcards from his jacket pocket. Still impossible to decipher the scrawl of his predecessor's given name. Illegible on its own, the first part of the signature was further throttled by the pulled noose of the Bleaney's Y. Derek Bleaney? Eric Bleaney? Earnest Bleaney? Edrich Bleaney? Ernie Bleaney?

Was he just imagining it or did the signature grow more flamboyant with each extra week on the franking date? Testament to Bleaney's improving spirits perhaps, or warning sign – those loops and leaps describing a nonentity's struggle to assert himself against encroaching disaster.

One by one the others sheltering got up and braved the rain. The last to go left a newspaper. *The Frinton Courier.* Yawning, Arthur picked it up. Four whole pages of boarding houses. What was the name of the establishment that had contacted Mr Bleaney? Fairview or something. They all had similarly anodyne names. He probably wouldn't be staying there now anyway. Would need to be somewhere he wasn't known. Would he pass the girl off as a daughter or a bride?

It was still raining when Arthur left the shelter and headed inland. The boarding houses of Frinton rose above him like a great rampart. Passing a jungle of *no vacancy* signs, he watched the holidaymakers hurrying as best they could through the rain to their lodging, gazed at every pale face caught at a high window, and even pried through net curtains into the dining rooms. At one attic aperture a wistful young woman stood with her head in her hands. She finally looked up. Not Bleaney's bint.

It had *really* begun to piss down when Arthur realised the

truth. Giving up his assistant librarian had been an act of colossal and breath-taking tom-fuckery. Why was he wasting his time with the ghosts when he could be with the living?

A ragged, almost sprint took him fifty yards to the nearest phone box. It was the customary red. Riding a reckless wave of nostalgia for the cream of wheat phone boxes of home, he yanked the door open. Dialled the cherished number. Heard the ringing two hundred miles away. 'Niamh, I love you,' he practised, as the ring-ring in the dentist's house continued. 'I love you more than anything else there is.' Ring-ring, ring-ring. The phone continued unanswered. He tried again two minutes later. And then two minutes after that. Five minutes. Ten. 'Niamh I love you.' A mantra now, the words accompanied the beating rain as he swept along the seafront in search of another phone box. Ring-ring, ring-ring. Still no one at home. She must be out with Ernie. A mental picture expelled him from the box, and sent him lurching to the sea wall. The tinker's daughter being rogered by the Soviet poster boy.

Before he could realise that it was a silly thing to do, Arthur had jumped.

He hit the sand. A juddering pain, and then he was rolling over a surprising number of times.

The drop had been further than expected. Gingerly he got up. A wave broke a few paces away. Was the tide coming in? If so, had he jumped twenty minutes later, a twisted ankle might not have been the worst of it! Was it suicide if one hadn't entirely meant to end it all? Or at least for only a second.

Arthur stood there staring at the sea. Seething with the rain, for a while it seemed to keep its distance until a finger of surf reached decisively towards him and lapped at his feet. Yes, the tide was coming in. He kicked off his shoes. Pulled his socks off. A fizz of salt lapped over his toes. Surprisingly, not too cold. Shoes tied round his neck, Arthur watched the water advance. Soon he was rolling up his trousers. 'I grow old, I grow old,' he whispered, instinctively reaching for T.S. Eliot. 'You shall wear the bottom of your trousers rolled,' the sea seemed to reply mounting his calves. The last time he'd paddled like this had been with Niamh. Niamh, Niamh, Niamh! The sea took up her name as it reached further and further in until the librarian couldn't roll his trousers any higher, and he had to step back. To think he'd once paddled with her. To think one night he had been inches from kissing her. To think that he had then walked away. To think that even now 'orrible Ernie might be… Arthur howled at his own sickly moon. The water broke over his trouser tops, the sea whispered, 'and what's more, you shall grow old alone.'

'J'accuse Arthur Merryweather,' the head librarian suddenly declared as he took another step back from the ocean's terrible hunger, 'of being an incontestable twat.' Well, how else to describe himself? When fate called a truce and offered him the chance (blessed be even the remotest chance) of forming a genuine attachment with a girl from the Forest of fucking Arden, he'd taken fright and acted like a prize pratt. All at once, an unbearable despondency vaster far than any ocean.

A boisterous wave sent the librarian stumbling. Bloody hell, if he wasn't careful he'd be in. He backed yet further from the sea only to find – the wall. Good god, he'd have to look lively; wouldn't do to be trapped.

Hobbling along the remaining spit of sand, he searched for egress from the beach. There didn't seem to be any. No, wait. There were some stone steps over there. To reach them, he'd have to wade through that channel. Deeper than it looked, Arthur had only hazarded a few yards when he lost his footing. A shock of really deep water. 'Stop!' a voice commanded from the seawall. 'There's no way through there.'

'What shall I do?' the librarian returned, voice cracking.

'There's a metal ladder on the wall. Over here.'

Retracing his steps, Arthur blundered over to the voice. 'Where?'

The voice was directly above. 'Here, Mr Bleaney.'

Scrabbling desperately over to the barnacle-encrusted seawall, Arthur's fingers found rusty iron. Sea shredding at the bottom rung, he ascended. 'You won't find your brother that way,' said 'Mr Fun', reaching down to pull him up.

For the first time in two decades Arthur willingly shook another man's hand. 'You saved me,' he said, standing on the esplanade.

'Mr Fun' shrugged. 'Anyone would have done the same.'

The wild will to live, which had taken over from Arthur's despair, became embarrassment. And then the need to get away. Quickly. 'For your collection plate,' he said, fumbling a ten shilling note from his wallet.

Barefoot, Arthur had already begun to hurry away when he heard. 'Good luck.'

He turned to face his saviour. 'Beg pardon?'

'Finding your brother.'

'Oh, he's gone. I just found out. He's not here.'

Still barefoot, Arthur stopped at the first phone box. Bullishly he pulled the door open. Again and again no answer. Suppose Ernie really was lifting aside the *cave crucifix* right now? Grinding his teeth, he smashed the receiver down. Craning around in wrathful agony, he caught a madman's eye challenging him through the phone box window – his own reflection. He put his shoes back on, and walked away.

A sea fret was swallowing Frinton-on-Sea (or was it night-fall?) as Arthur headed for the station. Once in London, he'd catch a train north. There was always the night mail. W.H. Auden wasn't the only one who could travel with the letter and the postal order. He'd be under the Merryweather maple by morning. As he had said, Mr Bleaney had gone. All that was left was Niamh.

The slamming of a coach door greeted the librarian at Frinton station. A whistle being blown. The train, about to pull out, was at the far platform. A fifty-yard dash; if he half-killed himself maybe he could make it. 'Don't bust a gut, mate,' a British Rail man with a huge brush called. 'There's another one in half an hour.' Halfway to the now moving train, the librarian gratefully capitulated, and then subsided into a wheezing, heaving heap. Well, he wasn't Roger Bannister.

After half an hour's wait, a different British Rail man came down the platform with the same brush. 'Come on, cock, let's be having you.'

'Beg pardon?'

'You can't stay here all night. I'm locking up.' Arthur explained what the man's colleague had said. 'Did he have a brush?'

'Yes.'

'Oh, you don't want to listen to him. Doesn't know his arse from his elbow. We only let him sweep up here. You'll have to come back tomorrow.'

'Tomorrow?'

'The next train to London is the half ten in the morning.'

Still the rain dowsed the quiet, unpubbed streets of Frinton as Arthur wandered along the seafront looking for a bed for the night. The first five hotels he approached had already locked their doors. The owner of a small temperance affair was finally persuaded to open up. Kitchen closed, not even a sandwich to be had. By lying about a family crisis, Arthur was able to gain access to a telephone. I really must be mad ringing up at this hour he reflected, listening to the familiar ring-ring of an unanswered call. Perhaps the troubadours *hadn't* been lying out of their arses, and love really was a kind of insanity. 'Hello, Thinness Road surgery 6781. How may I be of assistance?'

A craven impulse to resurrect Stanley Smallman was shaken off with surprising ease. The time for evasions was over. 'Hello,' said Arthur to the dentist. 'It's Arthur. Arthur Merryweather.'

'What the bejasus do you want?'

'Is Niamh there, Mr O'Leary?'

'At this time of night?'

'May I speak to her, please?'

'No, you bloody well can't.'

32.

Though he woke to a morning, grey as a bowl of semolina, Arthur Merryweather's mind had never been clearer.

Loafing along the esplanade he didn't even force himself to wait until eight o'clock. 'Hello, Thinness Road Dental Surgery,' said the dentist somewhat testily.

'Hello, Mr O'Leary.'

'Is that you again?'

'Yes, it is,' said Arthur, having to suppress a nervous giggle.

'What do you want now?'

'May I speak to Niamh?'

'She's out.'

'Out?'

'At Fr. Carrick's first Mass.'

'Well, can you tell her that I love her? I don't just mean a little. And if you bump into that fathead Fr. Carrick then tell him I agree, tell him I'll become a Catholic, down to the nth fucking generation of *issue*, or a bloody Wesleyan, Primitive Methodist with pink and white spots as long as I can love your lovely daughter,' he didn't quite manage to say.

Having to put in time before he could escape from Frinton, Arthur took his place among the lard-faced Pharisees strolling (or being wheeled) through the puddles to church, chapel and

Christian Philadelphian Worship Hall – whatever the hell that was.

England, recalling its vocation as the flooded corner of the European field, had resumed its habitual damp cheerlessness. Driven to a shelter, Arthur took out his *Lyflat* memo pad. Now that he'd surrendered to Eros, his pen flowed like fucking wine. After half an hour, he'd written a whole poem. No threnody to a lonely salesman; no still life suicide in an empty room, but a love poem! Of course he'd have to double check its worth by his 'Spartan infant' protocol, which involved exposing each new born poem to at least a day on the mountainside, but, all things being equal, he'd penned a fucking masterpiece. There, on the page, as clear as if it had been a sketch, lay a portrait of Niamh O'Leary. At last, Arthur Merryweather had taken his rightful place amongst the troubadours! The central image was the line on her brow he'd noticed the night they nearly kissed. In the poem it became a kind of cupid's dart: a flame stolen from the gods. Long used to accepting his mediocrity, the librarian was rather shaken by this visit of brilliance. Even longer used to the aloof demesne of 'I want to be alone', this novel need for another human being touched him more deeply than he thought possible.

On the way to the station, Arthur tried to dampen his unaccustomed high self-esteem. He couldn't. And what was this? Had his luck turned again – a tearoom was open. Alleluia for sabbath-breaking free spirits, and toasted teacake! A perfect way of killing the three-quarters of an hour remaining.

A girl took Arthur's order, and a colourful array of postcards his eye. He went over to the display. The final touch, a few postcards. One for his successful friend, one for his mother, one for Niamh, and one for the ghost who had brought him down here.

Arthur had written three cards when the refreshments came. 'Mum does all the jam,' the waitress said indicating the jars gracing each table. Arthur helped himself liberally, and then licking a finger wrote the postcard to his never-to-be-found twin brother. *Dear Mr Bleaney, you never knew me, I had the room after you at sixty-one Corporation Road. This won't reach you, but if it should, good luck and why not give Prestwick's Teatime Sauce a try? Best regards, a well-wisher.* It was addressed simply to, Mr Bleaney, the World, the Universe.

After this farewell to his predecessor, the librarian wrote three more words on the card to Niamh. Words he had never once written or spoken.

Postcards finished, something struck the librarian. He brought out Mr Bleaney's originals, and laid them out, one by one, picture up. Yes! He was right. They *were* the same as the ones *he'd* just written. Glancing over at the display, the librarian felt his nose hairs bristle. Mr Bleaney's postcards were *exactly* the same as those in the display. Yet, one supposed that the same postcards were available everywhere in Frinton. There wouldn't be an overabundance of choice on the East Anglian Essex coast.

Fr. Brown himself would have been happy with the deduction that Arthur made two-thirds of the way through his meditative Park Drive. Arranging the received postcards in calendar order of franking, he saw they formed the same pattern as on the display. Knowing the insurance agent's methodical character, what more evidence was required? They *must* have been bought here. Not only bought but written too, those smears on a couple of Mr Bleaney's postcards, which he had hitherto rather juvenilely speculated upon as being blood, were the thumbprints of a man consuming a jammed teacake as he wrote. Those homemade jams would have attracted Mr Bleaney as surely as any wasp. Inadvertently, Arthur had set the same seal on the foot of one of his postcards too. Yes, here, right at the end, having finally renounced him, he was closer to Bleaney than ever before. Shared the room, shared the bed, now shared the same raspberry jam teacake. What the fuck might fate arrange next – a tinkle of the shop bell, and the bastard coming to sit beside him? *Introibo ad altare Dei*, as Niamh's Mass might put it.

For a good five minutes Arthur actually sat tight and waited.

Rising at last he went to the counter. Wasn't there a good chance that the girl or the jam making mum would know the loyal customer? A good chance they would know when he was likely to pop in next. A good chance Arthur might, after all, be able to meet his ghost. 'Did you like the jam?' the girl asked.

'Yes,' said Arthur. He took a deep breath. 'I don't suppose you know…' A slight stammer. He smiled and started again. Then broke off once more. 'I don't suppose you know the way to the train station.'

The half ten train was actually the 10.23. Once again he entered Frinton station to the duet of guard's whistle and slamming carriage door. 'Hold that train!' he barked, driven to desperate measures. 'I'm a doctor.'

Before anyone could ask any questions, Arthur had hurtled down to the far platform, bullied open a door, and practically fallen into the three-quarters full compartment. The other occupants were too busy chatting their heads off to notice. He pretended to sleep. And if the yattering ladies club (or whoever his fellow travellers were) found this ill-mannered, then so fucking be it.

'I don't know what they do to get the sheets *so* dirty,' one of the passengers was saying, one with a poisonous feather in her hat.

'And would it cost them anything to flush a toilet?' a second demanded.

'Or rinse the scum ring from a sink.'

Obviously a coterie of landladies (better collective noun –

a Vim, a bed and breakfast, a Jeyes Fluid of landladies). Arthur tried not to listen to their carping about their guests. Easier said than bloody done however, as he heard, in horrifying detail, how dead bodies were dealt with in the hospitality trade. This was reaching a chilling climax when the compartment door slid open and another of their number entered. Judging by the smell of scented soap, she'd been to the toilet. 'Oh, hello, love. I hope we haven't offended you.' Arthur didn't realise she was speaking to him until she sat beside him.

Sitting up, he removed the hand shading his eyes. 'Beg pardon?'

'It's just that you always stay with us at *Fairview* when you stay in Frinton – ' she broke off. 'Oh sorry I thought you were someone.'

The vein on Arthur's temple pulled as tightly as the Y on his predecessor's signature. He took a deep breath. 'I don't suppose, by any chance, you thought I was Mr Bleaney?' he didn't say.

Dumbstruck, he watched the landladies rise in a body at the approach of the next station. 'I thought he was that odd chap,' the one who'd spoken to him 'whispered' to the others as they passed into the corridor. 'You know, always comes to us. Spends his holidays pushing cripples up and down the esplanade. Kind but picky.' She shrugged. 'Maybe he's snuffed it.' The train stopped; the Jeyes Fluid of landladies poured out. Travelling through the open window, their voices became audible again as they headed up the platform for the exit.

'Oh I know who you mean,' yet another landlady was saying. 'Always does the same circuit? So regular on the esplanade, you could set your clock by him? Well, you know what they say about him, don't you? They say he...'

A roar of steam from the engine drowned what they say about him. An impulse to get out and follow them. A sneeze.

Had he caught a chill yesterday? The train pulled out. Frinton, and Bleaney, fell free like a discarded crutch.

33.

'She isn't here,' the dentist said, opening the Thinness Road front door.

'Are you sure?' the librarian half demanded, craning to look past the dentist.

'I'm telling you she isn't,' the Irishman flared.

Either she was inside and complicit with her father's stone-walling, or she was out with Ernie. 'Where is she, Mr O'Leary?'

'Church.' Profound relief. A sneeze. Was the chill hardening into a cold? 'She's gone to Benediction.'

Yet more rain hosed Thinness Road as Arthur hurried away. Even the holy tree looked bedraggled. He knew the way to St Augustine's. He'd made it his business to map Niamh's world.

Church door snapping shut behind him like a spring trap, Arthur stepped into a candlelit twilight. In the shadows, a scattering of worshippers. High above, a muddy-brick cupola. Doleful singing. An organ toiling somewhere like a boiler. As his eye sought Niamh, it caught a glint of gold. The priest was raising what looked like a crucifix bathed in the rising sun. Clearly the nub of the hocus pocus, the congregation fell to their knees. Near the front, Niamh wore a black lace mantilla swathed round her head, her whole body stooped in peasant piety. He wanted to call out to her, shout, but the wide river of her religion flowed between them, that vast, moth-eaten musical brocade invented to pretend we don't die.

Arthur was opening the door to slip back outside and wait for her there when the singing took a different turn. All at once the whining dirge ended, and a sweet, plaintive, searching melody fell through the shadows like a shaft of light. In its beam Arthur half glimpsed himself standing at the altar. What was he doing? Of course waiting for Niamh, his bride. Now Niamh was standing there with him, holding their first child; second child. As the beautiful tune continued, Arthur watched life sift through the fingers of countless Sundays en famille until his casket stood at the front, being wept over by an elderly Niamh. Wearing the same, if faded, mantilla, she was flanked by square-shouldered sons, feisty tinker daughters and staring, red-eyed grandchildren. Arthur Merryweather had caught a vision of the future. Oh, one didn't need to believe in all the nitty gritty to take what faith offers. And why the fuck shouldn't he take it?

A resounding sneeze coincided with the abrupt silence. The singing was over. The prayers too. Arthur blew his nose.

The head librarian was again blowing his nose as his assistant passed. Clearly flustered, her nod was barely that of an acquaintance. In the headiness of the moment as he followed her out, he also blessed himself. Why not? Perhaps this church, so casually visited, might became one of the settings of his life. *Would* definitely if he bloody well had anything to do with it.

He caught her up in the car park. Instead of declaring his love, he grinned foolishly into the rain falling between them. Before he could speak, she was walking off.

Helplessly drawn after her, yet hobbling rather after yesterday's jump, Arthur managed to overhaul her again outside a fish and chip shop. 'What do you want?' she asked facing him at last.

'I came to Benediction because,' he began.

'If you're going to mock the faith then – '

'No, I'm not. I came because I wanted – '

'To snigger.'

And she was striding off once more. It hadn't meant to be like this. There was a bewildering hardness about her. All at once, declarations of love seemed a long way away. 'What was that hymn?' he called desperately.

'You're not really interested, Arthur.'

'I am. It was lovely. The last one.'

Niamh was still walking, but slowly enough now to encourage Arthur to come beside her. 'Are you limping, Arthur?'

'Yes.'

'Tantum Ergo Sacramentum,' she said. 'The hymn.' A searching glance. 'There's a couple of lines in there for you.'

'What are they?'

'Præstet fides supplementum, sensuum defectui.'

'Which means?'

'Sight is blind before God's glory, faith alone may see his face. Now go on, have your laugh.'

'I'm not laughing.'

'No, you'll go home and write a poem about how superior you are.'

They'd reached town, and were crossing the square. *I'll do it before we reach the statue*, he promised himself. They reached the statue. *I'll do it before we reach the theatre*, he promised himself. They reached the theatre. *I'll bloody well do it before we reach the phone boxes*. 'Niamh,' he said, stopping at the phone boxes and gently taking her arm. 'I've been thinking.'

'What's come over you, Arthur? Why have you been ringing my father up? He's says you've turned all queer.'

'Perhaps I have.'

'Fr. Carrick said you pretended to be someone called Stanley Smallman.'

'Yes, I did.'

'Why?'

'Because I love you.' Had he said that? Her face suggested he had.

There again the strange eating up of distance he'd experienced that evening in his flat, and there once more his lips within tasting distance. This time he didn't lurch away. She didn't. He wouldn't, even if a thousand Teesdales appeared, all shouting their heads off. He closed his eyes. She still didn't move away, he could feel her breath. He whispered her name. No, she hadn't moved away. He kissed her. For at least two seconds she persisted in not moving away, in fact – was kissing him back. Then a gulf reared between them. A resounding slap. Pigeons rose all around the municipal square.

They walked to the trolleybus in silence. Niamh got on, and was taken away. Arthur retired to the Royal Station Hotel with its high chandeliers and ugly quartets of upholstery. By his second drink, he had recovered enough to wonder whether the slap was really as final as he had thought at first. A shock reaction? The instinctive resistance of a virgin? The pulled puppet string of her infernal religion? She was so hard to read. Might as well fucking understand *Finnegan's Wake*.

Well, a slap couldn't be interpreted as encouraging, however one considered it, but the kiss. The kiss. The kiss! Plus, as the trolley pulled away she'd looked back. That was both biblical *and* hopeful.

It had all been going so well. Had his breath smelt? Repeatedly ringing up the dentist had obviously been an own goal. Then ferreting her out at church. She was always rather touchy about her faith. One ought to have built up to it more. *Wooed* her.

Sinking into a desolation, Arthur plunged his hands in his pockets. There they encountered – redemption! His *Lyflat* memo notebook, complete with the fresh poem. Of course, that's how he should have gone about it. Softened her up with the poem first, done a bit of Cyrano de Bergeracking. Hadn't she seemed a bit put out on the night of the Top Table club do when she'd read his poems and found none about her? *I'm no poet. If I was, you'd be what I wrote about.* The grammar might be faulty, but the logic was bloody bull's eye. And what's more, now he'd actually written one about her! Real as rain, the poem told her how he felt, better than he could ever hope to say.

It wasn't too late. Arthur opened the notebook and fumbled for a pen. Quick, get a copy written out, and sent to her first class. That would do the trick. Bugger that, hand deliver it. Tonight. Now!

Arthur had only copied out the first verse when he laid his pen down. The poem had failed the 'sounds like a prick' test. It lay dead on the hillside. To call it utter rubbish would be flattery. How could he have been so wrong? Taking his spectacles off he rubbed his eyes. A sneeze. On top of everything else he'd only gone and caught a fucking cold.